**"YOU KN...
STAY," F...**

Rolling over in the tousled bedclothes, she pulled the sheet over her body. "I live at home with my mother. I can't do as I please. Mama would have a fit if I traipsed in some morning after staying out all night with a strange man."

"Hey," Adam objected. "I'm no strange man. I'm the guy who's crazy about you." Playfully he tugged at the sheet.

Francy averted her gaze. Crazy about her? What did that mean, she wondered. It was obvious he liked making love to her. But would he be so crazy about those aspects of herself that she'd kept hidden from him? Francy was pretty sure she knew the answer to that one, and it was a resounding no.

A crazy fling, that's all this was. All it could ever be....

## ABOUT THE AUTHOR

Jane Silverwood decided to write about dyslexia
after listening to a radio interview. "Imagine not
being able to read a newspaper, a street sign or
even a restaurant menu," she comments. Life is
very hard for a dyslexic. The difficult part is
telling other people—Francy's dilemma in *Beyond
Mere Words*. A sensitive and talented author,
Jane has written more than thirty novels under
her own name as well as the pseudonyms Anne
Silverlock and Alexis Hill Jordan.

## Books by Jane Silverwood

**HARLEQUIN SUPERROMANCE**
282–THE TENDER TRAP

**HARLEQUIN TEMPTATION**
46–VOYAGE OF THE HEART
93–SLOW MELT
117–A PERMANENT ARRANGEMENT

# Jane Silverwood

# BEYOND MERE WORDS

## *Harlequin Books*

TORONTO • NEW YORK • LONDON
AMSTERDAM • PARIS • SYDNEY • HAMBURG
STOCKHOLM • ATHENS • TOKYO • MILAN

Published July 1988

First printing May 1988

ISBN 0-373-70314-7

# CHAPTER ONE

"GOD, WHAT A HUNK!" one legal secretary whispered to the other.

"Yeah," her bespectacled friend agreed. "Guess he's going to celebrate tonight."

"Wish I were the one he was celebrating with."

"Don't we all."

Avidly the two young women gazed at Adam Pearce's rangy figure as he strode rapidly down the corridor and through the doors of the Ellicott City courthouse. Stopping only briefly to field several reporters' questions, he took the steps to the sidewalk two at a time. Then, a broad grin lighting his ruggedly handsome features, he slid behind the wheel of his sleek black Mazda RX-7 and backed it from its designated parking space.

Once beyond the limits of the historic little town, which was the county seat, he accelerated east toward Baltimore. It wasn't easy to hold the sports car down to the posted speed because what he really wanted was to shout "Yahoo!" and make the needle on the speedometer jump through the roof. He'd just prosecuted and won an important case and he was high on his success.

Tapping one long finger against his leather-covered steering wheel, Adam reached out with the other hand and turned on the radio. It was set at an all-news station, and for several minutes he listened with half an ear while accounts of international disaster and intrigue spilled from the sports car's stereo speakers.

Adam was well into the city when he heard his own name mentioned. "This just in. Howard County Prosecutor Adam Pearce has won another dramatic victory. In a much-publicized murder case that has gone unsolved for five years, Pearce assembled the evidence to prosecute Gary Johnston. Accused of the slaying of sixty-five-year-old shopkeeper Thelma Murdock, Johnston pleaded not guilty by reason of temporary insanity. But after a dramatic courtroom battle, the twenty-five-year-old gas-station attendant was convicted late this afternoon.

"During the six years of his tenure, Howard County's prosecutor has become something of a legend," the newscaster went on. "It's even rumored that he may be a candidate for the House of Representatives. With his movie-star looks and bulldog tenacity—"

Adam had heard enough. Pushing a button, he switched to a classical music station. The soothing strains of a Chopin nocturne poured out, and he settled back into his car's comfortable leather seat to negotiate five o'clock traffic.

Baltimore's renovated Inner Harbor was his destination. There, in an elegant new thirty-story high rise overlooking the waterfront, Barbara Kains had recently purchased a condominium. Adam planned to accept her invitation to stop in for a celebratory drink.

The building and location suited her, he reflected as he pulled into the underground parking garage adjacent. It was dramatic, upbeat and fashionable—which pretty much described Barbara, too. The niece of a family friend, Barbara owned a small art gallery and involved herself in fund-raising activities for several worthy organizations in which Patricia Pearce, Adam's mother, also took an interest.

It was Patricia who'd introduced Barbara to Adam. And like a lot of women before her, Barbara had wasted no time letting Adam know that she was attracted. She had showered him with party invitations and then invited him to dinner at her place. After some initial hesitation about getting involved with anyone his well-intentioned but overenthusiastic mother was trying to shove at him, he'd begun dating her.

In the past couple of months Adam had settled into seeing Barbara pretty much exclusively. This was partly because it had been so easy and partly because it made a lot of sense. At thirty-five he was getting tired of playing sexual roulette with women who didn't really interest him. Barbara was good to look at, and since they came from similar backgrounds and enjoyed all the same sorts of things like cool jazz, Oriental food, ballet and coffee and croissants for breakfast, they got along fine. In fact, as his mother had pointed out to him only the other night, they were ideally suited.

"Why don't you marry the woman?" she'd asked in her blunt way. "You like her, don't you?"

"Of course I like her. I like her a lot."

"Well, then?"

"I guess I was hoping there might be a bit more than just liking the woman I got married to."

Patricia had laughed and stirred her tea. "Passion, I suppose you mean. You men are all alike. Well, let me tell you something, Adam. You're just the same as your father. The only thing you're ever really going to feel passionate about is your work. What you need is a wife who can give you a comfortable home and a smooth path to the kind of success you really lust after. Barbara would be perfect.''

*Much as I hate to admit it, maybe my mother has a point,* Adam thought as he buzzed Barbara's number. Had a woman ever given him the kind of high he'd just experienced in the courtroom? If things went on so pleasantly between him and Barbara, why not eventually propose to her? She'd given him good reason to bet that she'd accept. And it was getting to be time he settled down.

As the elevator carried Adam up to the seventh floor where Barbara had her condo, he tried to imagine what domesticity would be like with such a paragon of femininity. They both had their careers, of course, so they wouldn't plan children for at least five or six years. But he could imagine that Barbara would handle motherhood with the same crisp efficiency that characterized everything she did. Really, he acknowledged, she'd be the perfect helpmate. An attractive, ambitious, well-educated and socially adept wife like Barbara could do nothing but enhance his career. And he didn't doubt for a minute that she'd make a beautiful home for him, and give him children as healthy, good-looking and intelligent as herself.

Adam wondered if he shouldn't stop malingering and pop the question sometime this weekend. At his age, if the woman of his dreams hadn't shown up, she probably didn't exist. What was so great about bachelorhood that he couldn't bring himself to give it up? And what had happened to all that euphoria he'd been experiencing only a few minutes earlier?

"Adam, darling," Barbara cried when she flung open the door to his knock. "I spent the afternoon with my ear glued to the radio. I heard all about your court-room triumph. You were fantastic today.''

Adam cast an admiring glance at the inviting picture Barbara made in her green silk pajama-style slacks and overblouse and then grinned and strolled into her mar-ble-floored foyer. "I don't know about fantastic. Inci-sive, maybe. Or possibly persuasive and magnetic.''

Laughing, Barbara playfully tweaked his tie. "You were all of those. They said your closing arguments were mesmerizing, and obviously the jury thought so, too. Oh, darling, I'm so proud of you.'' She reached up to bestow a peck on his lean cheek. "But what a horrible little man that Johnston is. I'd hate to meet him in a dark alley,'' she added with a shudder.

"Johnston is safely in prison, so there's no need to worry.'' Adam turned toward the living room where Barbara had installed an elegant little bar. "I have to admit I've been looking forward to unwinding. Mind if I pour myself a drink?''

Since Barbara usually let him mix their cocktails, the question was rhetorical. Tonight she surprised Adam by putting a restraining hand on his arm and saying in a low voice, "Oh, darling, I'm so sorry. I never dreamed the verdict would be in this quickly, so I let the slip-cover person come at five. She's still in there.''

"The slipcover person?''

"Yes. Now that it's spring, I thought I should try for a lighter look. Well, I decided to have slipcovers made for the club chairs to match the Nile green in the dra-peries.''

Adam nodded, vaguely remembering that she'd said something about changing her decor according to the seasons the last time they'd been together. Barbara had impeccable taste, of course, but since Adam's idea of decorating was putting a leather easy chair in front of the fireplace and leaving it there, he really hadn't paid much attention. His profession was so fraught with challenge and turmoil that he tended to be a traditionalist about the other aspects of his life. That was one of the things beginning to attract him about marriage, after all—stability, security.

"The person I'm having do the slipcovers got here rather late and she hasn't finished yet," Barbara was saying. "It's annoying, of course, but from what I can tell, she does seem to be doing an excellent job. Do you mind bringing our drinks into the dining room while I get the cheese and crackers? Then we can relax at the dining-room table."

Shrugging his agreement, Adam watched Barbara hurry into the kitchen. When she was out of sight he crossed the hall and sauntered into the living room. But he hadn't taken more than a few silent steps on the plush mushroom-colored carpet when he paused, arrested by the sight before him.

A petite young woman wearing faded jeans and a pink cotton knit sweater knelt on the floor. As she reached out to pin fabric in the crevice of the chair she worked on, she unconsciously presented Adam with a view of a rounded bottom fetchingly molded by straining denim. Maybe it was just the angle, but her hips tapered to an unbelievably narrow waist—the kind of waist that a man's hands naturally itched to span. Around her shoulders spilled curls so thick, glossy and dark that they made Adam think of a blackbird in flight.

All that he could glimpse of her face was a slice of small, firm chin. Wanting to see more and also to warn her of his presence, he cleared his throat and murmured, "Excuse me."

Her head jerked around, and suddenly he felt an odd sensation in the pit of his stomach. Under brows as luxuriantly feathery as moth wings, startled, widely spaced, velvety dark eyes fenced by impossibly long lashes stared up at him. For a long moment it was only the eyes that he took in, and during that time Adam forgot everything—where he was, what he was doing. For all he knew he might even have stopped breathing. It was only when she reached up to brush a lock of hair off her forehead and take some pins from between her luscious lips that Adam was yanked back into reality.

"Sorry if I startled you," he said.

"That's okay. I didn't hear you come in." With a faint shrug, she turned back to her job, and after another second or two, Adam continued toward the liquor cabinet. As he got out the vodka, he directed several surreptitious glances at the kneeling young woman. While her fingers, bare of anything that looked like a wedding ring, worked deftly, a ray of late afternoon sun warmed the top of her head, bringing out glints of purple and blue in her rich black curls.

Again, he cleared his throat. "I'm just mixing a drink for myself and Miss Kains. Can I offer you something? A martini or a glass of sherry?"

She shot him a brief, surprised glance. "No thanks. I don't drink."

"Never?"

"Now and then a beer or a glass of wine. But never while I'm on a job. I'm just about finished now." She leaned back on her heels and surveyed the chair in front of her. Then she stuck several unused pins into a large cushion, dropped it and a pair of sheers into a bag and pushed herself to her feet.

All the while Adam watched in fascination, quite unable to take his eyes off her. She was short, he realized—no more than five two or three. And though she was slim, she was certainly not skinny—no, indeed, not with those seductively flared hips and what looked beneath the loose folds of her sweater to be a very well-rounded bosom. As she leaned over the chair to remove the cut and pinned fabric, he could feel his pulse revving like a sports car about to tackle the Indy 500.

At this the part of Adam still operating with something like his customary cool and calculating logic registered astonishment. What was going on here? He hadn't experienced such instant physical attraction in over a decade, he thought. Moreover he liked his women tall, sleek and well-dressed. To find himself suddenly so drawn to a stranger in jeans who wasn't even his type was unnerving.

Absentmindedly Adam unscrewed the lid of a jar of olives. "I would have absolutely no idea how to go about putting slipcovers together," he commented. "How did you get into the business?"

"Oh, it's a family thing. My father used to do it for a living, and I just grew up knowing how." She was very busy, folding up the pinned fabric and putting it into a large plastic bag, and she answered his question distractedly, as if her thoughts were on something else altogether.

Adam wasn't used to being treated so casually by young women, and he felt piqued. "As a matter of fact, I've been thinking of having a couch slipcovered," he heard himself say. "Can you give me your name and telephone number so that I can contact you for an estimate?'' When the words were out, he blinked in amazement. The last thing on his mind was redecorating his bachelor apartment. He liked it just the way it was.

She reached into one of her back pockets, and as Adam's eyes followed the movement of her hand sliding over her derriere, his palms tingled slightly.

"Here's my card,'' she said, coming over to him.

Tempted as he was to touch her fingers, he took the small white rectangle without giving in to the urge. Eagerly his eyes scanned the card's print. "Francesca Rasera," he read aloud. "Beautiful name."

"Thanks."

"I'm Adam Pearce."

"Oh. Glad to meet you."

"Glad to meet you, Miss Rasera." Since his trials often made the newspapers these days, a lot of people were familiar with his name. He waited for some sign of recognition from Francesca, but there was none. She'd gone back to her cleaning-up activities.

"Well," she said, stuffing a few last scraps of fabric into one of her bags and then slipping on a loose linen jacket, "I'm all done here."

He was about to answer when Barbara walked into the room and looked quizzically from Adam to Francesca and back. "Darling, what's taking so long? Was there something you couldn't find in the liquor cabinet?"

Adam glanced down at the cocktail shaker sitting on the bar. He'd forgotten all about Barbara and hadn't even started on the martinis. "No," he mumbled, "I got sidetracked. I've never seen anyone cut slipcovers before."

"It is fascinating," Barbara answered, her eyes narrowing slightly. Then she turned to Francesca. "All done?"

"For now," she answered cheerfully. "I'll come back in two weeks to fit the finished product to your chairs."

"That will be fine." Graciously but firmly Barbara showed the other young woman to the door.

When Barbara returned a few minutes later carrying a carefully arranged tray of cheeses and crackers, Adam had finished mixing their drinks. He looked up to find her standing in the middle of the room eyeing him with an arch little half-smile hovering about her lips.

"Since when did you become interested in how slipcovers are made?"

"Since ten minutes ago," he replied. "Those chairs are going to look great in here. In fact, I'm getting jealous. Maybe I should think about having my place redecorated, too."

Barbara set the tray on the coffee table, sank gracefully down into the couch and patted the cushion next to her. She waited until Adam had settled himself and then said, "I know what you found so intriguing. It wasn't really the slipcovers, it was the pretty little Sophia Loren type, wasn't it?"

Adam lifted an eyebrow. "You mean Miss Rasera?"

"Of course I mean Miss Rasera, and I don't blame you a bit. She's charming, and such hair and eyes. But she's not for you, I'm afraid."

Adam took a sip of his cocktail. "Oh," he replied. "Why is that?"

"For one thing, her family live in Little Italy, and I happen to know that she didn't finish high school. Which is a shame, really, because she seems quite bright. But can you imagine what your mother's reaction would be if you brought home a woman like that?" Barbara laughed and then reached forward to spread some soft cheese on a wheat cracker. "If you're really serious about fixing up that rattrap bachelor apartment of yours, leave it to me. I've been longing to get my hands on it for months. Now, what are we going to do to celebrate your victory this weekend?"

Politely Adam accepted the cracker she proffered. "I don't know. Guess I'll leave that to you." One thing they weren't going to do, he thought, was get engaged. He slipped a hand inside his pocket and fingered the sharp, crisp edges of Francesca Rasera's business card.

FRANCY EYED the colorful advertisement above the bus seat on the other side of the aisle. It showed a stunning blonde offering a cigarette to a blue-eyed macho type, and it reminded her of Barbara Kains and the gorgeous guy she'd had at her place. What a pair those two had made—straight out of a daydream about the beautiful people. She cocked her head as she continued to study the poster opposite her. You didn't need to be able to read the print above the blonde's head to understand the advertisement's message. Still, a wistful expression came into Francy's large dark eyes as she switched her scrutiny from the handsome, self-satisfied looking couple to the black letters.

Fifteen minutes later Francy climbed off the crowded bus, shifted her bags over her shoulder and trudged up the busy avenue.

On the next block she paused in front of an imposing gray stone building and then, after taking a deep, steadying breath, began to climb the dozen marble steps that led to its ornate brass doors. Marvin Paley Public Library, the chiseled inscription above them read. But

Francy didn't look at it. Just as always when she went into this building, her nerves jumped and her heart thudded.

Inside, she took another steadying breath and directed her rubbery legs toward the circulation desk and Mrs. Surrey, the kindly librarian who presided over it.

"Hello there, Francy," she said, looking up with a quick smile as she saw the dark-haired young woman approach. "Are you returning those tapes so soon?" When Francy nodded and handed over a half dozen cassette recordings of fiction works, Mrs. Surrey shook her graying head and commented, "I can't get over how quickly you zip through those. Why, you must have listened to half the tapes we own. How did you like the Hemingway?"

Francy's beautiful eyes began to glow. "Oh, I loved it. *For Whom the Bell Tolls* is a wonderful story."

"And the Faulkner?"

"I liked that, too. Though it was a little hard to follow at times."

"*The Sound and the Fury* is easier to listen to than to read," Mrs. Surrey agreed. "I don't blame you for preferring to just hear it. How was the Shakespeare?"

"*Midsummer Night's Dream* was beautiful, but sometimes the vocabulary..."

The older woman nodded. "Now there's a case where it's really better to read the text while you listen to the actors speak the lines. Would you like to check out a copy of Shakespeare's works?"

The glow faded from Francy's eyes and she looked down at her hands. "No, I don't have time," she mumbled. "I'd just like to take some more tapes of his plays."

Mrs. Surrey shot her a quizzical glance and then lifted a typed list and placed it on the counter. "Choose the ones you want, and I'll get them for you."

Swallowing, Francy gazed at the black print. It seemed to blur before her eyes, making no more sense to her now than it had in first grade when her teachers had tried, unsuccessfully, to persuade her to read. Like her father before her, she'd never been able to do it. At first they'd called her lazy and stupid. It wasn't until much later that she'd been told she had a learning disability—something she'd just have to overcome. Except that she'd never been able to.

Steeling herself, she looked up at Mrs. Surrey. "I don't know which ones I want. Would you choose for me?"

"But I'm not sure I remember which of Shakespeare's plays you've already listened to."

"*Hamlet*, *Macbeth*, *The Winter's Tale*, *Much Ado About Nothing* and now *Midsummer Night's Dream*," Francy recited tensely. She supposed she should really tell Mrs. Surrey about her reading problem. It would make these visits to the library so much easier. But she hated people to know. She could imagine how Mrs. Surrey would look at her—the amazement and disbelief, and then the pity. Even the thought of it made Francy's skin crawl.

"Well, how about some histories? *Richard II* and *Henry IV* and *V*?"

"That sounds fine." Francy's smile was relieved.

As Mrs. Surrey checked out the tapes for her, she glanced longingly around the library, her gaze lingering on the shelves of books that would always be a mystery to her. Then, with another grateful smile, she took the tapes, thanked the librarian for her help and hurried toward the exit.

Outside, Francy adjusted her bags and headed east. As she walked, several young men lounging outside a barbershop cast admiring glances at her and shouted an invitation. After waving a dismissive hand, Francy paid them no mind. She'd lived in this neighborhood all her life and knew they meant no harm.

When she came to an empty storefront she paused, shaded her eyes and peered inside. The sign on the front door was easy enough to recognize. It said For Rent. The space, formerly a tailor shop, had been empty ever since old Mr. Fiorelli keeled over in front of his sewing machine a month and a half ago and had to be taken to a retirement home. Like most stores in the area, the shop had been there forever and needed cleaning and repainting, but it was a prime locale and was bound to rent soon. Closing her eyes, Francy pictured the windows filled with fabrics in bright colors—with perhaps a chair half reupholstered just to show how skills like hers could make a worn-out piece of furniture fresh and beautiful again.

"You still thinking about opening a shop in this place?" a gravelly voice asked.

Francy turned and smiled at Gus Venturo, the middle-aged proprietor of the Italian grocery next door. He had come out to take in the baskets of fruit and vegetables displayed on the sidewalk.

"I'd like to," Francy admitted, "but it's a big step."

"How's business?"

"Good. Lately I've got more orders than I can fill, and I'm working all the time."

"Tell you what," Gus said, coming up to her and laying a confidential hand on her shoulder. "How long have I known you now?"

Francy laughed. "Just ever since I can remember." This was no exaggeration. Her mother had always bought fresh produce at his shop and whenever she had stopped in with Francy, Gus had produced a crisp apple or a plump peach or banana to give to the dark-eyed little girl.

Now Gus nodded sagely, wiped his square hands on his long white apron and handed her a choice-looking pear from the top of a bushel basket.

Smiling, Francy accepted the fruit and waited to hear what he had to say.

"You're a good girl, smart and hardworking," he began. "The way you took over your papa's business when he died and supported your mama and your sister's kids was wonderful." Gus cocked his head. "What's Teresa doing with herself these days, by the way?"

Francy shrugged. "Just the usual."

Gus rolled his eyes. "She used to be the prettiest girl in Baltimore. Broke my heart when she got married to that no-good Tony. Anyway," he went on, "what I wanted to say is that you're never going to get anywhere working at home. If you want to make something of your business, you got to expand. You got to have a store where customers can go and feel comfortable, you got to branch out with different services—interior decorating maybe. And you got to start advertising."

Francy nodded. She knew all this. For a year now she'd been telling herself that the time had come to take "the big step." She knew all about fabrics and making draperies and slipcovers. She could practically reupholster a chair or a couch with her eyes closed. The only thing she lacked was confidence—confidence that a person who couldn't read contracts or decipher a simple memo could make a go of it in business. But this wasn't something she could discuss with Gus Venturo. After a few more friendly words, she waved goodbye to the grocer and turned down the street toward the brick row house where she'd lived all her twenty-five years.

Inside, she set down her burdens and inhaled deeply. The garlicky aroma of simmering spaghetti sauce triggered a Pavlovian response in her stomach and she walked back to the kitchen sniffing happily.

"Smells good, Ma. Where's Teresa and the kids?"

"Out shopping." Mrs. Rasera turned her curly gray head and beamed. "How'd it go today?"

"Went great." Francy dipped a finger in the spaghetti sauce and licked it appreciatively. "Mm, *bono, bono!*"

Her plump little mother bustled across the room to the sink where the customary mountain of pots and pans had steadily built through the afternoon. "That Miss Kains has been good for business, huh?"

"She's been like a spring rain in the Sahara," Francy replied, pressing her palms together and rolling her eyes upward as if thanking heaven for its bounty. "I've gotten so many new customers through her. She knows a lot of *House Beautiful* type people, I'll tell you."

"Rich people like her, then," Mama agreed cheerfully. "She sure don't hold back on her place."

"You're right about that," Francy answered, straddling a kitchen chair and pushing her thick, wavy hair off her face as she settled down to eat Gus Venturo's pear. "Everything in that condo of hers looks like something out of a magazine. And she's a one-woman fashion show herself. You should have seen the slinky outfit she had on today—clingy green silk with little touches of gold. And you should have seen the guy she was trying to impress. Oh, boy, was he something."

Mama turned up the heat under the huge pot of water. "She had a man over while you were cutting her covers?"

"The job took longer than I expected, and he came in when I was nearly done," Francy explained.

"So what kind of man does Miss Kains invite up to her apartment?" queried Mama.

"A dishy yuppie type straight out of *GQ*, what else?" Francy bought all the most popular magazines and spent what spare time she had studying the pictures in them and struggling to decipher their printed legends. There was a need in her to know and to understand. For years now her secret sorrow had been that that need would never be satisfied.

Mama obviously didn't recognize the popular men's magazine to which her daughter referred. "What type is that?"

Closing her eyes, Francy visualized the gorgeous man who'd taken her by surprise that afternoon. "Tall, lean and very distinguished looking. Cheekbones you could carve a Thanksgiving turkey with, eyes like a clear blue winter sky, and browny-gold hair with just a hint of silver at the temples. Dressed in an expensive three-piece suit and wearing a gold watch that looked like the real thing. His name was Adam Pearce."

"Sounds just right for Miss Kains."

Francy grinned impishly. "Yes, but he wasn't above flirting a little bit with me."

"He flirted with you?"

"A little bit. Or maybe I was just imagining things."

Mama frowned anxiously. "Oh, Francy, be real careful. Miss Kains will get mad if her boyfriend flirts with you. You don't want to lose her as a customer."

"I don't think there's anything to worry about," Francy replied. "I'm not exactly Mr. Pearce's type."

Mama bristled. "And why not?"

"Oh, come on, a guy like that wouldn't take someone like me seriously. Oh, sure, he might like to fool around a little bit. But Miss Kains is the kind of woman he'd bring home to mother—and I'm smart enough to know it."

Shrugging, Mama began to throw handfuls of pasta into the boiling water on the stove. "It's time you found someone and got married," she muttered. "Look at your sister. By the time Teresa was your age she had two babies and another one on the way."

"Yes," Francy replied, "and because her louse of a husband was too busy running around with other women to support his family, she and her four kids are now packed in with us like sardines. No, thank you, that's not for me."

"Why are you talking that way?" Mama said disapprovingly. "You know that you love Teresa's babies."

"Yes, I do," Francy agreed. "But I want to make a life for myself. I don't want to be completely dependent on a man the way she was. And why are you throwing so much spaghetti into that pot? Who's coming to dinner, the Salvation Army?"

"It's just us and Teresa and the kids," Mama said.

Francy grinned. "Oh, then, come to think of it, maybe you should put more in just to be sure we don't run out."

Josephine waved a dismissive hand at her daughter. She knew perfectly well that despite Francy's criticism, she loved her older sister and adored her noisy nieces and nephews.

As Francy got up from her chair to set the table, a smile turned up the corners of her soft mouth. But she hadn't taken more than a step or two when the phone rang.

"I'll get it," Mama said and reached to the right of the sink for the receiver. "Hello."

Francy waited to see who it was. You could never tell. Customers called at all hours of the day.

Slowly her mother turned and held out the receiver. There was a quizzical expression in her bright eyes. "For you. A Mr. Adam Pearce."

# CHAPTER TWO

"HELLO, MR. PEARCE," Francy said, summoning up her most businesslike manner. "What can I do for you?"

The pause that followed was brief. Yet something about that infinitesimal hesitation combined with the husky baritone she heard vibrating on the line immediately after made the tiny hairs on the back of Francy's neck lift. Silently she admitted to herself that ever since she'd laid eyes on Mr. Adam Pearce that afternoon, he hadn't been long out of her thoughts. There was something very satisfying about hearing from him again this way.

"I suppose you're wondering why I'm calling you so soon after we just met."

"Well, yes." Determined to disguise the wings of excitement fluttering in her stomach, she made her voice curt.

As if he understood her motives exactly, he sounded faintly amused. Was he laughing at himself or at her? she wondered.

"I'm home now," he said, "and looking around at what I now realize is a very drab apartment. I'm badly in need of your decorating skills, Miss Rasera. When can you give me an appointment?"

Francy glanced at her mother. Josephine Rasera was over at the stove, pretending to stir the spaghetti sauce.

It was obvious to her youngest daughter that she'd fixed her attention on the telephone conversation. Her gray curls bristled like radio antennae receiving enemy signals.

After clearing her throat, Francy asked evenly, "How soon would you like it?"

"As soon as possible. As soon as you have an opening in your appointment book."

"I don't keep an appointment book, Mr. Pearce. But I have a very good memory. Would Thursday the eighteenth at four o'clock work for you?"

"Works fine," he agreed smoothly, giving her his address. "I'll see you then."

"Yes, see you then." Francy hung up the phone and stood blinking at it.

"So," Mama began the instant she heard the receiver hit the cradle, "was that Miss Kains's boyfriend?"

"Yes. At least, that's the man I saw in her apartment this afternoon."

"He didn't waste any time getting in touch."

"No," Francy conceded. "He says he's in a big hurry to have his place redone."

Josephine made a rude noise in her throat. "He's in a big hurry for something, all right." Abandoning the spaghetti sauce, she faced her daughter, arms akimbo. "Miss Kains is a good customer. Do you think it's so smart to make appointments with her boyfriend?"

"Ma, he's asking for an estimate on some work, not a date. It's a job, and I can't afford to say no to one of those. Not when I'm thinking about expanding the business."

"Why are you still talking about that? I thought we already decided it was too risky. You're doing okay the way things are."

"Maybe, but I won't go on doing okay if I start turning down jobs. Besides, I don't really know that Mr. Pearce is Barbara Kains's boyfriend. All I know is that she had him up there for drinks."

Far from placated, Josephine declared, "I got a bad feeling about this, Francy. You be careful."

"Aren't I always? Listen, I was born careful. For heaven's sake, you don't have to warn me about Adam Pearce. I know his type, and I know he's not for me. If the guy tries anything funny I'll give him the cold shoulder."

And with that Francy marched out of the kitchen and into the small dining room. Relieved that her mother hadn't tagged along to pursue the debate, she took several deep breaths. Then she went over to the heavy carved sideboard, scooped up a handful of knives and forks and began to slap them down around the mahogany table.

In a moment, however, Francy slowed her pace and started arranging the cutlery with care and precision. All the important meals she could remember had been eaten around this table. As far as she knew it had been in the family since newly married Louis and Josephine had first come over from the old country and settled in the Baltimore ethnic neighborhood where they had put down roots.

Now the roots were deep and the memories were thick. Her hands still filled with the fine old silverware that had been her mother's dowry, Francy paused behind the carved chair at the head of the table. On those rare occasions when her older brother, Paul, came home for a visit, he would sit in it. Otherwise, since the day Francy's father had died of a heart attack five years earlier, the chair remained empty. Lovingly her hand stroked the polished wood.

Then, with a sigh, she continued around the table, methodically arranging place settings while her thoughts drifted back to that phone call from Adam Pearce. *What's it all about?* she asked herself. She hadn't missed the gleam in his eye at Miss Kains's apartment. *Does the guy really want his place decorated, or does he just want to get me there so he can make a pass?*

Francy was used to men making passes at her, men who only wanted to amuse themselves. Up to now her luck with the opposite sex hadn't exactly been the greatest. The ones who'd been serious about Francy were the ones she couldn't take seriously herself. The others, the kind of men who really attracted her, had only wanted a casual flirtation. She shook her head. If that's what the hunky Mr. Adam Pearce had in mind, he was in for a disappointment, because her casual-flirtation days were over.

LONG AFTER ADAM HUNG UP the telephone, he stood with his hands in his pockets, looking out the window but not really seeing the busy avenue below. *Am I crazy or what?* he asked himself. A couple of hours earlier his life had seemed on course. He'd gone to Barbara's apartment filled with elation, expecting to invite her out for a special dinner and possibly even to stamp his future into the expected mold by proposing marriage.

Instead, after a hurried and uncomfortable cocktail, he'd made a feeble excuse to leave and had sped home so that he could pick up the phone and hear the warm sound of Francesca Rasera's contralto voice.

Really that was no way to treat Barbara, and he was ashamed. But he'd felt like a lowlife accepting her hospitality and pretending to listen and make the proper responses to her small talk while all he could think about was Francesca. What was it about that young woman that had sent him off the deep end? She was very pretty, but then so was Barbara and most of the other women he'd dated in his long history as an eligible but elusive bachelor. Had he responded so strongly to her because he was emotionally off kilter after all the turmoil of the trial? He didn't know. All he knew was that he had to see her again. And if that meant a steep bill for her decorating services, then so be it.

Smiling ruefully and shaking his head at his own folly, he turned away from the window and sauntered into his small but well-equipped kitchen. Adam had taught himself to be a better than average cook, but tonight he didn't feel up to dealing with pots and pans. Instead he took a gourmet frozen dinner out and put it in the microwave. After setting the timer, he leaned against the counter and folded his arms over his chest to wait.

*Some celebration,* he thought. Yet this simple meal by himself at home was about all he felt up to. This and maybe some long overdue quiet reflection about his life.

He was just settling down to eat his microwaved shrimp and chicken Cantonese when the phone in the kitchen shattered the quiet mood. "Never fails," he muttered as he got up to answer it.

"Adam," an imperious female voice on the other end declared. "I didn't expect to find you at home on this of all nights."

"Then why did you call, Mother?"

"To congratulate you, what else. Darling, I'm so proud. Did you see yourself on the evening news?"

Adam shook his burnished head. "No, I'm afraid I missed myself. How was I?"

"Very handsome and forceful. Very young Kennedyish. Turn on the ten o'clock news this evening. I'm sure they'll repeat the story."

"By that time I'll probably be in bed. I'm exhausted."

"Oh, pooh! I'll make a videotape so that you can see what I mean. I've told you this before, but I'll say it again. You're extremely photogenic. And it's such a lucky thing."

Adam raised a hand to his forehead and rubbed the crease that had appeared above his nose. "I'm afraid you've lost me, Mother. What are you talking about?"

"This is a mass-media society we live in," Patricia retorted coyly. "These days people who run for national office need to be photogenic."

"Yes, but if I remember correctly I'm not running for national office."

"You will be. Oh, Adam, don't you see that this is the perfect moment? With all the wonderful coverage you've gotten out of this trial, your name has been in all the newspapers, and your face has been on everyone's television news show. Now is the time to strike."

"Strike?"

"There's a man I want you to meet. His name is Ben Catlett."

Adam lifted an eyebrow. "The Ben Catlett who ran Sam Spendry's race for governor?" Adam knew Catlett's work and his reputation. A PR genius who was still a force to be reckoned with in state politics, every now and then he came out of retirement to mastermind a campaign for a candidate in whom he believed. And when he did, the result was always spectacular success.

"The same," Patricia returned confidently. "The man's a brilliant organizer who knows Maryland politics inside out, and he's very interested in you."

Adam straightened. "How do you happen to know this?"

"Because I've already talked to him. We met in Bermuda at a party the Kitteredges threw. He spends his summers there now. Adam, Catlett is going to be in town on business. I've taken the liberty of setting up an appointment on the twenty-eighth for the two of you to meet for cocktails at my place. You will come, won't you?"

Adam hesitated. For years he'd been resisting the high-handed manner in which his mother tried to run his life and make decisions for him. On the other hand, he couldn't deny that he was interested in meeting Catlett. *No point in cutting off my nose to spite my face,* he thought. "All right," he agreed. "The usual time?"

"Yes, and wear the Harris tweed sport coat I gave you for Christmas. You look like Robert Redford in that."

"If you don't mind, I think I'll wear something that lets me look like me."

A moment later Adam hung up. *I really need to do some serious thinking,* he realized as he walked back to the table where the now less than appetizing shrimp and chicken Cantonese waited. *Funny how everything can be going along predictably and then in a matter of hours it all gets turned upside down.*

AROUND THE DINNER TABLE knives and forks clinked as seven eager pairs of hands dug into the fragrant

mounds of spaghetti Josephine Rasera had heaped on
their plates.

"Good, Mama," Teresa said and then added, "Mike,
Jerry, stop making faces at each other. See how your
sister Jenny eats like a little lady?" Teresa then turned
her attention to her youngest daughter, five-year-old
Rosy. "No, no, don't eat with your fingers. You use
your fork like this—see?"

While Teresa ministered to the little girl, Francy
watched, half amused and half distressed. When she'd
been eleven, everyone had told her that she was going
to be the image of her gorgeous eighteen-year-old sister. Well, she knew that she looked a lot like Teresa had
in those days. Unfortunately, Teresa now bore hardly
any resemblance to her younger self. The past ten years
had been hard on everyone in the Rasera family, but on
the eldest daughter it really showed.

Childbearing and just plain lack of interest had made
Teresa's body thick and shapeless. Disappointment in
a marriage gone sour and the apathy that resulted had
remodeled the contours of her once lovely face. Long
ago her handsome dark eyes had lost their sparkle.
Where once she had been ready to take on the world,
her interests now were confined to housework, coping
with her boisterous children and anesthetizing herself
with television soap operas and game shows.

Francy loved her older sister. It hurt to look across
the table and compare Teresa to the glowing young girl
she'd been on her wedding day twelve years earlier. It
also reinforced Francy's determination not to let the
same thing happen to herself. Long ago she had decided that she wanted to be a woman who could take
charge of her own life.

"So, what do you hear from Paul?" Teresa asked.

Mama smiled and reached into her pocket. "I got a letter just the other day."

She passed it across the table and Teresa put down her fork so that she could glance through it. "Great," she commented after scanning the neatly typed lines. "He just performed successful open-heart surgery on Vera Cechetti, the famous opera singer. And he and that snooty Boston socialite wife of his have season tickets to the ballet." Teresa lifted her palms and rolled her eyes ceilingward. "Very cultural. What is it with this family? Paul went to Harvard on a scholarship, and the way he writes you need a dictionary to make it through one of his letters. Yet Francy here, who as far as I'm concerned has more brains than all of us put together, was never able to learn how to read a word and can hardly write her name. It doesn't make sense."

Shrugging, Mama reclaimed the letter. "Paul takes after me. Francy is more like her papa. God knows my Louis was a smart, wonderful man—kind and good and a real artist in his way, too. Yet he could never read a word. It was some kind of a..." She waved her hand in the air, at a loss for the correct term.

"A learning disability," Francy supplied. Though she'd winced when Teresa had brought up the subject of her reading problem, she knew that her older sister had no idea how sensitive she was about her failures and meant no harm. "The Rasera curse," Francy muttered. For that was how she thought of the humiliating inability that had plagued both her and her father.

"If it's a curse, thank God I haven't got it, and neither do any of my kids," Teresa said, complacently spearing a meatball. "Mike and Jenny are doing great in school. Aren't you guys?"

"Yeah, Ma," eleven-year-old Mike agreed between forkfuls. His nine-year-old sister's mouth was already full, so she merely nodded her agreement and smiled sweetly.

"And what about this little devil?" Josephine asked, pinching six-year-old Jerry's plump cheek. "How's he doing?"

Teresa shrugged. "Okay, I guess. You're doing okay, aren't you, Jerry?"

"Yeah, sure." The curly-haired little boy concentrated on his plate, his long black lashes hooding the expression in his dark eyes.

Francy adored all her sister's children, but Jerry was her favorite. It was just after Rosy's birth, when Jerry was barely a year old, that Teresa's troubles with her husband had come to a head and they'd separated. Prostrate with misery, Teresa hadn't been in any shape to do more than care for her newborn, so Francy had taken over with Jerry. She'd gotten up in the middle of the night with him, fed him, changed his diapers, rocked him to sleep and made sure that he got all the love and affection that his mother was too preoccupied to give him.

Since that time Francy had always had a special bond with the youngster. Lately she'd sensed that something was bothering Jerry. Now she studied his lowered head, a worried little frown creasing the skin between her eyebrows. First grade had been a crisis in her life, she recalled. That was when she had realized that she was different from the other kids—that there was something important they could do and she couldn't. Could Jerry be having similar troubles? *Oh, surely Teresa would know if he were,* she told herself. Still, she decided to talk to him as soon as possible, that night if she could find the opportunity.

An hour later, after Francy and Teresa had washed up in the kitchen and Teresa had joined their mother and the other children in the living room to watch their favorite TV shows, Jerry tapped Francy on the elbow.

"Aunt Francy?"

"Yes, honey." She paused with her foot on the first step of the narrow staircase.

"Where are you going?"

"Up to my room. I've got some new tapes to listen to."

Jerry cocked his head. "Don't you like television?"

"I like it okay, but there are other things I like better." She reached down and took his hand. "Want to come up with me? While I listen to my tapes we could play a game of checkers."

Jerry flashed her a big grin. "Okay, that sounds neat."

Upstairs Francy opened her door, flicked on the overhead light and beckoned the little boy in. Her room was small, but it was special. The rest of the house had been decorated in her mother's taste, which ran to heavy mahogany furniture and rather florid colors. Francy's private hideaway was different.

The color scheme had been dictated by a piece of stained glass she'd found in a flea market and mounted in her window. The subtle blues and pale golds in its geometrical pattern were echoed by the wallpaper, which had a rich cream background flecked with tiny flowers and finished with a gold design border. For her balloon curtains, slipcovered easy chair and bedspread she'd chosen a coordinating dark blue floral. The effect was cool and elegantly feminine.

"Your room is so pretty," Jerry commented admiringly. "Just like you are."

"Why, thanks, Jerry." Francy gave his ebony curls a friendly tousle. "How about you set up the checkers on the bed while I get my tape going?"

"Okay," the youngster agreed. Since they'd played many times before he knew where the game was kept and went to get it.

Meanwhile, Francy dug her library tapes out of her bag. Too bad she'd only taken Shakespeare this time, she thought. At six years of age, Jerry would probably have preferred something else. On the other hand, now that she'd gotten the hang of Shakespeare and had even memorized many of his lines, she was anxious to hear all his works.

"How come you like to listen to that stuff?" her nephew inquired when the tape was going and they'd settled down to begin their game.

"Because the stories are exciting and the language is beautiful," said Francy. "Just listen to what the king is saying." She paused and then quoted, " 'The edge of war, like an ill-sheathed knife, no more shall cut his master.' Aren't those wonderful words?"

"Yeah, I guess," Jerry muttered and appropriated two of her red checkers.

"Someday you'll be able to read all of Shakespeare's plays."

"I don't care about reading. The stuff in books is dumb."

"Jerry!" Francy's eyebrows snapped together. Absentmindedly she jumped one of his men and plucked it off the board. "There are wonderful things in books. Sometimes I feel as if the whole world is locked up in books where I can't get at it."

"Then why don't you go read them?" Jerry demanded.

"Because I can't. Don't you think I would if I could? Believe me, I'd give anything to read. But when I was your age in school and they tried to teach me, I couldn't learn. And believe me, I tried."

"School is dumb. I hate it," Jerry declared. "I wish I could drop out."

Francy studied her young nephew with a growing feeling of alarm. Though he was scowling down at the checkerboard, she knew he wasn't really thinking about the game. "Is there something wrong in school?"

"Nah."

She reached out and nudged his tense little shoulder. "This is your Aunt Francy asking, Jer. You having trouble with any of your studies?"

He hung his head. "Maybe a little."

"What does your teacher say?"

"Miss Taylor hates me."

"No one could hate you. Tell me what she says."

"Just that I'm not concentrating."

"Have you told your mom about this? Has she talked to your teacher?"

"I didn't give her any of Miss Taylor's notes."

"Jerry!" Francy cupped his chin in her palm and lifted it so that his big eyes met hers.

"Mom is too busy taking care of us kids to go to school and talk to Miss Taylor," he mumbled. "Besides, Mom gets mad if she misses her TV shows."

Francy couldn't help feeling a little shocked by this remark. She knew Teresa had let herself slip into a rut, but surely it wasn't so bad that even her six-year-old had noticed. "The only thing your mother might get mad about is that you didn't show her your teacher's notes or tell her that you were having problems.''

Though Jerry didn't answer, the misery in his expressive eyes and drooping shoulders made Francy's heart ache. "Jerry, listen, hon. Don't you worry. I'll talk to your mom about this. And if she can't find time to get to your school, I will. How's that?"

He shrugged and looked away. "Okay, I guess."

Ignoring his I-don't-care act, Francy leaned forward and gave him a big hug.

"Hey," he protested, "you're messing up the checkerboard."

"Sorry about that. Guess we'll have to start all over from scratch."

"Just when I was winning," Jerry said with a grimace. But despite his complaints, he looked happier and more at ease now than he had a few minutes before.

While he rearranged the game board, Francy switched off the tape player. "I'll save Shakespeare for later. How about a little music?"

"Yeah."

"What would you like to hear?"

"Madonna."

"Sorry, sport. Best I can do is some vintage Beatles."

Half an hour later the muted strains of "Norwegian Wood" played in the background and they were deep in their game. After Francy beat Jerry, they started a new game and she let him beat her. She had lost all track of time when Mama's voice echoed in the stairwell.

"How about we all have some ice cream in the living room while we watch the evening news?"

"Hey, yeah!" Jerry yelled and scrambled off the bed so quickly that he sent the checkers flying. While he raced out the door Francy glanced down at her watch and was surprised to see that it was ten o'clock. "Almost my bedtime," she muttered as she got to her feet, stretched and headed toward the hall.

Downstairs in the cluttered little living room Mama, Teresa and the kids were already sinking their spoons into heaping bowlfuls of Heavenly Hash.

"There's some left for you in the freezer," Mama said when Francy strolled in.

"No, thanks. I've got to watch my figure." Francy found a spot next to Jerry on the couch and focused her attention on the television set where scenes of a row house fire were being shown.

"Thank heaven my figure-watching days are over," Teresa muttered, taking an extra large gob of the gooey frozen treat she was eating.

Francy eyed her sister. "Why do you say that? Why shouldn't you be watching your figure now just as much as before?"

"Isn't it obvious? The only reason to diet and primp is to attract a man. Since it's too late for me to do that, I can relax."

Francy scowled. "There are other reasons for taking care of yourself than attracting men. And even if there weren't, why is it too late for you? You talk as if you're ready for the old-age home when you're only thirty-two."

"Age is just part of it," Teresa argued stubbornly. "What man is going to be interested in a woman with four kids?"

"Kids don't scare everybody. There are a lot of men who'd find you attractive if you'd just make an effort," Mama interjected.

Teresa snorted and pointed her spoon at the television screen. "Oh, yeah? Well, the day a hunk like that guy calls for a date is the day I'll go on a diet."

After throwing up her hands to express her frustration, Francy returned her gaze to the local news show to see who Teresa was talking about. The image that greeted her made her jaw sag and her eyes widen.

"Another stunning victory for Howard County's crusading young prosecutor," the newscaster intoned as Adam Pearce, looking for all the world like a young god in a gray flannel suit, stood on the steps of a courthouse with the sun glinting off his windblown hair.

Casually and good-humoredly he fielded reporters' questions. "I think that justice has been done at last," he told one newsman. And, "No, I have no immediate plans to run for any other office," he assured another.

"Hey, Francy," Mama said when the story was over. "That isn't by any chance the same Adam Pearce who called you this afternoon?"

With an effort Francy cleared her throat. "Same guy, Ma," she managed to croak.

# CHAPTER THREE

FRANCY CHECKED HER WATCH. She had plenty of time to make it to Adam Pearce's place—even if this conference with Jerry's teacher lasted an hour. With a last glance at the bus stop where she intended to catch a ride out to Catonsville later in the afternoon, she turned up the cement walk that led to St. Edward's.

*This place gives me the creeps,* she thought as she walked into the old brick elementary school where she'd been a student herself. Maybe other people felt a pleasant nostalgia when they revisited their grade school. Francy felt sick.

Turning right, she made her way along the polished tile corridor with its lining of pint-size green metal lockers. Even the smells were the same—chalk, old wax and the evocative fragrance of bologna sandwiches confined too long in damp paper bags.

Heading for the room where Miss Taylor taught first grade, Francy was glad that she wasn't wearing jeans. When she'd topped her narrow gray linen skirt with a cream-colored blouse under a red sweater vest, she'd told herself that she was dressing up for Jerry's teacher and not Adam Pearce. Then she hadn't quite believed herself. Now she did. For this interview, she was going to need all the confidence she could get.

"Mrs. D'Alessio?" Miss Taylor, who was sitting at her desk glancing through some papers, looked up at Francy and smiled tentatively.

"No, I'm Miss Rasera, Jerry's aunt. My sister was going to come, but yesterday she came down with the flu. So, she's home in bed and I'm here."

The lay teacher, a pleasant young woman with short brown hair and metal-rimmed glasses, looked uncertain. "When your sister called, she said she wanted to discuss Jerry's progress."

"Yes." Francy dropped her bag and shoehorned herself sideways into one of the student desks. She'd forgotten how small they were. Sitting in one brought back vivid memories of a little girl, helpless and tongue-tied with misery as she huddled before a baffled nun who couldn't understand why she kept reading what sounded like gibberish. "How's Jerry doing?" she asked.

"I did send several notes home with him."

"Yes, but those never reached us."

Miss Taylor's mouth turned down at the corners. "I see."

"Jerry's only six years old," Francy said rather defensively, "and he's scared."

The teacher blinked. "There's nothing to be frightened of here in first grade."

"For some kids I think maybe there is," Francy commented dryly. "Tell me about Jerry."

The other young woman began to seesaw her pencil back and forth between her neatly manicured fingers. "Well, for a while, I thought he was very shy. He was quiet as a mouse and would start to cry whenever he was called on. But now I'm beginning to wonder if he doesn't have a problem with hyperactivity."

"Hyperactivity?"

"Yes, obviously he's a very bright little boy, but his attention span just isn't what it should be, and he's not keeping up. I'd certainly hate to hold him back from second grade, but he's really not ready to do second-grade work. Here, let me show you." Miss Taylor pulled out a couple of pieces of paper from the pile on her desk. "Tuesday the kids were asked to copy some short sentences from the board. This is what I got back from Jerry, and this other was done by one of the little girls who completed the assignment correctly. As you can see, Jerry's letters are very malformed and he's got the words so garbled that they're unrecognizable."

Francy stared down at the two examples. Even she could see that her nephew's blotched scribblings looked all wrong. With some trepidation, she faced Jerry's teacher. "Miss Taylor, if Jerry isn't doing good work in your class, it's not because he's hyperactive or—or un-motivated. It's something else." As Miss Taylor arched an eyebrow, Francy took a deep breath. "Let me tell you about my father and about what happened to me when I went to school here."

It wasn't easy for Francy to admit to this bespecta-cled young woman that she couldn't read, nor was it pleasant to unearth childhood memories of confusion, failure and humiliation. Those were things she'd spent the last ten years doing her damnedest to overcome. But for her nephew's sake, Francy let it all spill out. When she finished, Jerry's teacher looked stunned.

"You mean you still can't read?"

Francy shook her head. "Oh, simple things, you know. I can pick out words like in, out, entrance, exit, bar, restaurant. And I can identify the ladies' room and find hamburger and coffee on a menu. But I couldn't begin to read a book, or even a newspaper article."

"Well, that certainly does shed a different light on Jerry's problems." Miss Taylor frowned. "It sounds as if you and your nephew have a learning disability. I'll have him tested by the psychologist."

"Psychologist?"

"That's the first step in diagnosing a problem like dyslexia," Miss Taylor explained.

"Thank you," Francy told her a little doubtfully.

Now, forty-five minutes later as the bus jounced along Frederick Road, heading west to the end of the line, Francy muttered the word "dyslexia" under her breath. She'd heard it used before in connection with her own problem. Maybe she still wasn't quite sure about its technical definition. But one thing she knew it meant was that she, and now probably Jerry, were different from everyone else, different in a way that made life in a big city one heck of a tough proposition.

Take this trip out to Adam Pearce's place. Francy knew Baltimore's neighborhoods and could go most anywhere she wanted on one of the city buses. But Adam Pearce lived west of Catonsville, which meant she was going to have to do some walking and hope against hope that she didn't get lost.

Teresa had looked his address up on the map and described how to find it. And Francy had memorized her directions along with his street name and number. But it was unfamiliar territory and it wasn't as if she could look it up on a map for herself. If somehow she got turned around, she'd be out of luck.

Luck was with her, however, and, after checking the rings she wore on each of her hands—the red stone for left and the blue stone for right—she turned down a shady street and found the place just where Teresa had told her it would be. It was a big old Victorian house that had been converted into apartments. As Francy climbed the steps to the wraparound veranda, she studied the fanlight over the oak front door appreciatively. Then, realizing that there was yet another ordeal to get past, she peered down at the typed names under the various buzzers to one side of the door. Which one belonged to Mr. Adam Pearce?

Again, luck was with her. Just as she stood debating between buzzing apartment number three and apartment number five, a low-slung black sports car pulled up to the curb and Adam Pearce got out of it. With his gaze fixed on her, he quickly strode up the front walk.

"Hi, there. Have you been waiting long?"

"No, I just got here."

"I was delayed at the office. Something I couldn't help. All the way home I worried I might miss you."

He wasn't lying. She could see from the expression on his face that he really had worried. He stood next to her now, close enough so that she had to arch her neck slightly to look at him. His eyes were just as blue, his features just as ruggedly patrician, as she had remembered. As a kid he must have been a towhead. Now his hair was a color that made her think of autumn leaves and crisp weather. Embarrassed by the mushy train her thoughts were taking, Francy dropped her gaze and glanced around the yard.

"It's nice around here," she said. "The dogwood and azaleas are really something."

"Yes, we've been having a pretty spring," he replied without taking his eyes off her averted profile. Fishing out his keys, he let her into the downstairs hall. "My apartment's this one on the left." He unlocked it and pushed open the door. "I hope I didn't leave it in too much of a mess."

"Don't worry about messes. They've never bothered me."

His living room wasn't untidy, though. In fact it was so painfully neat and uncluttered that she suspected he must have had a cleaning lady in the night before and not touched it with human hands since. "This is the room you want to do something with?"

"Yes."

Francy walked to the center of the polished strip oak floor and did a slow turn, pausing to study the old-fashioned double-hung windows with their varnished woodwork and the brick fireplace in the opposite corner. Hands on his trim hips, Adam stood behind her. When she was facing him again, he smiled. "Can I get you something to drink?"

"No, thanks."

"Not even a cup of coffee or a cola? What about a glass of ice water?"

It had been a long bus ride out here, and Francy really was thirsty. "Ice water would be good, thank you."

"Coming right up."

As he walked out of the room, Francy's dark eyes followed him warily. Just how was this going to turn out, and exactly what did he have in mind? In her business she didn't usually have to deal with men. Women were the ones who liked to redecorate. Not that his place couldn't use it. She glanced at the worn sofa and the pair of shabby leather wing chairs in front of the fireplace. Then she crossed to the windows. The drapes were so faded by the sun that it was hard to guess what their original color might have been—maroon, maybe? Two steps to the right brought her up short in front of

a floor-to-ceiling bookcase. It was packed with fat, inscrutable tomes, which she wished she could identify.
*This guy must be very brainy,* Francy thought. His library looked as if it had been brought down from the
mountaintop by Moses right along with the Ten Com-
mandments.

"It's not as bad as it appears. Dusty old law books
are not what I read for pleasure."

"What?" Startled, Francy looked over her shoulder
and then blushed guiltily. Adam was coming toward her
with a cut-glass tumbler in which ice tinkled invitingly.
In his other hand he held a coffee mug.

"I keep those reference books here because sometimes when I'm working at home I need to use them,"
he explained. "But if you're looking for a key to my
personality, you should check out the shelves next to the
fireplace before you give up on me. Those have some
real literature on them. Shakespeare even."

"Shakespeare even? You mean 'The elegance, facil-
ity, and golden cadence of poesy?'" At Adam's blank
look, she added, "That's a line from *Love's Labour's
Lost.*"

He lifted an eyebrow. "I'm impressed."

"Don't be. I have something very close to a photo-
graphic memory." Which was what you needed for
survival if you couldn't read, Francy thought, secretly
pleased at being able to dredge up that line from a tape
she'd been listening to the previous evening. Accepting
the ice water, she took a sip. "I know that you're a
lawyer," she volunteered. "I saw you on television the
other night. They called you by a fancy title."

"State's Attorney for Howard County?" He grinned.
"But don't you be too impressed. All it means is that I

get smaller paychecks and dirtier jobs than anyone else who graduated from law school in my class.''

Francy eyed him curiously. "I think it must mean more than that. Were you elected?''

"Yes.''

"Well, that's pretty impressive, isn't it?''

He shrugged. "Maybe, maybe not. I'd like to think I was voted in because of my excellent qualifications. But I suspect that family name had something to do with it. The Pearces have lived in Howard County and dabbled in local politics for over a century.''

It figured, Francy thought. He looked like the kind of guy who came from an old family with money. Not that her family wasn't old. The Raseras went back to the Renaissance when they'd been artisans in Florence. Money, however, was another matter. She continued to study Adam, absorbing the unconscious aura of confidence he gave off—half attracted by it, half resenting it. She wouldn't be surprised one bit if he'd grown up on a country estate with picture-perfect horses grazing behind spotless white rail fences. To Francy, who'd spent her twenty-five years in the concrete heart of the city, a life in a setting like that seemed about as alien as a picnic on Mars.

"Well, anyway," she said aloud, "you must be doing a pretty good job or they wouldn't be singing your praises on television. Congratulations." She lifted her water glass to his coffee mug and then waved her free hand at the draperies behind the sofa. "Now, what did you have in mind for me to do here?''

For the first time Adam looked slightly uneasy. Shifting his weight, he glanced around his living room. "I'm not exactly sure. I guess I was hoping you'd tell me. What do you think the place needs?''

The phrase "a complete overhaul" hovered on the tip of Francy's tongue. But she bit it back and said instead, "Well, it's not decorated at all, if you know what I mean. But it's up to you how far you want to go. For starters, you could just get new drapes and recover your sofa. That wouldn't cost too much."

"I think the cost is something I can handle. What would you do if this were your place?"

Francy glanced at him warily. Was he telling her that money was no object? She cleared her throat. "If I had a free hand and some leeway in my budget, I'd repaint and paper a couple of walls for texture. Of course, that couch needs reupholstering. Then I'd give the windows a different treatment and add one or two new pieces of furniture." She made a sweeping gesture. "You have to admit that what you've got here is kind of sparse."

"Point taken." Chuckling, Adam pushed back his open linen herringbone jacket and slipped one hand into his trousers pocket. Francy couldn't help notice how flat his belly was and how trim his hips were in contrast to his broad shoulders. Dragging her eyes away from him, she fixed her gaze on the small Oriental rug in front of the fireplace. It was old and rather frayed around the edges, but she could see that it was good. Francy had an eye for such things. Did he buy it himself, she wondered, or was it a family castoff? Most likely the latter, she guessed. The Pearces probably stuffed treasures like that away in their attic and forgot they even had them.

"I guess from the looks of this place, it's pretty obvious to you that I'm a bachelor," Adam was saying.

Francy snapped her gaze back to his. Something in the way his blue eyes crinkled around the corners told her that he was looking for more than a purely professional response. Better squash any fanciful thoughts right away, she decided. Aloud, she said, "I knew that you were a bachelor when I saw you in Miss Kains's apartment. No wife would stand for her husband having drinks alone with such a beautiful woman."

As she had expected it would, Adam's smile slipped slightly. "Barbara and I are old friends. Our parents have known each other for years."

"You're certainly lucky to have a classy lady like that for a friend," Francy returned primly. "She's been very nice to me. A lot of my referrals have come through her, and I'm very grateful."

"I see." Adam started to cross toward the chairs in front of the fireplace. "Why don't we sit down and talk some business?"

"Sure."

When they were both ensconced and facing each other over the rug Francy had been admiring a moment earlier, Adam said, "I'd like you to go ahead and redo the whole room."

Francy blinked. "You mean, do all the things I said—paint, paper, new curtains, the whole works?"

When he nodded, she felt a small knot of excitement in her stomach and took a deep breath to steady herself. This was the kind of job she'd been dreaming about landing—one where she wouldn't be just sewing up drapes or recovering a piece of worn-out furniture, but actually decorating. It opened up all kinds of possibilities. She could bring a camera and take before and after pictures that would be useful demonstrations for future sales. It would be a chance to show what she could really do and a step toward the kind of jobs she would want to take on if she opened a full-service shop.

On the other hand, if she were redoing his place rather than just getting a few measurements for piece-work that she could take home with her, this would have to be one of several visits. It would be necessary to see quite a bit of Mr. Adam Pearce, something her instincts told her might not be such a great idea. For though he'd been the soul of polite discretion thus far, she knew he was offering her this job because he was interested in her. But then again, she could be wrong, couldn't she? And if she wasn't, that was his problem, not hers, right?

"Well, thanks," she said, "but if you're really serious, there are some things we need to discuss."

Adam balanced his coffee cup on his knee. "Fire away."

"Budget, for one thing. How much money did you plan on spending?"

"That's up to you."

"I'd rather you gave me your price range. That way I know what I have to work with."

"All right." Casually he named a figure that made her eyes widen.

"That sounds more than adequate. I'm sure we'll be able to transform this place. But how would you like it changed?"

"What do you mean?"

"I mean, what sort of look do you feel comfortable with?"

His blank expression was almost comical. Adam Pearce might be a whiz in the courtroom, but clearly when it came to making his own apartment livable, he was out of his depth.

"Let's start with colors," Francy suggested. "What are your favorite colors?"

He gazed into her eyes. "Brown is nice."

Francy refused to bite. "Brown can make a nice neutral background, but you'll want something to go with it. Name another color you like."

As he took a thoughtful sip of his coffee, his clear blue gaze continued to play over her. "Red is good."

It took an act of will for Francy not to look down at the way her red sweater vest molded her breasts, then dipped in where it was belted at her waist before it flared out softly over her hips. Under her gray linen skirt her stockinged legs rustled faintly as she shifted in the chair and recrossed them. "Red and brown. Well, that's something to work with. I think I have an idea what style of furnishings appeals to you. Tell you what. I'll select some fabric and wallpaper samples and bring them out for your approval in about a week's time. Does that sound okay?"

"That sounds fine," Adam said, setting his coffee cup down on the hearth and rising to his feet just as she began to do the same. He held out his right hand.

There was no way she could avoid the handshake. Besides, she was half-curious to know if Adam Pearce felt as good as he looked.

If his skin had been cold and clammy, she would have been relieved. It wasn't, of course. As he enfolded Francy's small hand in his, his grip, warm and firm, lingered long enough to let her know that she hadn't been imagining things. He didn't just like her for her slipcovers.

"Well, now that we've finished our business, do you have to go right away?" he asked. He consulted his watch. "It's almost dinner time, and since I haven't got anything in the house, I'm going to have to go out, anyway. Won't you join me? We could talk some more about my favorite colors over a good meal."

It was tempting, very tempting. But Francy had promised herself that she wouldn't make any foolish mistakes. This guy was not for her. "No, I have to get back." She made a show of checking her own watch. "You're right about the time. If I'm going to catch the six o'clock bus back into town, I'd better hurry."

"You took the bus out here?"

"I take the bus everywhere. I don't drive."

He looked shocked. "But the line doesn't even run out this far, does it?"

She shrugged. "Four blocks. That's not much. I'm used to walking."

"I had no idea that getting out here would be such an ordeal for you." He glanced down at her feet, which instead of being encased in her customary sneakers sported a pair of high-heeled dress shoes.

Francy felt her cheeks begin to glow. It had been crazy to wear such impractical shoes when she'd known she would be doing some hiking. Other than that they made her feet and legs look tremendously sexy, she had absolutely no justification for them.

"It doesn't look to me as if you could make it more than a block on those. At least let me give you a lift to the bus stop."

Still, Francy hesitated.

"Come on," he said, scooping his car keys up off the battered coffee table, "it's on the way to that restaurant, anyway."

It was really impossible to say no, Francy told herself as she let him guide her out the door and down the walk to his black Mazda. Besides, what could it hurt?

But when she had settled into the Mazda's cushiony interior, she knew that if she wanted to keep the atmosphere between herself and this dishy client professional, accepting the ride had been a mistake. There was something undeniably intimate about half-reclining in a sports car's cozy space with an attractive man. "Very nice car," she said as he slid in behind the wheel next to her.

"Thanks." After he turned on the ignition, he reached over to adjust the gear shift, his fingers coming within fractions of an inch of Francy's stockinged knee. Though Francy managed not to shrink back, she felt her neck go warm. Thank heavens Adam didn't appear to be aware of the effect he was having on her. "My hat is off to anyone who can get around without a car these days," he said as he pulled away from the curb.

"It's not so bad. You'd be surprised what you can do when you don't have much choice."

"I suppose you're right." Glancing over at her, he failed to notice that another car, fifty yards down the block, was pulling away as well. And during the five-minute drive to Francy's bus stop, Adam didn't notice that the other car kept pace with him.

"Are you sure you won't reconsider about dinner?" Adam asked as he stopped to let her out.

But with her hand on the door handle, Francy shook her head. "No, thanks. But you have yourself a nice meal."

*Sure,* Adam thought as once again he pulled away from the curb. In his rearview mirror he glanced back at Francy. She wasn't watching him. Instead, she had her head turned the other way, to where a city bus was looming into view two blocks down the road. He couldn't allow his gaze to linger long, but in the split second before he returned his attention to his driving her image burned itself into his memory—the glossy curls spilling around her shoulders, the slim, curvy little figure, elegant now in her different clothes and with her legs shown off by the sexy shoes.

He'd half hoped that when he saw her again he'd find that he wasn't interested anymore. *Thinking about asking Barbara to be my wife would probably have made me go off the deep end over any reasonably attractive female,* he'd told himself. *It was just my subconscious telling me that marriage to Barbara would be a big mistake.*

But now Adam knew it was more than that. The moment he'd seen Francy standing on his steps he'd recognized that she was just as special as he'd first imagined. And when she'd walked into his living room, he'd had no doubts at all. How much had he told her she could spend to fix the place up? Inside the car Adam's laughter boomed. "I must be out of my mind," he said out loud. Maybe, but money didn't seem to matter. All that mattered was getting to know Miss Francesca Rasera a whole lot better.

Trouble was, she didn't seem particularly eager to get to know him. Was she really as disinterested as she appeared, he wondered. She wore no wedding or engagement ring, but that didn't mean she didn't have someone. Maybe she thought he wasn't her type. After all, he'd thought the same about her. But not for long, he reminded himself with a rueful shake of his head. Not for long. Well, somehow he was just going to have to make sure that she didn't think it for long, either.

Instead of going to the restaurant where he'd wanted to dine with Francy, Adam picked up a hamburger, milk shake and French fries at a fast-food outlet and drove home. With the white bag of food sitting next to him in the passenger seat, he mulled over the problem of

Francy's strictly business attitude. She'd made a big thing about Barbara and how much she owed her. Had she refused his dinner invitation because she thought he was involved with Barbara? Well, up until very recently he had been, hadn't he? *I'd better go see Barbara and let her know exactly where I stand,* Adam decided as he parked the car in front of his apartment house. Frowning as he thought about this not-too-pleasant chore, he got out and carried his dinner up the walk to the front porch. Unaware of the car that had followed him to the bus stop, then to the fast-food chain and back to the street where he lived, he climbed the porch steps with his head down and a scowl digging a groove between his eyebrows.

## CHAPTER FOUR

SEVERAL DAYS LATER Adam's black sports car took the curves and climbed the hills that dipped softly into wooded valleys ablaze with white dogwood. Considering all the development going on in Howard County, a few years from now there weren't going to be many unspoiled roads like this one left, he mused. The thought saddened him. He loved the verdant Maryland countryside.

Slowing at the next bend, he put on his signal and swung left into a tree-lined entrance that would have been all but invisible to anyone who hadn't known that it led to Spruce Valley Farm.

Four generations of Pearces had been born, lived out their lives and died under the sharply pitched roof of Spruce Valley Farm's main house. An eighth of a mile past the gate the trees ended and Adam's car purred along the open road past a checkerboard vista of orchards and rolling fields dotted by peacefully grazing mares and their frisky new colts.

The oak-shaded house stood at the end of a circular driveway, set at some distance from the barn and other outbuildings. A three-story pale-pink stucco architectural anomaly, it was decorated with a wealth of improbable Victorian gingerbread and topped by a pagoda-shaped tower with a widow's walk. Judge Zachariah Pearce, Adam's ancestor and the worthy gentleman who in 1856 had originally emigrated to the then wilds of Howard County and built the house, had had whimsical tastes.

"Hello, anyone around?" Adam called out after he had pulled his car to the side of the gravel driveway and climbed out. Pausing briefly at the back of the house to glance at the deserted pool, which glistened invitingly under the late-afternoon sun, he then pushed open the kitchen door and looked around. Judy, his mother's part-time cook, came rushing into the room. Judy had known and felt free to scold Adam since he was a gap-toothed nine-year-old snitching freshly baked ginger snaps off her cookie trays.

"Where've you been?" she demanded. "Your mother is fit to be tied."

Adam checked his watch. "I'm only fifteen minutes late."

"Yes, but you don't keep a man like Ben Catlett waiting. That kind of man doesn't wait on anybody."

"Oh, Lord, I suppose that's his Mercedes out front," Adam said with a grimace. Shooting Judy a brief salute, he made his way down the center hall to the east parlor. There, in a sunny corner by the lace-curtained windows, he found his mother and her distinguished guest.

Patricia Pearce was a handsome woman. She was tall and regally slender, and her pale gold hair was artfully arranged around her face. She wore a blue silk shirt-waist, which like everything around her, struck exactly the right note of relaxed elegance.

The man she entertained presented a sharp contrast. Short, with thick shoulders, a tough, pugnacious face and a bald, bullet-shaped head, there was nothing casual or elegant about him. Despite his expensive hand-tailored suit he looked absurdly out of place in the fragile cabriolet armchair upholstered in pale green, pink and cream silk on which he seemed to perch uneasily.

"Mr. Catlett?" Adam said after he had greeted his mother. Holding out his hand, he strode across the room. "Sorry I'm late. The sheriff caught me on the way out of the office, and there was no way I could put him off."

"Don't worry about it. I've been enjoying talking to Patricia. Your mother is a very interesting and intelligent woman."

As the two men shook hands, Catlett's shrewd gray eyes swept over Adam assessingly. Adam did his best not to let the other man's inspection unnerve him. But in the space of thirty seconds he felt as if he'd been taken apart and put back together again. And he didn't much care for the experience.

After Adam had fixed himself a Scotch on the rocks and they'd all exchanged a few pleasantries about the beautiful spring weather, Catlett got down to business.

"I'm sure Pat has told you why I wanted to meet you."

Adam glanced briefly at his mother. "Yes, sir. She said you were interested in discussing the possibility of my running for Congress."

"We're both so pleased and flattered that you might consider managing his campaign," Patricia put in.

Catlett's eyes were fixed on Adam's face and missed nothing. "I'd like to hear what Adam has to say about the idea."

Adam swirled the ice in his glass. "Well, my mother's certainly right about the flattered part. It's a great compliment to have a man with your reputation take an interest in my career.''

"Fine, but it's not my interest that counts. It's yours," Catlett stated baldly. "Pearce, so far you've done very well for yourself. A lot of young men with your looks and money would be lolling around a pool between tennis matches or devoting their lives to improving their golf swing. Instead, you've graduated with honors from Harvard Law School, distinguished yourself as a criminal lawyer with a very prestigious law firm and racked up a truly impressive record as State's Attorney for Howard County. Have you decided where you want to go from there?"

"No, I haven't," Adam answered candidly.

"You must have had some political ambitions when you ran for county office."

Adam considered that. "I thought I would make a good State's Attorney, and I think I have. But that's a long way from wanting to go to Washington."

"Yes, it is," Catlett agreed. "And winning a Congressional campaign won't be easy. Though with Rand retiring next year, you'd have a better chance than might otherwise be the case—especially with all the favorable media coverage you've been getting lately." He steepled his thick fingers over his knee. "But strategy is not what I'm here to discuss. As I'm sure you've guessed, I wouldn't be sitting in this chair if I didn't think you had a chance to win. It's your opinion that really matters, though. I need to know whether or not you're willing to make a commitment to a long, tough, uphill battle to get elected to a seat in the U.S. Congress. Because if you're not, I might as well be on my way."

While Patricia looked tensely from one man to the other, Catlett set down his half-finished drink and waited for Adam's response.

Balancing his own drink between his cupped hands, Adam leaned forward in his chair and regarded the man across from him. Catlett would make one hell of a used-car salesman, he mused. But he refused to allow himself to be pressured—not over a decision as big as this one. "I'm afraid I can't give you an answer this afternoon," he said. "I need to do some thinking."

"Then do it." Catlett stood and reached into his pocket for a card. After scribbling a telephone number on the back, he handed it to Adam. "But don't take more than forty-eight hours," he warned. "That's how much longer I'm going to be in the Washington area."

Adam looked down at the card and then up into Catlett's blunt-featured face. "All right," he agreed. "I'll call you before tomorrow night."

Still, Catlett stood there eyeing him thoughtfully. "You know, I haven't been entirely honest with you," he suddenly said.

"Oh?"

"It's not just your record and your recent good publicity that intrigue me and the party leaders in this state enough to make us think you could be a winner."

"No."

"Unless I'm much mistaken, Pearce, you're a genuine Sir Lancelot, and that's a rare type in this day and age."

"Sir Lancelot?" Adam didn't know what to say. "I'm flattered, but I don't think anyone else sees me as a knight in shining armor."

"That's where you're wrong. The cleanup you've been conducting in this county is tempered by the sense that you have no personal axes to grind. You're that rare thing, a man who grasps at power because he wants to use it as a tool for justice and who, without the justice, doesn't give a damn about the power. If I and my friends in the party sense that purity of purpose about you, that integrity, I think the voters will, too. These are times when a knight in shining armor coming down the road would be a very welcome sight."

A few minutes later Ben Catlett was gone. As the throaty roar of his Mercedes Benz receded down the driveway, Patricia Pearce eyed her son. "For heaven's sake, why wouldn't you give the man an answer here and now?"

"Because I don't yet know what the answer is. I wasn't being coy, Mother. I'm really not sure what I want to do."

Exasperated, Patricia got to her feet. "Really, Adam, you know as well as I do that you were born to lead. Catlett was right about you. Ever since you were a little boy, you've been determined to fix the world. You don't really imagine that you'll be content to stay in Howard County prosecuting petty criminals for the rest of your professional life, do you?"

"Some of the criminals I've put behind bars haven't been so petty. This Johnston guy, for instance, was a real cold-blooded type. And I'm dealing with a case now that would make your hair stand on end."

"The child-abuse thing?"

"Yes."

"All right, but most of these messes you untangle are small potatoes. Howard County isn't exactly the crime center of the East Coast. You need more of a challenge."

"I'm not so sure of that. So far I've been content with the way things are."

Patricia dropped two cubes from the silver ice bucket into her drink and declared sternly. "Really, Adam, stop playing games. I know you. You could never be content to stay where you are. This is not an opportunity you can pass up."

"You could be right. But it's a big step and I'll have to think about it."

"Stubborn," Patricia muttered under her breath, and then shot her son a narrow-eyed look. "Speaking of which, what's going on between you and Barbara?"

Startled by the abrupt change of subject, Adam gazed at her warily. "Why do you ask?"

"Because she invited me to lunch yesterday and started pumping me about you. What's Adam up to? That sort of thing. Good Lord, I expected her to know the answer to that question better than I. So maybe you'd better tell me what's going on. Have you two quarreled?"

"No." Adam walked to the window. "I've stopped seeing Barbara."

Patricia's jaw dropped. "Stopped seeing her? Why?"

"Because I realized that our relationship wasn't going anywhere for me, and I decided it wasn't fair to take up any more of her time." He sighed. "I tried explaining that to her as diplomatically as I could. I guess she didn't understand."

"Oh, I think she understood. She just isn't ready to accept it yet. And neither am I." Rapidly Patricia crossed to where her son stood staring moodily out at the front lawn. "What's gotten into you? This isn't like you, Adam. Barbara is a lovely young woman who would make you a perfect wife. How can you treat her so shabbily?"

"I'm not proud of it," Adam admitted. "In fact, I feel guilty as hell. But I didn't have much choice."

Patricia circled around so that she could look her son in the eye. "Choice? What are you talking about? A few days ago I expected you and Barbara to get married and give me some grandchildren. What happened to make you act like this?" Her eyebrows snapped together. "Have you met another woman?"

Adam's jaw squared. "Mother, this is not really something I care to discuss."

"You have, haven't you! Who is she? What's her name? Where does she come from?"

"Why do I feel like I'm being grilled?" Adam queried irritably. "All right, yes, I've met someone. But I don't intend to give you her pedigree."

"If you were willing to dump Barbara because of this woman, you must know something about her. What's her family like?"

Adam set his empty glass down with a clink, pushed back the front panels of his sport coat and thrust his hands into his pants pockets. "All I know is that they're Italian."

"Italian?"

"And they live in Little Italy," he added, suddenly enjoying himself.

"Little Italy?"

"Yes, and they make slipcovers."

"Slipcovers? Slipcovers!" Patricia crossed her arms over her chest. "Adam, it's not that I want to interfere in your personal life. But if you're going to run for Congress, you must be very careful about the people who are close to you. It's not only you the media will take an interest in. They'll want to know all about your love life. You have to consider whether this young woman is really an appropriate companion."

Adam started to laugh. "As a matter of fact," he said, "I think she's very appropriate. Trouble is, she doesn't seem to see things my way."

Patricia stood, blinking. "What do you mean?"

"I mean you have nothing to worry about because so far the lady won't give me the time of day. Speaking of which—" Adam checked his watch. "It's getting late. I'd better be going."

"You won't stay for dinner?"

"Not tonight." Good humor suddenly restored, he dropped a light kiss on her scented cheek. "I need to think, and I need to do it on my own. I appreciate all your efforts on my behalf. And don't worry—whatever the right decision is for me, I'll do my damnedest to make it."

"See that you do. Adam, this is a turning point."

A quarter of an hour later, the black car was back on the road, smoothly eating up the miles. As the country air from the open windows fanned Adam's cheek and whipped through his gold-tinged hair, he reflected on what had just occurred at Spruce Valley.

Despite his initial resistance, he'd been impressed by Ben Catlett's blunt manner. With his extensive connections and background in state politics, the man had to know what he was talking about. "Decision time," Adam muttered. And this was a big one. "Just what do you really want to do with yourself, Pearce? Do you really want to be a leader of men? Do you really need to fix the world?"

It was tempting to say no, to tell himself that his mother was wrong and that he would always be happy with the kind of position he presently held. After all, the last few years as county prosecutor had been pretty rewarding, hadn't they?

Adam sighed. Yes, they'd been rewarding, but that was because of the things he'd been able to accomplish. Think of how much more he'd be able to do if he were in Congress. The possibilities opened out like an unfolding fan. Patricia Pearce wasn't the only ambitious one in the family. As usual, and much as he hated to admit it, she had his number. The more he thought about it, the more he realized that he couldn't let this chance slip by. If he did, he might be kicking himself for the rest of his life.

*Might as well call Catlett tonight,* he told himself. *No point in keeping the man waiting for another twenty-four hours when I already know the answer to his question. Yes, I want him to be my campaign manager. And yes, I do want to tip my lance at a few of those rotten windmills spinning around in that crazy world out there.*

"No wonder Jerry hates this place," Teresa commented as she and Francy walked down the hall toward the room where they were to meet the reading specialist, Mrs. Geddes. "Why don't they paint the walls a cheerful color instead of this dreadful green, for heaven's sake?"

"It's not the color of the walls," Francy said. "If poor little Jer is having the kind of experience that I had here, he'd hate it even if they had it fixed up like Disney World."

Teresa cast her younger sister a sympathetic glance. "You had a pretty rough time back then, I guess."

"You might say that," Francy said dryly. "You know how shy and self-conscious some six-year-olds are. Can you imagine standing up in front of a class and being asked to read when the marks on the page make no more sense to you than hen tracks? Before I started first grade I thought I was a pretty normal little kid. It came as a shock to find out that I wasn't. I'll never forget how I felt standing there with a book in my hands while I listened to the kids laugh at me. What a nightmare!"

"Yeah," Teresa agreed with a sigh. "But you never said much about it at home. And when you did, I know the folks didn't take it very seriously. They just figured you were like Pop and that school wasn't so important for a girl, anyhow."

Francy made a face. "All my life I've been trying to hide the fact that I can't read," she admitted. "In elementary school I led a life of crime, copying other people's papers, memorizing passages that we read over and over in class so that I could make it sound as if I was reading, too. And when none of those tricks worked, I was like Jerry and tore up the notes from the teacher. Lucky for him we found out early. Maybe if he's really got a problem, this lady, this reading specialist can do something."

"Well, I certainly hope so," Teresa declared. "But maybe there's nothing wrong. Maybe we're making a big deal out of nothing."

Mrs. Geddes was no older than Miss Taylor had been. A pretty redhead with a friendly smile, she got up from her desk when Francy and Teresa peered through her classroom door and introduced themselves.

"I have Jerry's test results right here," she said after she had shaken each of their hands and showed them to a seat. She tapped a pile of papers and then took one out from the bottom and handed it to Teresa. "Your Jerry is a very bright little boy, but I'm afraid there's no doubt that he's dyslexic." She leaned over and pointed at the line on the test page Teresa held. "Look at the way he's reversed those letters and keeps confusing b, p, d and g. That's a sure giveaway."

"But all kids do that sort of thing," Teresa protested.

"Yes," Miss Geddes agreed, "but not so consistently. I'm afraid that Jerry is going to have to work harder in school than other children do. But," she quickly added, "that doesn't mean he won't be able to learn everything he needs to know. With dyslexics it just all takes a little extra time and patience."

"Dyslexic," Teresa muttered. "What does it really mean, anyhow?"

The redheaded young woman hesitated. "Basically, it's the inability of otherwise normal children to read. For decades the affliction has been debated by psychologists, neurologists and educators, but it's generally agreed that it's the result of a neurophysiological flaw in the brain's ability to process language and that in a substantial number of cases it's probably inherited."

Teresa and Francy looked at each other. Then Teresa rubbed her forehead. "You mean there's something wrong with my son's brain?"

"Not in the way you're thinking," Mrs. Geddes assured her. "Jerry has a fine brain. In fact some of the most brilliant people in our western culture have been dyslexic—Yeats, Flaubert, Einstein, even Leonardo da Vinci. The dyslexic brain just works a little differently from the way most of ours do. Instead of the language center being on the right side only, Jerry's centers are located on both the right and the left. As a result, signals sometimes get crossed between the two the way they might in an overburdened switchboard.''

Francy listened intently. "That's just the way I felt when I was trying to read," she exclaimed. "As if everything was jammed up in my head and confused. Sometimes my head really hurt, and not because I had a headache." At Mrs. Geddes's interested look, Francy blushed and then shyly admitted that she had had learning problems in school and was still a nonreader. To her relief, the redheaded teacher appeared neither shocked nor horrified.

"Since Nancy Taylor told me about your situation, I've been anxious to meet you," she said frankly. "When you were in school there wasn't any help for dyslexics. In fact, the problem wasn't even recognized. You were probably told that you couldn't read because you were lazy and stupid, right?"

"Something like that," Francy agreed.

Mrs. Geddes gave her bright curls a distressed shake. "Well, thank heavens, we're not in the dark ages anymore, and all that's changed. I'm going to put Jerry into a special reading program that I know will help him. But he's not the only one we can do something for. Right now the education department is sponsoring a new program in the city to identify adult dyslexic nonreaders. Evening classes start in two weeks. Can I put your name down for the one I'll be teaching Tuesday and Thursday nights?"

Francy shrank back into her chair. She hadn't been prepared for anything like this and felt frightened and confused. The humiliation she'd suffered in school was something she wanted behind her forever. The thought of having to go through all that misery again made her stomach roil. "Jerry's a little kid. He can still learn. But it's—it's too late for me," she stammered.

"It's not too late," Mrs. Geddes corrected gently. "Oh, it'll be a lot harder, I admit. But if you still want to learn to read, it's not too late."

Francy shot her sister a panicky look. "I'm too busy. I haven't got the time."

Ignoring that, Teresa smiled at the teacher. "Put her name down. I'll make sure she's not too busy."

"But...but..." Francy sputtered in protest.

"Just put her name down," Teresa repeated calmly. "I'll see to it that she gets to class on time."

"Thanks a lot," Francy said a few minutes later as the two sisters walked out of the elementary school and into the afternoon sunshine.

"Oh, come on. You know you're dying to learn to read. Well, this is your chance," Teresa retorted. "You really *should* thank me."

"It'll probably be awful," Francy predicted. "I'll just be wasting my time. I'll be made to feel like a stupid fool all over again."

"That's some terrific attitude you have there," Teresa countered. "Just who do you think is going to be in this class, anyway? A bunch of Rhodes scholars? They're going to be people with the same problem as you."

"I don't think anyone has it as bad as I do," Francy returned darkly.

"Yeah, well, I bet you're wrong about that. You're always criticizing me, saying that I've retired from life. Well, I think you should try this class, and I'm going to make sure you do no matter how many appointments you pretend to have. Which reminds me—when are you going to be seeing Mr. Wonderful again?" As they proceeded down the avenue, she gave her younger sister a sharp look.

"I suppose you're talking about Adam Pearce," Francy muttered.

"Who else? Have you worked up a presentation for him?"

"I've picked out several wallpaper and fabric samples, if that's what you mean."

"That's what I mean. You know this is a big chance for you. You've always wanted to expand into decorating."

"Yeah."

Again, Teresa shot her younger sister a look. "Yeah, but you don't want to decorate this particular guy's apartment, right?"

"I didn't say that."

"You don't need to. It's obvious that you're uptight about going back to see him. You've been moody ever since he first called you."

"When did watching *Days of Our Lives* turn you into a psychiatrist?"

"I don't have to be a shrink to figure you out. I'm your big sister, remember. And as long as I'm at it—it's pretty clear that this guy is interested in seeing you. But just how attracted are you to him?"

Francy flipped a strand of long dark hair off her shoulder. "Not attracted at all."

Teresa hooted. "Come on, I saw him on television, remember? He's gorgeous. You'd have to be blind not to be interested."

"All right," Francy conceded, "he's very good-looking. And really, he seems to be very nice. But he's not my type."

"Then what does it take to be your type? Don't tell me you only like Italian men. I happen to know that you never miss one of Robert Redford's movies."

Francy laughed. "It's not a question of nationality, it's a question of background. I like men I can be comfortable with, men I don't have to pretend to be something I'm not with. Adam Pearce is a lawyer with a fancy society background. He's just out of my league." Before her sister could ask any more questions, Francy came to a sudden stop and pressed her nose against the glass of the empty storefront next to Gus Venturo's grocery store. "The For Rent sign is still up," she muttered.

"You still talking about opening a shop in that hole in the wall?" Teresa shook her head. "It looks so dingy in there, spider webs every square inch. It'll probably be months before they unload the place."

The door of Venturo's grocery banged open and Gus poked out his head. "That shows how much you know about a good business opportunity. There was a guy around here looking at it only yesterday."

Both women turned and stared at Gus.

"If you want that place, Francy, you'd better get a move on." Though the middle-aged grocer addressed his comment to the younger Rasera sister, his gaze was fixed on Teresa. "How are you doing, Teresa?" he queried. "It's been a while since I've seen you around."

She gave him a self-conscious smile. "Oh, well, you know how it is with four kids."

"No, being a bachelor and all, I don't know. Wish I did." He gazed at her for a moment and then shook open a paper bag and began to fill it with fruit from the baskets stacked in front of his store, heaping pears, apples and grapes into it as if it were a cornucopia and he the god of plenty. "Here. A little gift to your kids from me," he said, "in remembrance."

"In remembrance?" Teresa stared at him.

Gus nodded. "In remembrance of that time when you sold me a kiss at the St. Francis day bazaar. I suppose you've forgotten."

It was obvious that Teresa had. As she accepted Gus's offering, she looked nonplussed. "Gus, that was at least fourteen years ago."

The middle-aged grocer shrugged uncomfortably. "Seems like yesterday to me." Then, his thick neck reddening, he turned to Francy and awkwardly changed the subject. "I wasn't joking. Yesterday a couple of guys came around here to look at that store. I heard them talking about a drapery shop just like what you got in mind."

Francy frowned. "Were they anybody I know?"

"Don't think so. But tell you what, Francy. If you're serious about this place, you better let the owners know. It can't sit around much longer."

"Thanks for the advice, Gus," she answered abstractedly.

After Teresa had thanked him again for the fruit, the two sisters proceeded down the street toward home.

"You know what?" Teresa said after several minutes of silence.

"What?" Francy, who'd been deep in her own musings, gave her sister a questioning look.

"I'd forgotten all about the bazaar when I sold kisses."

"Well, no wonder. It was a long time ago. I mean, you were just a teenager."

"Yeah. But hearing Gus talk about it brings it all back. I wore a white eyelet dress with blue ribbon and my hair was in a French twist. And you know what?"

Francy shook her head.

"Gus Venturo wasn't a bad kisser."

## CHAPTER FIVE

NERVOUSLY ADAM PACED back and forth. From time to time he checked his watch and then peered out the living-room window. She was fifteen minutes late. Maybe, he told himself, he should have checked the bus schedule. But whoever heard of a business person in this day and age depending on buses to get around to appointments? It was crazy.

This whole situation was crazy. And nuttier than anything else was his own behavior. All week he'd been looking forward to going over wallpaper and fabric samples with Francesca Rasera. When she'd called the night before to set up this appointment, his spirits had soared. Minutes after he'd hung up the phone, he'd rushed out to an all-night grocery and laid in a stock of food big enough to feed a whole army of petite Italian girls. In the desperate hope that he might be able to tempt her to stay for lunch, he now had wine along with a pasta seafood salad cooling in the refrigerator. Flaky croissants were set out and ready to pop into the oven, and he'd polished up the kitchen as well as his best china and stemware.

"Pearce, the gourmet seducer," Adam muttered to himself as he glanced out the window again. His hands curled on the sill. And there she was, marching down the street carrying a bag that looked to be about half her size. God, she was sweet. All those rich black curls spilling over her shoulders. Dressed in pink cotton slacks and a matching jacket, she was as fresh and sassy as a peppermint stick. How would that full little mouth of hers taste, he wondered. Well, today he intended to do his damnedest to find out.

When she buzzed his apartment, Adam was ready and waiting. "Hi, there," he said as he threw open the door and took the bag she was carrying out of her arms. Up close she looked a little less like that tasty stick of cool peppermint. A faint frown wrinkled her brow and her forehead was slightly damp, as if she'd been walking faster than was wise in this warm weather.

"Sorry I'm late," she said. "The bus was delayed."

"Nothing to worry about."

"It's not good business practice to keep customers cooling their heels. When I set up an appointment, I like to be on time for it."

"Must be pretty hard, relying on public transportation."

Francy nodded. "Yes, sometimes it is." She had followed him into the middle of his large living room and now stood watching nervously as he set her bag of samples down on the oak table. Clasping her hands behind her back, Francy took a deep breath and willed herself to calm down. She was so anxious to treat Adam Pearce in a businesslike manner that the bus's being late had rattled her more than was reasonable. Now that she was here, the thing to do, she told herself, was to marshall her wits and behave as calmly and professionally as possible.

That, however, was not going to be easy—not with the way he looked this morning. Francy had seen Adam in suits and sport coats and knew that he was about as attractive as any man had a right to be. But this morning, dressed in faded jeans and a well-washed white sweatshirt, he made her feel all jittery and light-headed. The bleached whiteness of the shirt showed up the breadth of his shoulders and the healthy gold of his skin. The snug denim emphasized the sinuous masculinity of his long legs and lean hips.

*You should wear jeans and sweatshirts all the time,* Francy felt like blurting. But then again, maybe it wouldn't be such a good idea. If the guy went around looking the way he did right at this moment he'd have women piled up at his feet.

"Well, I can see that you've brought a lot of stuff to show me," he said, turning and favoring her with a glinting smile that made her blink several times in rapid succession. "Before we settle down to work, can I get you a cup of coffee?"

When Francy shook her head, he said, "Okay, let's get to it."

"Okay, let's do that," she replied briskly.

At first, the materials in Francy's bag might have seemed jumbled together and haphazard. But they weren't. She had taken a lot of time and care in selecting the samples she wished to present to Adam. As she arranged them on the table, coordinating colors, patterns and textures and suggesting possible combinations, he was visibly impressed.

"They all look good," he said, gazing at the several different choices she was offering him. "I was afraid that it would be too..." He paused to wave his hand in the air.

"Too decorated, too *House and Garden*?" Francy supplied. She smiled. "I tried to pick things that would suit you and make you feel comfortable."

He chuckled. "Sounds as if being an interior decorator means you need a degree in psychology as well as
a sharp eye for color and design."

"Sort of," she answered seriously. "Part of doing a
good job for a client is getting a sense of who he, or she,
is, his personality and tastes."

He gazed at her steadily, a faint smile hovering at the
corners of his mouth. "And just who do you think I
am, Miss Rasera? May I call you Francesca, by the
way?"

Francy picked up one of the samples and smoothed
it out. She didn't really want him calling her by her first
name. That made things too intimate, somehow. But
she couldn't bring herself to say no, either. "Sure."

"And please call me Adam."

"Okay."

"But I've interrupted you. You were going to give me
your analysis of my personality."

"Was I?" Francy met his questioning look with a direct one of her own. He was hard to resist, she acknowledged. How old was he? Thirty-four, thirty-five?
That meant he'd had time to charm a lot of women. No
wonder he was in such good practice.

"Well, I was hoping that was what you had in mind."
His blue eyes were as bright and as alluring as tropical
seas.

"Okay." Francy fingered another piece of fabric.
"You're young, but no kid. You're used to being surrounded by quality, and your tastes are sophisticated."
She gave him a brief, sideways glance. He was listening
intently. "You're obviously successful and obviously
smart." He lifted deprecating hands, which she ig-
nored. "From the looks of this room, and the general
way you come across, I guessed that you didn't want

anything too startling or trendy. I figured you'd go for something attractive, but comfortable and low-key. The textured browns with touches of red and blue seemed right for you. But if they're not, just tell me and we'll start over.''

"They're perfect, but I haven't quite made up my mind which combination I'll go for." He glanced at the clock on the mantel. "I know it's early for lunch, only eleven-thirty. But I never got around to having more than a cup of coffee for breakfast this morning, and I'm hungry. I wonder if you'd join me in the kitchen for a bite to eat while I think over my options.''

Francy had purposely tried to get here in plenty of time this morning so that lunch wouldn't become an issue. Now what was she supposed to do? Tell him to starve?

"Sure," she responded hesitantly. "But I'm really not hungry. I'll just watch you eat.''

"That'll make me feel like a glutton, but suit yourself." Smoothly he rose out of his chair. "Kitchen's back this way. Why don't you bring those samples along so that I can think about them while I'm feeding my face?''

By the time Francy gathered her materials and carted them into the kitchen, the buttery fragrance of warm croissants had begun to waft seductively from the oven. Adam had already set the table for two. An open bottle of Chablis stood in the center, along with a carafe that held the long pale green stalks of three irises. Their delicate shapes and rich indigo color were centered with bright golden hearts.

"You've set a place for me," Francy observed a bit accusingly.

"Only in case you should change your mind. You certainly don't have to eat anything if you don't want to." Adam was rummaging around in a drawer.

"Is there anything I can do to help?"

"Yes, on that shelf behind you there's an unopened tin of paprika. Would you hand it to me?"

Francy turned to stare at the spice shelf. She could easily recognize the paprika in her mother's kitchen. But Adam used a different brand and nothing looked familiar. Her hands went cold. *Don't panic,* she told herself. *It must be that red one.*

But when she handed the red container to Adam, he frowned at it. "This is red pepper, not paprika."

"Oh, sorry." Francy tried to keep the distress out of her voice.

"Doesn't matter." Adam crossed to the shelf and pulled a different tin from it. "The salad might not be so good if I put a layer of red pepper on top of it, though."

"No." She pretended to laugh, but her heart was pounding, and when he pulled out a chair and looked at her expectantly Francy dropped into it weakly. While she sat trying to gather her wits, Adam took out the croissants and put a small basketful of them in front of her. They smelled delicious. Then he set down the bowl of pasta salad.

"Are you sure I can't offer you some of this?"

"Well, maybe just a little."

"Ah, then you're not going to make me eat alone, after all." He dished them each out a liberal portion. "Wine?"

Hastily Francy covered her goblet. Enough was enough. "No, thanks."

Adam merely smiled while he filled his glass and then forked up a succulent pink shrimp. After a moment's hesitation, Francy began to eat as well. The salad was excellent, and all at once she was ravenously hungry.

As they ate, they talked about neutral topics: the weather, the national and local news. She asked Adam if he had any hobbies, and he told her that he liked golf, tennis and horseback riding. When he queried her about her interests, she merely shrugged.

"Where I live we don't do things like golf, tennis and horseback riding. And my job keeps me pretty busy."

"But there must be something you like to do for recreation."

*Yes,* she thought, *I like to listen to tapes of the books I'll never be able to read.* Through her lashes she glanced furtively up at the handsome man seated opposite her. What if she'd told him the truth when she made the mistake about the paprika? What would his reaction be if he knew he was having lunch with someone who couldn't even read a simple newspaper article? Shivering slightly, Francy pushed a noodle around on her plate. "I like to cook," she said, "and sometimes I take my bike out and peddle around. Last year I took a ballet class. That was fun."

"But mostly you spend your time sewing curtains and slipcovers for other people?"

"Most people I know have to work pretty hard to make a living. There's nothing unusual about me."

"Now there I have to disagree," Adam said. Casually he reached over and filled her wineglass before topping up his own. Francy opened her mouth to protest and then closed it again. A drop of wine wouldn't be so bad right now.

"You," Adam continued, "are one of the most un-usual women I've ever met."

*That was probably true,* Francy thought and gazed at him nervously. There was no way he could have guessed her secret, was there? "What do you mean?"

"I mean that you're responsible and creative and very independent. Yet you're nothing like any of the other career girls I've run into over the years. There's a soft-ness as well as a toughness about you." He swirled the wine in his glass. "I don't know how to put it exactly. You're just very different. Tell me something, Fran-cesca. You're obviously hardworking. Are you ambi-tious as well? Do you hope to do something with that creativity of yours, more than what you're doing now?"

Francy felt her face go warm. "Yes," she admitted. While she watched her host's expression, she thought about the line he'd just handed her—tough and soft and different, come on! What was it about him that made her want to tell him her life story, anyway? Usually when men said absurd things to her, she laughed. But she didn't feel like laughing now.

It wasn't just that he was so attractive. She had dated several men who were, in their own way, as handsome as he. There had been Mike with the flashing dark eyes and drawling humor. And Sam—Sam had been an ex-perience, all right. But Adam had something special that made him different from the other men Francy had known, a way of looking at a woman as if he was really taking her in, as if he were truly interested in the per-son behind the set of features she presented to the world. Of course it could all be an act to encourage her to make a fool of herself, but... Suddenly Francy found herself telling him about the shop next to Gus Ventu-ro's grocery store.

"It sounds ideal," Adam commented. "Why don't you go for it?"

"Because I know my own limitations. To run a shop you need more than skill with a sewing machine. Frankly I don't have much formal education. I doubt that I could handle the paperwork."

Instinctively she knew that he didn't like the reference to her lack of education, but he showed no outward sign.

"Other people can do that for you. Most businessmen I know have accountants and lawyers." His smile was encouraging. "I would be glad to give you whatever legal advice you might need."

"Thanks." Suddenly embarrassed at the way she'd revealed her dearest fantasy to him, Francy put her fork down and glanced at the fabric samples she'd arranged on one of the kitchen counters. "You said you were going to think about your decorating scheme. Have you made a decision?"

Grinning at her, he pushed back his plate and rose from his chair. "Let me see," he said, as he ambled over to take another look at the swatches of material. After a moment's deliberation, he picked up a textured tweed and a dark red linen. "This for the draperies, and this for the slipcovers, I think."

"Ah, I guessed you'd go for those."

His grin widened. "That's right, I'd forgotten. You have me all figured out." When she didn't answer, he added, "You know, Francesca, now that I think about it, I'm a little insulted."

"What?" Over the top of her half-empty wineglass, Francy shot him a wary look.

Turning, he leaned against the counter and regarded her with that easy assurance that both attracted and irritated her. "When you said you didn't think I'd be interested in anything superstylish or trendy, you made me feel that I was rather boring. Is that the way you see me—dull and conservative?"

"Oh, there's nothing dull about you," Francy answered without thinking.

He cocked his head, his eyes brightening. "I wonder how you mean that."

Francy put down her glass. No point in fencing around like this, she thought. Might just as well get it out into the open. "Mr. Pearce, Adam, let's be straight with each other. You're a very attractive man, and you're single. That means most women are going to find you fascinating."

"But not you." He held up a hand. "Okay, Francesca, let's really be straight. The moment I saw you, I was attracted. But as far as I can tell, I don't interest you at all." He glanced at her ring finger. "Are you involved with someone?"

"A man?" Francy shook her head. She was feeling a little breathless at the sudden turn their conversation had taken. "No, I'm not involved with anyone, but that doesn't mean I would be willing to poach on another woman's property."

"Another woman's property?" Adam straightened. "Now let me see if I can figure out what you mean by that."

"It's no big secret. When I first met you, you were having drinks with Barbara Kains."

"Francesca, I'm not Barbara Kains's property."

"The two of you seemed pretty chummy," Francy answered stiffly.

"We are friends." With his blue eyes pinned to her flushed features, Adam moved closer. "That's all we are," he continued. "And all we're ever likely to be now that I've met you."

Francy blinked up at him. Then suddenly apprehensive and feeling very much at a disadvantage, she pushed her own chair back and jumped to her feet. But that only made things worse because as she straightened he took another step forward and suddenly their faces were within inches of each other. Francy could feel the heat from his skin, smell the cool fragrance of his after-shave. As she stared up into his tanned face, she could see the thick gold lashes that framed his clear blue eyes. His slim nose was arrow straight and his mouth was cut so cleanly that it made her think of sculpture. Some of the statues of saints she'd seen in church had had mouths like that.

Adam appeared to be having a similar experience. "God, you're a lovely little thing," he said, reaching out to capture a lock of dusky hair between his thumb and forefinger. "Your eyes are like mahogany velvet."

"They're just plain old brown." Francy's breath lodged in her throat, and the words came out sounding strangled.

"Plain old beautiful," he murmured. His grip tightened slightly on the curl, and his head began to incline toward hers. Francy knew that in a moment they'd be kissing. Did she want that? Yes, she did, every bone in her body seemed to plead. No, she did not, her slightly befuddled brain managed to dictate. Only a fool would allow a client to kiss her on what should be a business visit. And she was not going to let herself be made a fool of!

"Do you need help cleaning up these dishes?" Francy whirled, almost knocking over her chair.

Adam was so startled by her abrupt withdrawal that he didn't release her curl and she lost several hairs in the process.

"No," he said, staring down at the ebony strands still wrapped around his finger. A few feet away Francy stood feeling angry and ridiculous and rubbing the spot near her ear where they'd been torn free.

Adam looked at her. "Did I hurt you?"

"No. Well, maybe a little."

"I'm sorry."

"It was my fault."

"No," he countered, "it was my fault. I wanted to kiss you. I thought you were willing."

"Yes, I know." She glanced away. "Adam, please, I don't believe in mixing business with pleasure."

He sighed. "Francesca, I don't know how else to say this. I'm very attracted to you. I want to get to know you better. Won't you let me take you out? There's a musical down at the Lyric tonight. I could get tickets. We could have dinner beforehand."

Instead of answering him, Francy skirted the table and headed for the pile of fabric samples on the counter. "Thanks for the invitation, but I have too much work to do," she said, not looking at him as she began gathering them up.

"Do you have too much work tomorrow night?"

"Yes."

"And the weekend after that?"

Francy turned, clutching her materials to her bosom as if for protection. "It's going to be the same story then, too, I'm afraid. I'm just too busy. Look, if that's the only reason you're having me do this work for you, then let's just forget it."

A grimness settled around his jaw. "It's not the only reason."

"Are you sure about that?"

"Yes, I'm sure."

He was lying, she thought. Right here and now she should resign from the job. Why wasn't she going to?

FOUR DAYS LATER Francy turned left off Pratt Street and walked down the wide brick steps between the two glass-roofed shopping pavilions that anchored Baltimore's renovated Inner Harbor. It was a glorious day. Overhead, screaming gulls wheeled and barrel-rolled in a cloudless sky of eggshell blue. Beyond the promenade the water sparkled and sailboats bobbed gently on its glistening surface, looking a little like bright new toys intended for playful children. The cheerful weather seemed to infect everyone with good spirits. People smiled and laughed as they strolled past Francy on the brick walkway.

Normally Francy would have been in a good mood, too, since this was one of her favorite places in Baltimore. But today as she trudged along carrying an enormous plastic bag over her shoulder, she hardly seemed to take in the festive scene. Her smooth olive skin was pale. Faint shadows lurked around her eyes, and even her black curls seemed to droop.

Since her hasty departure from Adam Pearce's apartment the preceding Saturday, she'd spent almost every waking hour hunched over her sewing machine. She told herself that she'd been right to refuse his invitation, but that didn't make her feel any better about it. What would it have been like to go out on a real date with him? It wasn't as if she was seeing anyone else at the moment. By being so sensible, was she cutting off her nose to spite her face?

Decisions and turning points seemed to plague her on all sides. Her first class was tonight. Should she go? And then there was the shop. She had to make a decision about whether or not to go ahead with that, and she had to make it soon.

Burying herself in work hadn't answered any of the questions nagging at her brain, but she had managed to finish up quite a few back orders. Now she was headed toward Barbara Kains's high-rise apartment building with a delivery.

A few minutes later as she rode up in the elevator, Francy shifted the bag full of completed slipcovers from one shoulder to the other and sighed. She wasn't looking forward to this visit. Her feelings didn't make any sense, she told herself. The covers she was delivering were in great shape. And there was no reason to feel guilty because Adam was flirting with her. He'd said that he and Barbara Kains were only friends and, in any case, Francy hadn't submitted to his kiss or taken him up on any of his dinner propositions. She'd been thinking about him almost nonstop, though, and when the tall blond young woman opened the door and gave her a friendly greeting, Francy felt her cheeks going pink.

"Come on in. I'm dying to see how the covers look."

"I think they came out pretty well. But when I put them on, that will be the moment of truth."

Francy never allowed a customer to fit new slipcovers to furniture. Putting the completed product on a chair or sofa was almost as much an art as making the slipcovers in the first place. While Francy worked at it, Barbara stood in the entry watching her. She was wearing a mushroom-colored raw silk skirt with a loose fitting blouse in a complementary shade of taupe. The outfit was set off by a gold leather belt and the equally bright gold of her smoothly cut hair. Standing there with one shoulder negligently propped against the wall, she looked cool and elegant.

Suddenly, in her navy blue cotton slacks and slightly stretched red cotton knit sweater, Francy felt frumpy. Even her fingers, normally so quick and deft, seemed to grow awkward. With Barbara's watchful eyes on her, she had to struggle over one recalcitrant cover more than should have been necessary.

*Why do I care that I'm not dressed as nicely as she is,* Francy asked herself irritably. *Maybe I couldn't afford to buy an outfit like that, but I could make it for myself if I wanted.* In fact, Francy knew that she could copy any Paris original down to the last dart if she felt in the mood to do it. But who had time for such nonsense?

"That looks wonderful." Barbara strode forward and ran an approving hand over a chair's smooth arm. "It really does fit like a glove. You're a very talented seamstress."

Warmed by the praise, Francy swallowed her irritation and smiled. "Thanks. I'm glad you're pleased."

"I am pleased. Very." She tilted her head. "Francy, it seems as if you're always rushing off to another appointment. Do you have a few minutes? I just made a pot of tea. Can I offer you some?"

"Well..." Francy checked her watch. She did have a little time to kill. And suddenly she felt guilty about her nonsensical reaction to Barbara. It wasn't her fault, after all, that she was rich and beautiful and made lesser women feel at a disadvantage. Really Barbara seemed like a very nice person. "Sure, a cup of tea would be good about now."

When Barbara came back she was carrying a large tray loaded down with crackers and an assortment of cheeses as well as a pretty flowered teapot and matching cups. "I always think it's nice to have a little something with tea," she commented as she set her load down on the coffee table.

"That looks good," Francy agreed. "Actually I could use a snack. I'm not going to make it home for dinner tonight."

"Oh?" Barbara sat down on the other side of the couch. "Why is that?"

"I'm taking an evening class."

"What sort of class?"

As Francy gazed into Barbara's green eyes, which were now bright with curiosity, she wished she hadn't brought the subject up. No matter how nice Barbara seemed, the last thing she wanted to confide to this tall sleek blonde was the fact that she was starting a class tonight for nonreaders. "It's kind of a literature course."

"Really? What sort of literature?"

Francy squirmed. "American, I think."

Barbara finished pouring the tea. "That's wonderful," she said as she handed Francy a cup. "I really admire people who try to better themselves. Didn't you tell me once that you never finished high school?"

"Yes." As Francy spread Gruyère cheese on a wheat cracker she wished she'd kept her big mouth shut. She'd let slip that bit about her education weeks ago when she'd been trying to figure up Barbara's estimate without her calculator and couldn't make the numbers come out right.

"Didn't your parents object when you dropped out?"

"They weren't happy about it, but a formal education isn't as important in my family as it is to some."

"I know what you mean." Barbara rolled her eyes. "If I hadn't gone to Vassar my folks would have died."

"You went to Vassar?" Carefully Francy balanced her teacup in its delicate saucer.

"Yes."

"My brother has a degree from Harvard, actually."

"Oh?" Barbara shot Francy a bright, interested glance. "That's wonderful! What year?"

"He got his undergraduate degree in seventy-two. He's a doctor now."

"Really? He must have been in Boston around the same time as Adam, then."

"Adam?"

Barbara nodded. "Yes, Adam Pearce. You must remember him. He was the gorgeous man who came to have drinks here with me when you were cutting the slipcovers."

"Oh, yes." With difficulty, Francy managed to swallow what was left of her cracker. Should she mention that she was doing some work for Adam Pearce? "I'm working on drapes for him right now," she said carefully.

"Oh?" Barbara's eyes narrowed and there was a brief but distinct hiatus while she absorbed this information. "I have to admit that I'm surprised. I didn't think Adam took the slightest interest in how his place looked. How lucky that you were here when he came up so that he could get a chance to be impressed by your craftsmanship."

"Yes," Francy mumbled.

Barbara leaned back against the couch cushions and regarded Francy with a small half smile hovering around her beautifully formed mouth. "Now there's someone who's really had to live up to family tradition. I don't think there's been a male Pearce who hasn't graduated from Harvard—not in this century, anyhow. Poor Adam—it isn't easy to be a Pearce."

"He looks as if he's doing all right at it," Francy commented.

Barbara chuckled. "Oh, he's doing a lot better than all right. All the Pearces have had to be perfect, it's a family tradition. But even so, Adam is their wonder boy." She shook her head as if remembering some private joke, and suddenly Francy knew that Adam had been wrong about his relationship with Barbara. He might think they were just friends, but that wasn't Barbara's idea. And she wasn't happy to hear of Francy's involvement with him, either. "He graduated summa cum laude and Phi Beta Kappa," she went on, proudly. "In law school he was at the top of his class and editor of the *Law Review*. And since he's gotten out he's been more or less setting the world on fire. He's the best prosecutor Howard County has ever had, and recently a little bird told me he might run for Congress."

"Really?"

"Really. And if he wins, which with his looks, brains and charisma, I don't doubt that he will, who knows? It wouldn't surprise me if Adam Pearce wound up being president some day."

Francy blinked. "President? Of the United States?"

"With a man like Adam, anything is possible."

"But he isn't even married. Bachelors aren't usually elected to the Congress, are they?"

Barbara shrugged. "Adam's been pretty elusive. But I don't think he'll stay single much longer, not if Patricia has anything to do with it."

"Who's Patricia?"

Barbara popped a cracker into her mouth. "Patricia Pearce is Adam's mother. And believe me, the matriarchs on those evening soap operas have nothing on her. She'll sweet-talk Adam into settling down with Miss Right—after the poor girl has passed Patricia's inspection, that is."

"She inspects his women friends? Adam didn't strike me as the mama's boy type."

"He isn't. It's just that Patricia Pearce is a very unusual mother."

Francy had lost her appetite. She set down her plate and gazed thoughtfully at Barbara. And just what kind of wife would Adam's mother think was Miss Right? But she already knew the answer to that. She would have to be a woman like him—a woman with brains and looks and breeding who dressed like Barbara and had graduated from a school like Vassar. Francy cleared her throat. "Well, thanks for the tea and crackers. I'd better be going."

"Oh, must you?"

"Yes." Francy nodded. "I really must."

AN HOUR LATER Francy stood in front of the entrance to Fort McHenry High School. According to her digital watch, the reading class inside the school had already been in session for five minutes now. Actually, Francy had been in front of the building for almost twenty minutes. Yet she hadn't gone in. Instead, she had paced slowly up and down in front of the long concrete walk which led to the doors. And she was still pacing.

When she'd left Barbara Kains's apartment she'd been feeling low. But as the bus neared her evening's destination, her gloom had thickened. *A far cry from Vassar,* she'd thought as she stepped down in front of the old city high school with its graffiti covered gate-posts and dust bowl of a front lawn. Schools always depressed her; she'd had so many painful experiences in them. Now the thought of walking into this one shot her through with panic.

*What am I doing here?* she asked herself. *What's the point of putting myself through any more misery? I must have been crazy when I agreed to this!* She knew exactly how it would be—hopeless. The teacher would start cheerfully enough. But when she discovered just what a stubborn case Francy's really was, she would grow irritable and then angry. The class would laugh behind their hands when Francy tried to stumble through a lesson and jeer at her in the halls. Still, despite this nightmare vision, she couldn't seem to make herself walk away, either.

Just then another bus wheezed up to the stop in front of the school. "Getting on?" the driver asked after he opened the doors.

Francy gazed at him mutely and then shook her head. "No," she said. When he'd pulled away and disappeared in a cloud of exhaust, she turned toward the entrance. Determinedly she walked toward the big double doors.

Inside the halls were dim and cool and the place wore a deserted air. A sign on the wall indicated in large red letters that Adult Remedial Reading was being held in room 106. Francy had no trouble picking out the word

"reading." That was one set of letters she always recognized.

After a moment's hesitation, she turned down the
main corridor toward the sound of voices. When she
reached room 106, she had to brace herself before she
peered through the door. The men and women sitting at
the desks inside looked just like ordinary people, no
different than herself.

"Why, Francy," Mrs. Geddes said, "there you are.
We've all been waiting for you." With a warm smile, she
came forward and took Francy's hand. "Come sit down
so we can get started."

# CHAPTER SIX

ON THE CROWDED PLATFORM, Adam stared along the empty track and tapped his foot impatiently. He set down his garment bag and shifted his briefcase to his left hand. Amazing how heavy a leather briefcase could get when it was stuffed with dry-as-dust legal papers. He was headed to New York City for a legal conference, one to which he wasn't looking forward and wouldn't be going if he hadn't agreed to be a panelist months earlier. Normally he enjoyed these getaways, but right now he had too much on his mind.

There was the Shosteck case with all its negative implications for the future of day care in the country. And then there were these puzzling grave robberies. He wasn't convinced that the police had given him the right suspect. Pun or no pun, it was something he needed to get to the bottom of, and quickly. Also weighing on his mind was the decision he'd made to throw his hat into the ring for the congressional race. In a few weeks he'd be going to Bermuda for an initial planning session with Ben Catlett. Finally there was the maddeningly elusive Miss Francesca Rasera.

As Adam's gold-flecked brows drew together in a frown, a headlight appeared in the darkness and the tracks below him vibrated with the approaching train's rumbling forward movement.

"Amtrak Patriot, service to Wilmington, Philadelphia, New York City and points north," a voice announced on the loudspeaker.

*Why, when he had tried to kiss her, had she run out of his apartment as if she'd spotted horns beneath his curls,* he asked himself. Okay, he could believe that a woman might just not be interested. That hadn't happened very often in Adam's life. But he wasn't a vain man, so he had no great trouble accepting the possibility. But not in the case of Francesca Rasera. All his instincts told him that when she looked at him she liked what she saw. So what was holding her back? Why wouldn't she give him a chance?

Hissing, the train bore down on the platform, and people swirled all around Adam jockeying to be in position when the doors opened. With his garment bag in one hand and his paper-crammed briefcase in the other, Adam moved forward to the edge of the platform. Strobe lights flashing, the train's cab slid within feet of him. Then suddenly, totally without warning, a hand on his back pushed hard.

"Hey, what—" As he struggled to regain his balance, something metallic hooked around his right ankle and yanked. Adam found himself falling forward, about to be crushed beneath the moving train. Behind him a woman screamed.

It was odd how everything seemed to happen in slow motion. Slowly he released his luggage. Slowly his arms flew out in front of him. In high school, Adam had been a basketball star. His rangy six-foot-two-inch frame hadn't qualified him for the college team, but he was a natural athlete and he'd kept himself in shape. Now all those hours in a gym rewarded him.

As he tumbled forward, his foot connected to the edge of the platform and he was able to give himself a push. At the same time one hand reached up and grasped the grab iron on the train's forward-moving cab. Holding on tightly, he was dragged a good fifteen feet, his ankle scraping painfully between the train's steel body and the concrete platform. But the straining muscles of his right arm were able to support his weight and keep him from being dragged beneath the wheels. At last the monstrous vehicle ground to a stop and Adam heard shouts of horror and the clatter of rushing feet. Hands reached out and helped him back to safety.

"Hey, fella, you almost bought it there, you know that?"

"Yes," Adam muttered beneath his teeth.

"What happened?"

"I don't know." As he stumbled to his knees, Adam was too shaken to focus on his questioner. "It felt like someone pushed me."

HESITANTLY FRANCY MOUNTED the steps to Adam Pearce's apartment. Under her arm there were several rolls of wallpaper and a package of unmixed paste. When she'd made this appointment to paper Adam's dining-room wall, he'd told her he would be out of town and that she could get the key from his landlady. But his black Mazda was parked in front of the house. Did that mean he was home?

Well, she'd soon find out. Squaring her shoulders, Francy buzzed his number. A moment later the door opened, and Adam peered around it.

"I thought you were going to be away," Francy blurted. All week she'd been telling herself that she didn't want to come in contact with him again. But that didn't stem the spurt of pleasure that coursed through her system at the sight of him. It was strange how some people could make you really see them. Adam was like that. Every time they met she found herself taking him in as if he were the only scenery around. He was paler than usual, she suddenly realized. And there were long red scratches on his cheek.

"My plans got changed. Sorry." He pulled the door open a little wider and beckoned her in.

It was then that she spied his bandaged foot. "What happened?"

"I had a little mishap at the train station. Nothing serious."

"Nothing serious?" She dumped the wallpaper on the floor and, arms akimbo, looked him up and down. "What happened? Your face is all scraped, and your arms are a mess."

Ruefully Adam glanced down at himself. "Well, as a matter of fact, I had a little run-in with a railroad train, and the train won." When he went on to explain, she was even more upset.

"But that's terrible. You could have been killed."

"I could have been ground into a very well-educated hamburger patty," Adam agreed, a smile twitching at the corners of his mouth. "Luckily it didn't happen."

Francy wasn't amused. "You say it felt as if someone pushed you?"

"That's what I thought at the time. But the platform was crowded, and people were stampeding toward the train. It was probably just an accident."

The frown didn't leave Francy's brow. "Is there anyone who might have a reason to want to do something like that to you?"

"Sweet little old *moi*?" Shrugging, Adam hobbled over to the couch and dropped down into it. "I've been asking myself the same question. Fact is, in my line of work you do make a few enemies. Most wind up safely behind bars. But not all. I just have to hope that this was an accident."

As he spoke, he studied Francy's expression with interest. She looked truly concerned. In fact, this was the first time he'd seen her show some real interest in him. Maybe all these weeks he'd been taking the wrong tack with her, he thought. Moaning faintly, he leaned down and rubbed his bandaged ankle.

"Does it hurt very much?" Francy queried anxiously. She couldn't get the image of Adam falling beneath the wheels of the train out of her mind. It was horrifying. Despite the warm day, she shivered. "You really shouldn't be walking around on that, you know. Why don't you put your feet up?"

"Moving is such an effort. My whole body is just one big ache." That was true enough, Adam reflected. At least when Francesca was around.

"Here, let me help you." She came forward and gently lifted his knees. "Now, just swivel around."

Groaning, he complied. "I don't want to lie flat on my back this way. I need a pillow or something."

"Of course you do." She gathered up three couch pillows and then gingerly slipped her hand behind his neck. "Lift up a little so I can put these behind your back."

"I feel so weak." With a sigh of contentment, Adam clasped Francy's slim waist and let his head fall forward so that it rested on the soft cushion of her bosom.

Francy stared down at the top of his silky head. Where his forehead touched her, her breasts seemed to burn. "Adam," she said a little breathlessly, "stop it. You're not that weak."

"Right now I am. You turn my bones to jelly." He snuggled closer. "God, this feels good. I'm getting better already."

It did feel good, marvelously good. She fought with a mad urge to clasp his head and pull him closer yet, to wind her fingers in his sunlit hair and drop comforting kisses on his brow. Instead, she pushed him away and declared sternly, "I was just trying to help. But you were taking advantage."

Cornflower-blue eyes opened to gaze at her with limpid innocence. "Me?"

"Yes, you." Clucking, she plumped up the pillows behind his head. "Is that all right now?"

"Yes, as long as I can get a good view from this angle."

"Of what?"

"Of you putting up my wallpaper."

When she cast him a suspicious glance, he met it with another of his guileless choirboy expressions. "I've always wanted to watch someone hang wallpaper. Especially a beautiful woman in tight blue jeans."

Francy got to her feet. "You're hopeless. And my jeans are not tight." She glanced down at herself. "Well, maybe they're a little snug, but I didn't think you were going to be home today."

"And here I was beginning to worry that you weren't writing love sonnets about me in your diary every night."

If he only knew how unlikely *that* was, Francy thought wryly. "Keep it up and you'll have me pushing you off railroad platforms."

Shaking her head, she picked up her materials and lay them out on the dining-room table. All the while as she moved back and forth she was hotly conscious of Adam's eyes on her. "And stop staring at me."

"I can't help myself." When she glared at him, he added meekly, "You'll find a bucket under the sink in the kitchen. You can use that for mixing up the paste."

"A minute ago you implied that you didn't know anything about hanging wallpaper."

"I helped my mother paper a bathroom once, but it was a long time ago."

Francy considered that. "Papering is a nasty job. You must be awfully fond of your mother."

"I didn't do it out of fondness. Bullying people into doing things they dislike is one of her main talents. If she'd been born a man, she'd be a five-star general by now."

"Does she bully you?"

Lazily Adam folded his arms behind his head. He was wearing a dark blue knit shirt that emphasized his muscular build and set off his golden coloring. "She tries."

"Does she succeed?"

"That depends."

"On what?"

"On whether she's trying to bully me into something I want to do anyway."

While Francy thought that over, she went into the kitchen and mixed up the paste. Back in the living room, she began moving furniture and spreading newspapers.

"If it weren't for this bum foot, I'd help you," Adam said. As before, his blue eyes followed her every move intently.

"I know you would. Don't worry about me. I'm stronger than I look."

"So I've noticed. In fact, you're a pretty tough little cookie, aren't you?"

She measured a piece of paper and then fished out her scissors. "I don't know about that."

"I do. You have the kind of toughness I've seen in some kids when they get out of prison. To survive in that environment, they've needed to acquire a certain veneer. But that's all it is, just a veneer. Have you been hurt, Francy? Did some man hurt you? Is that why you're so leery of me?"

She began to slop paste on the paper. "You never let up, do you?"

"No, never. I'm famous for my persistence. Don't you read the newspapers? Pearce always gets his man. Only in this case I'm hoping to get my woman."

His question about reading the newspapers made Francy's expression darken. "I've got a long afternoon ahead of me, here. Could we change the subject?"

"Okay," he agreed equably enough. "What would you like to discuss?"

Francy applied the sticky paper to the wall, smoothed it into place and then stood back to check her efforts. "I'm curious about this wallpapering you did. I would have thought that the Pearces could afford to pay a peon like me for that sort of job."

"We don't always have other people doing things for us. Sometimes we like to do things for ourselves. Right now I can think of several little tasks I'd like to take care of personally. But I'd need your cooperation." He sighed melodramatically.

Refusing to rise to the bait, Francy retorted impatiently, "It must be nice to be able to afford anything you want."

"There are lots of things I want that I can't get."

She turned to face him. "You know what I mean, Adam."

His expression sobered. "Where you're concerned, I don't know anything. To be honest, I wasn't sure you'd come back. After the way you ran out of here the other day, I worried that I'd seen the last of you."

Her gaze flickered away from his. If she'd had any backbone, it would have been the last. "I'd agreed to do a job for you. I'm not rich. I can't afford to turn down good money."

"Is that the only reason you came back? The money?"

Francy was too honest to lie. Sighing, she faced him again and said simply, "We come from different worlds. It wouldn't work."

"How do you know before you even try? I think you'd fit into my world just fine."

He was wrong, but Francy didn't feel like explaining why. Instead, she said, "You wouldn't fit into mine."

"How can you be sure?" He looked taken aback.

"You'd be about as comfortable having a spaghetti dinner with my folks in Little Italy as a prize poodle would be eating from a community dish in the dog pound."

His face reddened slightly, and she knew she'd angered him. "That's not exactly a comparison I appreciate." Curiously she observed his brief struggle for balance. He was very quick on his mental feet. Maybe he did have the makings of a politician. "Actually I see myself more as an Irish setter or possibly a golden retriever. And Italian cuisine is one of my favorites. I think you owe me an opportunity to prove that I can get along with most people. Invite me home for dinner, Francesca. Give me a fighting chance.''

"No."

"Why not?"

She gazed at him in exasperation. "Listen, could we—"

He threw up his hands. "I know, I know, could we change the subject. All right, what do you think about this weather we've been having?"

"I think it's great. I love spring." Doggedly Francy unrolled another length of paper and began slapping at it with her glue brush.

As she worked, some of the tension gradually left the air, and they began to talk about less volatile subjects. He asked about her family, and she found herself telling him a little about her nieces and nephews and her sister Teresa.

"That's tough," Adam said sympathetically. "Losing your father and then having to cope with your sister's problems—it can't have been easy."

"No, but it's been harder on Teresa than it has been on me. She misses Pop, too."

"What was he like?"

"Warm, kind, loving. He was truly a wonderful man. We all adored him." She patted the last strip of paper into place and began smoothing it with a damp sponge. "What was your father like?"

"Well, maybe not so warm and wonderful. Henpecked and uptight would probably be a more accurate description." When Francy shot Adam a startled look, he added, "The truth is that I never knew my father very well. He didn't spend much time at home, and he died when I was twelve. You see, Francy, in some ways your family's legacy is richer than mine. I'd give a lot to remember my dad the way you do yours."

Arrested, Francy stopped and stared. Either Adam Pearce was an awfully good actor or he meant what he'd just said. His expression was utterly sincere. "Maybe you have something there," she replied a little gruffly. Anxious to get back onto safer ground, she pointed at the freshly papered wall. "What do you think?"

"My reactions are mixed. I think it looks terrific, but now that it's done, I suppose you intend to go and leave me here all by my lonesome."

"As soon as I've cleaned up," Francy agreed. Already she'd begun picking up stray bits of paper. In a few minutes the part of the living room where she'd been working was tidy, and she'd pushed the furniture back in place.

"When will you visit the patient again?" Adam queried plaintively.

"When I've finished the drapes and slipcovers."

"You don't feel the least bit guilty about leaving me here a broken man?"

"You don't look broken to me." And he certainly didn't. Lying there stretched out on the couch he looked lean and dangerous and far too attractive for his or her good. Still, he had been badly injured and nearly killed. Francy took a step forward. "Is there something I can get you before I go?"

She braced herself for another of his flirtatious remarks. Instead, he bestowed upon her a sweet smile and said, "A beer and a ham sandwich would be nice. The stuff is in the refrigerator."

"Sure thing." Happy to be useful, Francy turned and headed for the kitchen. A few minutes later she emerged bearing the requested food. As she crossed the room toward him, Adam's blue gaze seemed to darken.

"Just set the plate and can of beer down on the floor," he told her.

When she'd done as he asked, he reached out and captured her hand. "Listen, before you go, I have something for you."

"What's that?" Francy eyed him warily. Where his hand covered hers, her skin tingled.

"Nothing that you need to look so suspicious about. What have I done to give you such a bad impression?" With his free hand he reached into his back pocket and withdrew a folded piece of paper. "Last week I had my secretary call about that shop you mentioned. The rent's not bad, actually." He glanced down at his notes and read a figure fifty dollars lower than the one Francy had expected. "Anyway, here's the information. If you decide to go for it, just let me know and I'll help you with the details."

She accepted the paper and stared down at the inscrutable handwriting that covered it. "Thanks," she finally managed. Folding it twice, she slipped it into her jeans pocket. "I . . . that was awfully nice of you."

"It wasn't nice of me at all." Instead of releasing her hand, he gave it a tug and suddenly Francy found herself perched on the couch next to him. "I was hoping," he told her, "for a reward."

Francy's heart accelerated and a breathlessness caught at her throat. All afternoon she'd been aware of Adam's steady gaze and the undeniable electricity that crackled between them. Every time she saw him it seemed to intensify. This morning she'd told herself that she was coming here to do a job—nothing more and nothing less. She should make it clear to Adam once and for all that she wasn't interested. But they both knew that would be a lie. "What sort of a reward?" she questioned huskily.

His mouth lifted at the corners and his eyes sparkled wickedly. "I want to prove something to you."

"What's that?" Francy instructed herself to pull back and put an end to this nonsense, but she couldn't.

"I can't tell you. I have to show you."

As he spoke, he lifted his hand, cupped her chin and gently guided her face toward his. When his long fingers curled around her jaw, Francy dissolved into mindless compliance. Her brown eyes stared into his sapphire ones. The blue was so intense that she squeezed her lids shut. A moment later she felt his lips on hers. Sweetly, gently, he kissed her and then with equal tenderness slowly touched his mouth to either corner of hers. Francy waited for more, wanting the feel of his arms around her, the demand of a more insistent caress. Surely this was just the prelude. Beneath her blouse her breasts felt heavy and something stirred within her. But there was no more. When, reluctantly, she opened her eyes, his face was inches from hers and he was gazing at her solemnly. "See," he said huskily.

"See what?"

"That wasn't so bad." His fingers stroked her cheek and then withdrew. He let his head drop back to the pillows and folded his hands over his chest. She realized that she was no longer his captive and so had no excuse to stay leaning over him this way.

Masking her disappointment as best she could, Francy stumbled to her feet. "I should get going."

"Of course you should."

She glanced down at the ham sandwich beside him and then at his bandaged foot. "Will you be okay?"

"Sure. It's not as bad as it looks. Tomorrow I'll be on my feet and back at my job."

"Maybe you should give yourself a little more time off."

Adam shook his head. "Too much to do. I'm a busy man—but not too busy," he added, "to help out if you should decide to rent that store. Will you call me if you do?"

Francy nodded. "Yes, yes I will." Swallowing the lump in her throat, she turned away. It really was time to go. If she stayed much longer she might do something truly foolish.


"So what did they say?" Teresa demanded.

"It's still available. The owner left the key with Gus Venturo. I can go take a look at it now if I want." Francy hung up the phone and reached for her shoulder bag.

"Are you going now, this minute?"

"Yes, yes, I am. It's time to stop dithering about this thing and make a move."

"Mama's not going to like it."

"I won't involve Mama. I'll do it on my own."

"Big talk, little sister."

Francy turned to look expressively at Teresa. "I know."

"Want some company?"

Francy's brow lifted with surprise. So far she'd been the only one who seemed interested in expanding the business. But now Teresa's eyes were bright with excitement. "Sure, I'd love to have you come."

"Just give me a minute to freshen up," Teresa replied with a grin, "and I'll be right with you."

Three quarters of an hour later the two sisters left the house. As they turned toward Linden Street, Francy shot Teresa a speculative look. Since the breakup of her marriage Teresa hadn't paid much attention to what she wore. Often she went to the store in shapeless caftans and comfortable but rather down-at-heel shoes. For this short trip, however, she had put on her best blouse and skirt, applied makeup and brushed her hair until it shone. On her feet she had strapped a pair of sexy high-heeled sandals that Francy hadn't seen out of the closet for years.

"When you said you were going to freshen up, I thought you meant you were going to put on lipstick, not turn yourself into the Italian version of Marilyn Monroe."

"A woman should always try and look her best, if only for her own self-respect." Teresa fired off a critical glance at Francy's jeans. "Why don't you wear skirts more often?"

"Because jeans are more comfortable, and I'm too busy to spend a lot of time dolling myself up."

"If you're serious about opening a store, you'll have to change your image. People aren't going to hire an interior decorator who looks like a refugee from a garage sale."

"That's true, I suppose." Francy looked sideways at her sister. A couple of weeks ago she had been trying to encourage Teresa to care about her appearance. Why had the tables been turned? "What's this sudden interest in fashion?"

"Oh," the older woman replied airily, "I just think it's time I started paying more attention to myself. I mean, thirty-two isn't really middle-aged yet, now is it?"

"Of course it isn't. And what's that got to do with anything? You're too hung up on age."

"You could be right. I saw a TV show on just that subject the other day—how to make the best of yourself at any age. It was all about good nutrition and proper exercise. Haven't you noticed that it's been a week since any dessert has passed these lips, and I'm only eating salad for lunch?"

Francy shook her head. "No." She'd been too occupied thinking about her illogical attraction to Adam Pearce, her renewed struggle to learn to read and the shop to notice much of anything.

Teresa looked piqued. "Well, I've already lost three pounds. Can't you see that this skirt isn't so tight around the hips?"

Francy eyed her sister's luxuriant figure. "You do look nice."

Mollified, Teresa smiled. "So do you, Francy. You've always been pretty no matter what you wore. If you decide to go into business and dress for the part, you'll be a knockout. Which reminds me, I've been meaning to ask how the classes are going."

"Not too bad," Francy replied cautiously.

"You think this time it might help?"

Francy held up crossed fingers. "I'm hoping. The atmosphere is different in those night classes. Everyone's got the same problem, so it's not quite so humiliating when we stumble and make mistakes. And the teacher is really nice and really patient. It's not like when I was a kid."

Teresa nodded. "Jerry likes his special reading class, too. He's been a lot less unhappy about school lately."

"I'm so glad. I wouldn't want him to go through what I did." Francy's reply was heartfelt.

They had arrived at the shop on Linden Street. Francy hurried forward and peered into its empty window. Then she motioned toward the grocery next door. "I'll get the key from Gus."

"No, I'll do that," Teresa countered quickly. "You just stay put."

A little puzzled, Francy watched as her sister teetered into the Italian grocery. Then she shrugged and returned her attention to the grimy window. Several minutes later Teresa reappeared with Gus. Smiling and joking with his usual good humor, he let the two sisters inside the empty little store. Beyond the threshold they both stopped, appalled by what they saw.

"It's even dirtier than it looks from the window," Teresa commented.

Francy wiped her finger along a dusty counter and eyed the stained and flaking walls.

"It needs a good cleaning, a little carpentry and a few coats of paint," Gus declared. Instead of going back to his store, he lingered in the open doorway.

"An awful lot of work," Francy muttered under her breath.

"Since when have you been afraid of hard work?" Gus stepped forward. "Listen, to get a pair of pretty neighbors like you two in here, I'll be glad to help out. We'll make a party of it. What do you say, Teresa? Are you game for a fix-up party?"

Teresa flushed slightly. "I say it sounds interesting. Count me in."

As Francy looked from her sister to Gus, her eyebrows shot up to her hairline. "Whoa, that's awfully nice of you guys, but I haven't decided to go ahead on this yet. There's more to be considered than scraping some dirt off the walls. I need to think about this."

On the short stroll back to the house, Francy glanced at her sister several times. "You know," she finally declared, "you surprised me back there."

"What do you mean?" Teresa didn't meet Francy's eyes.

"Since when have you been so enthusiastic about this shop? I've been talking about it for weeks, and you've never shown the slightest interest. In fact, all along you and Mama have been discouraging me from the idea."

"Well, I've changed my mind. I think it's time we took a step."

"We?" Francy gaped. For years now Teresa had been quite willing to sit back and let her do everything. How come she was suddenly so gung ho?

"Yes, we. I know you're afraid to rent this store because of the paperwork. But I can read, and in school I was pretty good at math. I can help you with the accounts."

"What about the kids?"

Teresa shrugged. "You know how Mama is. If we need help, she'll give it. Besides, they're all in school now. They don't need me home all the time."

Well, that was certainly a new idea for Teresa, Francy thought.

In front of the house, Teresa stopped and turned toward her younger sister. "Don't forget, I'm Papa's daughter, too. I may not be as clever with a sewing machine as you are, but I can do my share."

Francy stared into Teresa's face. It had been years since she had seen her look so animated. And she was right, Francy suddenly found herself thinking. It was foolish to imagine that she could manage a store by herself. But she and Teresa just might be able to do it together. "Well, if you're really serious."

"I really am."

Francy continued to search her sister's face. Then she nodded. "Okay, let's go in and talk to Mama."

That night Francy waited until the rest of the family was out in the living room in front of the television set. Then she called Adam. Her heartbeat accelerated when she heard his baritone voice on the other end of the line.

"Adam?"

"Francy?" He sounded surprised. "Is that you?"

"Yes. I've decided to go ahead and do it, Adam."

There was a brief hesitation. "The store, you mean?"

"Yes. Will you help me?"

"Of course I'll help you. Don't worry about a thing. When I've negotiated the contract and the papers are ready to sign, I'll call you."

She smiled and unconsciously wove the telephone cord around her ring finger. "I should really pay you for your help."

"I don't want money."

"Then I should lower the price of the labor on your drapes."

"I don't want that, either."

She had trouble keeping her voice steady. "Then how can I repay you?"

There was the briefest of pauses. "By letting me take you out for dinner. Will you?"

She ran the pad of her thumb around the edge of the receiver. "Yes," she finally said. "I'd like that."

# CHAPTER SEVEN

"DEFINITELY LOOKS AS IF someone's out for your blood, my friend." Clarke Burdette, an assistant prosecutor in Adam's office and a friend who went back to his grade-school days, held a crumpled scrap of paper between his thumb and forefinger. "You say you found this on your doorstep this morning?"

"Right under the milk." Adam propped himself against the edge of his desk and loosened his tie. "What do you think?"

"I think there's no way we can trace it, since it's just ordinary lined paper that you can buy in any drugstore, and the message was put together from words cut out of a newspaper." He returned his attention to the paper and read, "'You're dead meat, pretty boy, but first I'm going to make you sweat.'" The balding young attorney gave his colleague a concerned look. "Do you think this might have some connection with that accident you had on the train platform a couple of weeks back?"

"Unlikely, but possible, I suppose." Frowning, Adam took the note out of Clarke's fingers and stared at it.

"Maybe you should think about who might have done this."

"I am thinking about it. Trouble is, most of the candidates I come up with are in jail."

Clarke scratched his head. "There's the Townsend case. A lot of angry people are involved in that mess."

"Not angry enough to kill me, surely. At least not until the custody of the child has been awarded."

"How about that character who drowned his wife and tried to make it look like suicide? He's out on bond, isn't he? And he can't be very fond of you for picking holes in his alibi so quickly."

"Bittner? I suppose it could be him, but somehow I don't think so. I'm meeting his attorney later on this afternoon, as a matter of fact."

Clarke laid a hand on Adam's shoulder. "Listen, remember in high school how you appointed yourself public defender and went after that overgrown bully who was shaking down all the ninth graders for their lunch money?"

Adam laughed. "What's that got to do with this?"

"Well, when he and his gang cornered you in an alley, you were able to take the bunch of them apart. You've always been able to wade into a messy situation and come out in one piece. But now you're playing in a different league. Since you became State's Attorney in this county, you've ruffled a lot of feathers. Excuse the mixed metaphor, but when you stir up muck, a lot of weird things can come creeping out. Whether you think so or not, maybe you should call the sheriff and ask for some protection."

Adam's look of perplexity turned into a scowl. "And have some flat-footed oaf in a blue uniform following me around? Not on your life."

"We're talking about *your* life, buddy. That oaf might save it."

Adam pushed himself away from the desk and started sorting through the stack of papers he needed to read before the day was finished. "I'm sorry I bothered you with this, Clarke. I think it's probably just a prank to get my goat."

"There are laws against pranks like that. I'm wondering if I shouldn't request some protection for you whether you like it or not."

Adam shot his friend a warning grin. "Do something like that and I'll start pasting up poison-pen letters and sticking them under your door. I have an important date tonight, and I don't want any chaperons dogging me."

"Aha." Clarke folded his arms across his plump chest. "Who's the lucky lady? Barbara Kains?"

Adam's grin slipped slightly. "No."

"That's right. Janet told me you two had cooled off. Now let me see if I can guess who your new flame might be." Clarke tapped his forehead. "Is there, by any chance, some connection between her and this negotiation you've been carrying on about a store in Little Italy?"

"Very clever, Sherlock. The negotiations are complete. The contract has been signed. And tonight I collect my prize."

"YOU LOOK REALLY PRETTY, Aunt Francy."

"Thanks, Jer." Francy eyed her reflection, turning this way and that to see how the handkerchief hem on her skirt hung from various angles.

"Is that the dress you were sewing on last night?"

Francy's eyes sparkled. "Ran it up on my hot little machine in less than two hours, and it's an exact copy of a Rykiel." As she spoke, she studied the deceptively simple midnight-blue dress with satisfaction. Its cut was just right for her figure. She looked elegant yet feminine, restrained yet sexy. *Barbara Kains, eat your heart out!*

"Maybe you should sew dresses instead of curtains."

Francy turned away from the mirror and grinned at her nephew. He was sitting cross-legged in the middle of her bed, crayons and an abandoned coloring book at his side. "The day of the little dressmaker is over. There's more money in home decorating," she told him. "I did think once about getting into fashion design, though."

"Why didn't you? I bet you would have been good."

Francy made a little face. "It was just before I dropped out of high school. I was feeling pretty down on myself. It didn't seem as if I could do anything right. So I decided to play it safe and stick with the family business."

"Was that because you had dis . . . disalek . . ."

"Dyslexia," Francy supplied matter-of-factly. "Yes, it was, though I didn't understand it at the time. Lucky for you people know about dyslexia and understand it better now."

"Some of the kids say I'm dumb."

"That's not true," Francy declared emphatically. "Your teacher knows your reading problem has nothing to do with how smart you are. Some of the smartest people in history were dyslexic. It's just that their brains worked a little differently."

"I still hate school," Jerry complained, shifting his position. "Reading is a pain. It's too hard."

Concerned, Francy dropped down on one knee so that her face was level with her nephew's. "I know it's hard, honey. Believe me, do I ever know. But don't you dare give up on it, Jerry. I won't let you."

"You mean you'll beat me up if I quit?"

Jerry giggled when his pretty aunt suddenly distorted her face to make it look like one of the evil cartoon characters on television. "I'll use my magic thimble to zap you," she told him sternly. She gave him a sympathetic grin. "I just wish I could help you. But I'm afraid it would be a case of the blind leading the blind."

A little disconsolately, Francy thought back to her last class. Sometimes she felt sure she was making a little progress, but other days it seemed as if she was going backward. "It's bound to be a slow process," Mrs. Geddes had warned. "You just have to be patient and persistent."

*If I ever have children of my own,* Francy told herself glumly, *that's what I'll name them: Patience and Persistence.*

Just then Teresa bustled in. "Hey, you look great. Stand up and let me see."

Her good humor restored, Francy got to her feet and whirled so that the hem of her tulip-shaped skirt flared out.

"Very sexy. Your handsome lawyer will be knocked right off his pins."

"He's not *my* lawyer."

"Well, he's certainly not mine. And I don't suppose he negotiated that contract because he was crazy for a jar of Mama's homemade spaghetti sauce."

Francy rolled her eyes. "I wish you hadn't let her send that home with him."

"How could I hold her back? When he stopped by to drop off the contract, she fell madly in love with him. Let me tell you, the guy is quite some charmer."

Francy shook her head. She'd been out making a delivery at the time and had missed the momentous meeting. What had Adam thought of her house, she wondered. Had he been put off by its small dimensions and the row-house neighborhood where so many people lived separated only by narrow brick walls? It certainly couldn't compare very favorably with the kind of home he was used to. Francy frowned. What did it matter? She couldn't change herself or her family, even if she wanted to—which she did not.

"Where's he taking you?"

"I don't know."

"Some place nice, I bet." Teresa turned to Jerry. "Hey, Jer, you wanna come help out tonight? The other kids said they would, and Grandma's going to fix us a picnic to take along."

Francy shot Teresa an inquiring look. "What's up? Where are you going?"

"Oh, didn't I tell you?" Teresa replied cheerfully. "Gus and I are getting together at the shop to do a little cleaning. You know how he suggested we make a party of it. He's bringing a big fruit salad and ice cream for the kids."

"You're going to clean in that?"

Teresa glanced down at the modish new peasant skirt and ruffled blouse she was wearing. "A little dirt won't hurt this outfit."

"But don't you want to wait for me?"

"Nah." Teresa reached out to take Jerry's hand. "You've been working your head off these past few weeks. Go out and relax with Mr. Golden-Good-Looks. Next time you see the inside of that shop, you won't recognize it."

On those words, Teresa tripped out with Jerry in her wake, and Francy was left staring at the empty doorway. *Too much has been happening too fast,* she thought as she turned back to her bureau and fished out a pair of dangly silver earrings she'd been saving for a special occasion.

A few minutes later the doorbell rang downstairs and she heard the excited sound of her mother's voice mixed with Adam's smooth baritone. Francy took a last apprehensive glance at the mirror. She was too nervous to appreciate the warm beauty of the slender, dark-haired young woman reflected there. All she could see was the question in her deep brown eyes. *Why am I letting this happen? What good can possibly come of it?*

Just as she'd feared, when she went down to the crowded little living room her mother was already pressing more food on Adam. "Take this jar of meatballs home with you. Have it over some noodles. *Bella!*" Mama touched her thumb and forefinger to her lips and made a faint smacking noise. "You'll see what real Italian cooking is."

"Mama, Mr. Pearce is not undernourished." Hurrying into the room, Francy cast a worried look at Adam.

Crisp and elegant in gray slacks and a navy-blue linen sport coat, he was smiling genially down at her mother and holding out his hand for the large glass container she proffered. "I tried your sauce last night, and it was delicious. I can't wait to sample more of your home cooking."

It was then that he caught sight of Francy. The smile didn't leave his face, but the expression in his blue eyes changed subtly.

"Doesn't my Francy look pretty?" Mama demanded. "She made that dress herself. Such a smart girl. It couldn't be any better put together if it came direct from Paris."

"She couldn't be any more beautiful if she came direct from heaven," Adam said, and held out his hand.

Francy found herself walking straight to him, her own fingers outstretched. Then, with his arm around her waist, they said goodbye to her mother and went out into the warm evening.

He took her to Vivande's, an expensive restaurant overlooking the Inner Harbor.

"I would have thought you'd had enough of Italian cooking," Francy commented when he told her where he'd made reservations.

"I love Italian food. And I wanted you to feel right at home."

Francy was silent. Actually, she dreaded going out to high-class restaurants with a date who didn't know her problem. It was always such a struggle to figure out what was on the menu. In cheaper places you could get away with ordering a hamburger, but she wouldn't be able to do that at Vivande's. Could she just ask for spaghetti? But sometimes the really first-class Italian restaurants didn't serve anything so pedestrian. Or if they did, they paired it with some type of exotic sauce, and what you picked never jibed with what was printed on the menu.

Her heart sank when they walked into the place. It was definitely not a pizza joint, she concluded as she glanced around at the white marble floor, pink linen tablecloths and black leather chairs. In the center of the airy dining room, a string quartet in dinner jackets played soft classical music. Well, at least she was dressed okay, Francy thought as the maitre d' led them to a table by the window. He'd obviously recognized Adam on sight, and as several people looked up and stared with interest at the tall man at her elbow, it began to dawn on Francy that she was in the company of a local celebrity.

The table Adam had reserved looked out on the dark harbor, which glittered with lights. "Beautiful," Francy commented.

He appeared pleased. "This is a celebration, after all, so it should be a little special. In fact, I think we need to drink a toast. Why don't I order us a bottle of champagne?"

Before she could reply, a waiter came up and Adam requested the wine list. When it arrived, Francy worried that he might ask her to look at it, but he didn't. After studying it, he ordered something French the price of which, she suspected, would probably have made her feel faint.

"To new beginnings," Adam said after the waiter had popped the cork and poured them each a glass of bubbly.

Francy took a sip of the tart, exhilarating wine. "Actually, that's one of the names I've been considering for the shop."

"New beginnings?" Teasingly Adam smiled at her. "I wasn't really thinking of your new store when I made that toast, you know."

Francy toyed with the stem of her glass. "What were you thinking about?"

"About how good you look in candle glow," he answered lightly. "You should spend more time bathed in it."

"Bad for the eyes."

"*Au contraire,* it's not bad for your eyes at all. Right now they look like huge, mysterious pools—the kind a man would like to lose himself in."

Francy shifted her gaze to her hands. "I want to apologize for my mother. I'm sorry she pushed all that food at you."

"Why? Your mom's a charming woman and a wonderful cook. I'm looking forward to those meatballs."

Francy had to laugh. "Somehow, I don't think your mother goes around shoving food at total strangers."

"No," Adam agreed, "food has never been a big interest of hers. She's too busy managing the world to cook for it. Speaking of which, why don't we take a look at this menu? I'm hungry."

For several minutes now Francy had been casting surreptitious glances at the large, leather-bound document the waiter had ceremoniously presented to each of them. Not too happily, she flipped it open and stared at the incomprehensible markings inside. Realizing that she didn't see anything she even remotely recognized, her nerves began to jump. Shakily she set down her glass, and a little of the champagne spilled on the starched tablecloth. Through her lashes she glanced at Adam. He was scrutinizing the heavy vellum pages with interest, a little smile hovering around the corners of his mouth.

"Why don't you order for me?" he said, catching her by surprise as he suddenly glanced up. "You probably have a better idea than I do about which of these entrées is good."

Francy pressed her damp palms against the edges of her chair. "I don't recognize any of these dishes," she blurted.

Adam looked nonplussed. "You don't recognize them?"

*Calm down,* Francy told herself. She refused to give in to the panic that this sort of thing used to induce—the fear and doubt, the clammy skin and accelerated breathing. As a child when she had been called upon to read in front of a class she had stood there hyperventilating to the point of faintness, unaware that she was babbling nonsense as she struggled feverishly to make sense of the dreaded black squiggles on the pages of a book.

"I believe that the cuisine they serve here is northern Italian," she improvised. "My family is southern Italian, so it's almost as unfamiliar to me as it is to you. I think I'll have a salad."

"What kind of salad?"

"Just tossed is fine."

"A tossed salad?" Adam stared at her. "Are you on a diet?"

"Yes," Francy told him. It wasn't really a lie. Like most women, she was always on a diet of sorts.

"Oh, but tonight is a special occasion. Aren't you tempted by the linguine or black fettuccine with shrimp and scallops?

Francy relaxed. "I have to admit those do sound good. Maybe I'll have the fettuccine. How does that sound?"

"Better than a tossed salad," Adam growled as he returned his attention to the menu. "You women amaze me sometimes."

Hiding a smile, Francy heaved a small sigh of relief and took a sip of champagne. A moment later the waiter approached and Adam ordered her *fettuccine nere con gamberetti e cappesante* and *penne alla bisanzio* for himself.

Their dinners, when they arrived, were as attractively prepared as the restaurant itself. After they had eaten, Adam had espresso and Francy asked for a cappuccino.

"That was delicious," she said as she sipped her rich, frothy coffee.

"Yes, it was good. We should come here more often."

Francy cleared her throat. "Adam, because I went out with you tonight doesn't mean—"

"Doesn't mean you'll go out with me again?" A line appeared between his eyebrows. "You really know how to hurt a guy, don't you?"

To Francy's surprise, he actually did look hurt. "I'm going to be very busy trying to make a go of this shop," she said. "And, by all accounts, you're going to be busy, too."

"My job always keeps me on the go. What's that got to do with anything?"

"I wasn't referring to your job, exactly." She moved the crystal salt shaker back and forth, pressing little circular patterns into the tablecloth. "I heard that you might be running for office soon."

Arrested, Adam queried, "Where did you get that idea? I haven't made any public announcements."

"From Barbara Kains," Francy told him, a faint edge of defiance in her husky voice.

"From Barbara?" Adam focused on her sharply.

"I delivered her finished slipcovers a couple of weeks ago."

"And afterward the two of you sat around discussing my career plans?"

"Not exactly. She invited me to have some tea and while we were drinking it the conversation came around to you." Francy noted Adam's closed expression. "I think she was feeling me out, trying to find how much I knew about you. She really likes you, doesn't she?"

Adam's blue eyes narrowed. "I really like her, too, Francy. But I'm not dating Barbara anymore."

"Is that the way you normally treat women? Give them a rush and then drop them like the good old hot potato when you see someone you like better?"

"I'm not some sort of two-bit playboy, Francy." Adam's voice was rough. "I feel guilty as hell about Barbara, actually. But I couldn't go on seeing her after I realized how interested I was in you. So I told her we were through."

"Did you tell her the reason?"

"Just that I'd met someone else. Your name didn't come up."

"She knows, though. Women have instincts where this sort of thing is concerned." Francy studied Adam's defensive countenance. She was glad that she'd mustered the courage to ask him these questions. He was always so aggressive with her, like a quick-witted shelty effortlessly maneuvering a bewildered sheep. It felt good to be on the attack for a change. Francy pushed her cup around in its saucer. "You've always had it pretty easy with women, haven't you?"

There was a faint flush on Adam's square jaw. "What's that supposed to mean?"

"It means that you're the type of guy who's never had to worry much about rejection. I bet in high school you were voted most popular boy and your date to the prom was the homecoming queen."

When his flush deepened, Francy knew she'd guessed right.

"I don't see what my high-school record has to do with us now. What's the point?"

She lifted her chin. "The point is that you're thirty-five and still single. Pretty unusual for a guy as attractive as you. Barbara mentioned that you had a reputation for being elusive. There must be quite a string of disappointed ladies stretching through the years since your yearbook voted you most popular."

Adam rested his flattened palms on either side of his abandoned espresso, and his narrowed eyes were flinty. Suddenly, as she faced him across the table, Francy had a sense of what it must be like to confront him in a courtroom. It would be a very different experience from being wooed by the man over candlelight and champagne.

"I see what's been going on in your head," he clipped. "Let me make something clear. I'm not still single because I enjoy racking up notches for my bedpost. I'm not a deceiver or a heartbreaker. Truthfully, in college I never had much time to chase girls. I was too busy hitting the books. Francy, I haven't got where I am now because of my active social life, or because my rich family bought me a sinecure. I've had to work hard for what I wanted, and that's exactly what I've done. The reason I'm not married yet is because I've just never met the right lady."

With that he signaled for the waiter and told him curtly that he wished to pay the bill. While he signed the check, Francy eyed the harsh line of his mouth and the way his lids hooded the angry expression in his eyes. Part of her was sorry she'd attacked him. It really hadn't been fair. It didn't make much sense to treat a man like Jack the Ripper because he was handsome, successful, rich and eager for your company. Still, another part of her couldn't really regret that she'd asked him some of those questions. The answers had been too enlightening.

When they were outside strolling on the promenade next to the water, Adam asked in a tightly controlled voice, "Is there anything you'd like to do? Take a paddleboat out, stop somewhere else for a nightcap?"

She knew he expected her to say, "No. Take me home please." Instead she surprised him, and herself, by answering, "Yes. I'd like to ride the merry-go-round."

After a second or two of silence, he said, "All right. If I recall, it's at the other end of the harbor next to the Science Center. We'll have to walk."

"I don't mind walking. It's a beautiful night."

The breeze off the water brushed their cheeks gently, and the balmy May air was scented with the delicate perfumes of spring. Lampposts lit the promenade, casting puddles of soft illumination.

Despite the late hour, people still crowded the promenade. Many were couples, their arms entwined, their heads close together as though sharing some secret knowledge. Francy looked at them wistfully. It had been a long time since she'd felt that way, a long time since she'd allowed herself to acknowledge her attraction to a man so openly.

Now and then, as she and Adam made their way toward the Science Center, she stole a glance at him. She knew why she'd been so belligerent with him in the restaurant. It was because he scared her. Falling in love with a man like this would be such an easy thing to do. But he was too good to be true. It couldn't last.

When they reached the merry-go-round it was almost deserted. Only a few children perched on the antique horses. Weary parents leaned against the railing or sat on the benches that ringed it.

"Too late for most kids, I suppose," Adam commented as he stepped up to the ticket booth. When he returned he gave Francy two tickets.

"Isn't one yours?"

"No, both for you. I'll watch."

"Thanks." She walked through the gate and found herself a snow-white steed with flaring nostrils and a bejeweled golden halter. She'd always loved carousels. One of her earliest memories was of her father putting her on a wooden horse and whispering, "Hold on tight, *Bellina*. This is a magic horse, you know." Papa had been right, she mused now as she waited for the music to begin. That painted horse had been magical.

A moment later the calliope started and Francy's white steed began to pump rhythmically up and down. As the carousel picked up speed, she held tight to the brass pole, closed her eyes and inhaled the scented night air. It lifted tendrils of hair from her forehead, almost as if she were flying away to some place of enchantment. When she opened her eyes again, the lights reflecting off the water seemed to blur and run together.

It was an unusually long merry-go-round ride, and when it finally ended Francy was on the side opposite to where Adam had been standing. *By the time I've gone for my second ride, he'll be bored to tears,* she thought as she waited for the carousel to start again. But he suddenly appeared just ahead of her. To her surprise, he stepped onto the red-painted wooden planks and, casting a faint, sheepish grin in her direction, mounted the striped zebra at her side.

"I thought you weren't going to ride."

"I wasn't. But when I watched you, I realized I was missing something special."

"Did I seem to be having fun?"

"To put it mildly. You looked as if you had found the key to paradise."

The girl who operated the carousel pushed a lever forward, the bright wheeze of the music startled the night air, and the painted horses began their stationary whirl. Francy and Adam went up and down in a counter rhythm, slow at first, and then faster and faster until once again the world outside the flying wooden steeds seemed to blur and lose its substance. Francy grinned across at Adam.

"So, what do you think?"

"I think it's great. Now I see why you looked so blissful."

"Didn't you ever do this when you were a kid?"

"No, somehow this was an experience I missed."

*Probably too busy riding real horses to bother with the wooden ones,* Francy mused. But then she pushed the thought aside in favor of just enjoying this strangely perfect moment.

At last the music stopped, the carousel shuddered to a creaking halt, and suddenly the harbor and the sound of traffic on the streets surrounding it shattered the fantasy. Adam slid off his zebra and helped Francy down from her steed, his strong hands lingering possessively on her waist. When they left the merry-go-round, he steered her toward a shadowy bench at the water's edge.

"Can we sit a minute? There's something I want to say to you."

"Sure." She shot him an apprehensive look, but dropped obediently onto the slatted wooden seat.

He settled beside her, stretching a long arm along the top of the bench behind Francy's head so that he could turn and look into her face. "I've been thinking about those questions of yours, and I've realized there's something more I need to say on the subject."

"About your career?"

"In a sense. Francy, my career, my personal goals—those have always been the most important thing in my life. I'd never met a woman who interested me more, and I guess I'd about come to the conclusion that I was too self-centered to ever truly fall in love. At least not in the soul-shattering way the poets write about. Even so, I was considering asking Barbara to marry me."

Francy inhaled sharply. "You were?"

"Yes, I was. But then I met you. Francy, when I met you everything changed. I've never before been so instantly attracted to a woman. And the more I learn about you, the stronger that feeling gets. Give me a chance, won't you?"

She gazed back at him, her eyes suddenly burning in the darkness. Adam had never looked more appealing. The starlight silvered his hair and carved the angles and planes of his face into mysterious shadows.

"We have so little in common," she said weakly.

"Now there's where you're wrong, and I'm going to prove it to you." As he spoke, he reached for her, gathering her into his arms. "We're human, Francy. I'm a man and you're a woman, and we need each other."

She couldn't argue the point. The feel of his hands on her body, the intensity of his gaze—suddenly she was beyond words.

His head lowered and his mouth came down on hers. It wasn't like the undemanding caress he'd bestowed on her earlier. It was a lover's kiss, amorous and impassioned. As it went on and Francy's lips melted beneath the heat of his, one of Adam's hands curled around the back of her neck, bunching her thick curls between his fingers, while the other stroked the slender line of her back.

At the same time Francy's arms lifted. For a moment her fingertips rested on his shoulders. But then, they moved to his head where they clung, sifting restlessly through the short, crisp strands.

Adam had invaded the moist interior of her mouth, his tongue dueling intimately with hers. At the same time he pressed her even closer so that the tips of her full breasts tingled and grew hard against the fine material of his shirt.

Swept away by his fiery ardor, Francy quivered in his arms, kissing him with all her strength, oblivious of their surroundings. It was Adam who finally pulled back.

"My God, but I wish we were alone somewhere," he whispered huskily.

"Yes," Francy replied starkly. She was too aroused to care whether it made any sense. At that moment she wanted nothing more than to be alone with him, too.

"Let's get out of here."

"Yes." Actually Francy wasn't too sure she could walk, and when Adam pulled her to her feet she did stumble slightly. But with his strong arm around her, half supporting her weight, she did manage to get her rubbery legs under control. Together they headed for the parking garage where he'd left his car.

It was a seven-story concrete structure. Since the Mazda had been left on the sixth level, they took the elevator up. Inside the tiny, airless cubicle, neither of them spoke. They were still too galvanized by the strong emotions quivering between them.

Though the sixth level had been half filled when Adam had parked his sports car, it was now nearly deserted. As she walked next to him, Francy's high heels echoed hollowly on the stony floor.

"These places are eerie at night," she heard herself whisper.

"Yes, but necessary. There's no other way to handle the kind of traffic the Inner Harbor draws."

She knew that Adam's answer was only a half-hearted attempt at civility. Like her, he was really thinking about what would happen when they were safely inside his car. They would kiss again, of that she was sure. And afterward? Would they go to his place? Did she want him to take her there?

They rounded a concrete post so that the sleek black Mazda was suddenly fully visible.

"My God!" Adam stopped in his tracks.

Francy let out a little gasp. "What happened?"

Instead of answering, he sprinted toward the automobile. When he was within a few feet of it, he once again stopped short. He was still standing there, staring, when Francy hurried up behind.

"Adam, what is it? What's happened?" The question was nonsensical since she could see for herself what had happened. Someone had smashed the car's windshield. "How—how could anyone have done this?" she stammered. Shards of broken glass lay all around.

"With a baseball bat or a crowbar." Adam walked around the hood and peered through the gaping hole in the glass. Then he straightened, an even grimmer set to his mouth. "Looks like I won't be sampling your mother's meatballs after all."

"What do you mean?"

"Take a look and see for yourself."

Gingerly Francy approached and peered into the car. The jar of meatballs, which had been left sitting on the dashboard, was smashed. Looking horribly like blood, red sauce covered the driver's seat.

Francy shivered. "Oh, Adam, why would anyone do such a terrible thing to your beautiful car?"

Adam was picking out a slip of paper that had been jammed under the hinge on the headlight cover. Unfolding it, he read, "Judgment day is coming, Pearce."

"What does it say?" Francy queried.

"Nothing enlightening." Folding it again, he thrust it into his pocket. Then he took Francy's hand. "Come on, let's go back downstairs."

"What are you going to do?"

"Put you in a taxi. Then I suppose I'd better call the police and my insurance company."

# CHAPTER EIGHT

"SO, IT WAS JUST A VANDAL who smashed your boyfriend's windshield?" Teresa inquired.

"He's not my boyfriend."

Teresa rolled her dark eyes. "So, it was just a vandal who smashed up your gentleman friend's car? How's that?"

Francy grimaced. "All right, I give up. Yes, Adam shrugs the whole thing off. But sometimes I have the feeling there's more to it."

"That's because you worry about everything. He's right, it was probably just some kid on a spree. Well, now that the car's back from the repair shop, where are you going with Mr. Perfect tomorrow?"

Francy eyed her sister who was busily stapling on a mini-floral-print table skirt. Once the decorative skirt was in place the table would hold a selection of wallpaper sample books. "Why don't you just call him Adam? Why is it always Mr. Perfect, or Mr. Golden-Good-Looks, or something like that?"

From her kneeling position on the floor, Teresa glanced over her shoulder. "I don't know. I guess I just can't get used to the idea that you've got a guy beating down your door who looks as if he belongs on a movie set. I mean, from what I've seen of him and from what you've told me about him, he appears a bit unreal—

rich, handsome, successful. There's gotta be a fly in the ointment.''

"I know." Francy put down the hammer that she'd just used to tack up a picture and mopped her brow. "A lot of the time he seems that way to me, too. I mean, take what we did last weekend. A moonlight supper cruise on the Chesapeake Bay. There we were eating lobster, sipping champagne, with the water lapping around us, the stars overhead and the wind in our hair.''

"Sounds okay to me.''

"It wasn't just okay. It was perfect, like something out of a dream. Teresa," she almost wailed, "things like that just don't happen to me.''

"But they are happening," the young woman on the floor pointed out. "Why can't you relax and enjoy it?''

"Because I'm enjoying it too much, and it scares me. It's like I'm losing touch with reality.''

Teresa shot her sister a shrewd look. "You haven't let him get you into bed, have you?''

"No. I haven't done anything stupid." Francy began to run a damp sponge along the Formica countertop. "He hasn't been pushy the way some men are. In fact, he's been treating me as if I'm made of glass—you know, showing me a wonderful time, trying to let me get to know him better. You asked what we're doing tomorrow. He's taking me to an afternoon bull roast for the Howard County Police Department. I think he wants to introduce me to some of the people he works with.''

"Well, that's a good sign," said Teresa. "When a man shows you off to his friends and treats you with respect then you know he isn't just out for fun and games. He really likes you.''

"I suppose." Francy put her hands on her blue-jeaned hips and glanced critically around the shop. This was her and Teresa's last week of fixing the place. On Monday New Beginnings was scheduled to open its doors for business. "It looks good," she pronounced as she eyed the floral curtains around the display window where a reupholstered chair and a selection of fabrics and wallpapers were now attractively displayed.

"It was a lot of work."

"Yes, and I couldn't have done it without you." Francy gave her sister a heartfelt look of gratitude. "You've really been great."

Teresa laughed. "Don't look so darn surprised. I know how to make myself useful. And it's going to be my shop, too. We're partners." As she spoke, she scrambled to her feet and brushed dust off her navy-blue shorts. "I have to get back to the house and change clothes. Gus Venturo is taking me out to a movie tonight."

"He is?"

"Yes." Teresa began gathering up the debris that had accumulated around her while she worked.

"You and Gus seem to be getting along really well."

"We are." To Francy's amazement, her older sister's cheeks pinkened.

"Do you really like him?" Francy asked curiously. She thought the grocer was one of the nicest guys in the world, but couldn't imagine having a romantic interest in him. To her he seemed like a kindly uncle.

"Yes, I do like him. When you get to know Gus, he's really a sweet person. All those years he took care of his ailing parents. Oh, I know what you're thinking," Teresa added. "He's not handsome the way Tony was, and he's older. But when you've had your heart broken by a man like Tony D'Alessio, a steady guy like Gus begins to look good to you. Anyway—'' Teresa shrugged "—it's not as if we're running away to Acapulco together. We're just going to a movie. I think it's good for me to start getting out of the house. Even Mama agrees.''

Francy agreed, too. Lately Teresa seemed like a different person. She was taking an interest in things, was far more cheerful and had been absolutely wonderful about helping to get the shop ready for business. At last she seemed to be finding the strength to emerge from the shell she'd plastered over herself after the breakup of her marriage. If Gus Venturo had anything to do with that, then Francy was all for him.

"Have a good time,'' she told her sister. "I think I'll stay and put just one more coat of paint on those bar stools.''

"Okay, but don't work so hard that you're too tired for that bull roast tomorrow afternoon.'' Teresa began to amble toward the door. Just as she reached it, she turned and studied her younger sister's shadowed profile. "I bet I know what's really bothering you about dating this Pearce character.''

"Oh? Listen, there are a lot of things bothering me.''

"Yeah, I know, I know. He's from a different world. He's too good to be true. You're not his type. But that's not really it, is it? Have you told him yet about the reading?''

Francy clutched the paint rag she'd just picked up. "No,'' she admitted in a low voice.

"Don't you think you'd better?''

"I can't.''

Teresa shook her head. "Sooner or later he's bound to find out, you know.''

"I know," Francy said. She began to pry the top off a paint can. "Sooner or later."

THE MONSTROUS CRYSTAL chandeliers dangled from the ceiling of the banquet hall where the Howard County Police Department was holding its eighth annual bull roast and fund-raiser. The chandeliers, more appropriate to the wedding parties that usually filled the hall, now struck an incongruous note.

For the scene was nothing if not informal. The guests wore shorts and shirt sleeves and drank their keg beer from plastic cups. The cutlery was plastic, the plates heaped with potato salad, baked beans, corn on the cob and sliced tomatoes were paper, and the round tables were covered with newsprint. In one corner a loud band featured an accordionist playing oompah-pah music. In the center area of the room several couples attempted spirited if less than coordinated polkas.

"Hey, look at Lassovitch whirl his wife around out there," Adam commented. "Who would have guessed he had that much energy? Whenever I talk to him on the night desk he comes across like a zombie."

"That's probably because you come across like Dracula out for blood," Clarke Burdette retorted cheerfully. "I know how you are when you're trying to track down facts on a case."

Francy withdrew her gaze from the dance floor and looked from Adam to his friend Clarke and then back again. She felt like a detective trying to ferret out evidence herself. Seeing Adam in this setting, surrounded by people who worked for and with him was a revelation. It underlined her earlier realization that he was someone special, a local celebrity. People looked at him in a special way and treated him with a subtle but undeniable deference. She was particularly intrigued by his relationship with Clarke. Obviously the two men had known each other a long time.

"Oh, yes," Clarke agreed when she asked him about it. "The Lone Ranger and I go way back. We met in grade school, as a matter of fact."

"Why do you call him the Lone Ranger?"

Clarke winked at his pretty, brown-haired wife, Janet, and then shot Adam a wicked grin. "Shall I tell her?"

Adam, crisply handsome in white slacks and a striped blue and white polo shirt, appeared embarrassed. "Stow it. Francy's not interested in your stories about my schoolboy doings."

Clarke took a long swig of beer and then grinned across the table at the lady in question. "Oh, I bet she is. You're interested, aren't you, Francy?"

"Yes, I am," she told him sincerely.

"Well, I'm not." Adam pushed back his chair and got up from the table. "Think I'll go for seconds. Can I get you something, Francy?"

Hastily she covered her paper plate with her hand. "No, I'm full up. Think I'll stay behind to hear your friend's Lone Ranger story."

Adam rolled his eyes and swiveled on his heel. Clarke and Francy watched him stride across the polished floor. Then, with a conspiratorial look, the plump, balding young attorney leaned across the table. "Adam doesn't like me telling this tale to his lady friends because it gives them a fix on his true character. But you're too nice to go around imagining that this guy is some kind of normal human being. So I'm going to give you the scoop on Adam Pearce, boy vigilante."

"Clarke, really!" Janet protested with a laugh.

But Francy's eyebrows lifted expectantly. "I'm all ears."

Clarke took another large swallow of beer and wiped at his mouth. "Well, it was like this. When I first met Adam, I worshiped the ground he walked on. There was something about him that made you want to follow wherever he led. But sometimes that wasn't such a smart idea. I'll never forget a thing that happened when we were both about ten. Adam and I were riding our bikes home from a scout meeting one night. On the road we came across an injured dog. It was a big old black mixed breed that'd been hit by a car and left to die."

Francy winced at the image. "He was still alive?"

"Alive and in agony, moaning and yelping." Clarke shook his head, obviously visualizing the scene himself. "To tell you the truth, I was scared. A big dog like that frantic with pain, I figured he might bite. I wanted to leave him and go for help. But not Captain Marvel over there." He glanced across the room at Adam who was chatting with the group of men standing in line for more meat.

The Lone Ranger? Captain Marvel? Teresa wasn't the only one who didn't want to call Adam by his real name. "What did Adam do?" Francy asked curiously.

"Got off his bike and walked over to help the dog get out of the middle of the road. And of course the dog bit him, but that didn't stop Adam. He wasn't going to leave it there to get run over again."

"Did he save the animal's life?"

"No, the dog died," Clarke admitted, "but that's where the story gets interesting."

Francy cocked her head.

"Our friend Adam over there was so mad that any-one would run over a dog and then leave it in the road to die that he decided he was going to find out who did the dirty deed and bring him or her to justice."

"At ten years of age he decided this?"

"Yup."

"And did he?"

"In a manner of speaking. Overnight he turned into a junior Dick Tracy investigating the case. He even persuaded his friends to help him gather evidence. I wound up helping Adam interview everyone who lived on or might have traveled that road around the time the dog was hit. Well, eventually, thanks to Adam's persistence, we found out who did it."

"Who?"

"A Mr. Bentham Bradley, a rich friend of Adam's mother's who owned a place about the size of a French château and who liked to rip around the countryside in his bottle-green Jaguar. He was famous for that car, always wore a special little tweed hat when he roared out of his mile-long driveway with it."

"Adam was certain that this Mr. Bradley hit the dog?"

Clarke leaned his elbows on the table and plucked a handful of potato chips out of the plastic bowl in the center. "Oh, yes. He even sneaked into Bradley's compound and scraped blood off the edge of the front bumper. There were short black hairs stuck to it." Wryly Clarke chuckled at the memory. "Adam was not your average ten-year-old."

"No, I guess not," Francy agreed. "But there wasn't much he could do about his discovery once he found out, was there? I mean, he was only a kid."

"Yeah, that was the problem. How to bring Bradley to justice. Adam told his mother, but she ordered him to forget it."

"Did he?"

"Are you kidding? He decided to take matters into his own hands. That's where I bowed out. I didn't want to get into trouble. But Adam has never been one to avoid trouble, at least not where his conscience is concerned."

"What did he do?"

"He put sugar in Bradley's gas tank."

"Sugar!"

"Yeah, ruined the Jaguar's engine. Then he marched up to his mother and told her what he'd done and why he'd done it."

"He did?" Francy was fascinated. "What happened?"

Clarke shook his head. "Patricia was furious. Adam had to spend the next five years of his life paying for the ruined engine. In high school he was the rich kid in our crowd who never had money. But the point of this story, Francy," Clarke added, leaning further across the table and shooting her a conspiratorial wink, "is that he's no different now than he was then. Beneath the incredibly good-looking exterior of that Robert Redford type heading toward us with a loaded paper plate beats the heart of an old-fashioned knight errant."

"But that's good, isn't it?"

Clarke's expression had taken on a thoughtful cast. "Not necessarily. Oh, sure, guys like that are easy to admire, but in some quarters they're also easy to hate. They make enemies."

"Yes," Janet chimed in, "and I suspect that when they're on their high horse, they can also be tough to live with. If Adam ever gets around to marriage, his wife will have her work cut out for her.''

Clarke, who was gazing across the table at his approaching colleague, didn't seem to take note of his wife's playful comment. Instead, there was a faintly worried expression in his eyes. And suddenly, as Francy saw it, she was reminded of Adam's car with its smashed windshield and seats covered with red tomato sauce, which at first glance had looked so horribly like blood. Men like Adam Pearce make enemies, Clarke had just said. Adam had told her not to worry about the car, that it was just a vandal's doing. Had he been telling her the truth?

All during the rest of that afternoon Francy found herself thinking about Clarke's story. It was still on her mind when the party wound down and she and Adam were having a last slow dance together on the almost deserted dance floor. She knew Adam didn't want to talk about his boyhood exploits and was embarrassed by Clarke's beery stories, but she couldn't keep herself from asking questions.

"Did you mind having to pay for Bradley's engine?"

"Of course I minded," Adam muttered. His arm circled her waist, and they moved together in slow rhythm. "I didn't think a guy like that deserved to own a car. I still don't."

"Were you sorry you put sugar in his tank?"

"No, I hated paying for it, but I never regretted it. And I did learn a valuable lesson from the experience."

"What was that?"

"That it's better to seek justice within the system. That's really when I decided to study law. The law is a

weapon for good, but first you have to understand it
and know how to use it.''

Francy glanced up at his face, seeing with sharp clarity the strength and determination hidden just below the
surface. It might be the countenance of a convention-
ally handsome man, but beneath those easy, fair good
looks was something very unconventional, indeed. All
along she had sensed it. Now, for the first time Francy
was beginning to really understand it, and she was intrigued. For a split second she could picture the little
boy who'd felt so bad about a helpless victim that he'd
been willing to take on an adult, no holds barred.

When the bull roast broke up, Adam drove Francy
back to his place. She'd finished the drapes for his living room and wanted to hang them. Before starting up
the engine Adam cranked up the Mazda's sunroof.
Smoothly the low-slung car purred through the sultry
early June weather. As the fragrance of honeysuckle
and roses flowed through the open windows, they talked
of small things. At her urging, he told her anecdotes
about some of the people she'd met and described a
typical working day at the county office.

"Sounds as if you never rest."

"I keep myself busy."

"Have you always been a workaholic?"

"Always. But given the right partner, I know how to
play, too." He shot her a glinting smile that made her
flush slightly.

He didn't seem to want to talk about himself and kept
steering the conversation back to Francy and her con-
cerns.

"So, how's it going with your shop? Are you really
ready to open up Monday?"

"Yes, I think so."

"Nervous?"

"A little. It's a big step for me, and for my family."

"You can do it. You can do whatever you want."

How little he really knew about her capabilities, Francy thought. She glanced at his profile, noting the firm texture of his tanned skin, the way it was carved into planes and angles by his high, sharp cheekbones. His dark lashes were gold-tipped and behind them his eyes, studying the road narrowly, were a clear, clean blue, like the sky at high noon.

Then all at once his eyes weren't on the road anymore, but bored directly into hers. "Why are you looking at me like that?"

"Like what?"

"As if you don't know what to make of me."

"I like looking at you, Adam," she answered with sincerity. "And it's true, I guess. I really don't know what to make of you. I've never met anyone like you before. I can't quite believe that you're real."

Her whimsical remark didn't seem to amuse him. Instead, if anything, his jawline sharpened. Suddenly he reached out, took her hand and lay it palm down over his thigh. Beneath her flesh she could feel the flexed muscle and sinew, the pulsing heat. "I'm real," he said grimly. "I don't know what Clarke has been filling your head with. But I'm no Boy Scout or fairy-tale Prince Charming. I'm a real man who's been looking at you all afternoon, and wanting you."

After that they drove in silence, held in a bubble of taut feeling. Several times Francy wondered if she shouldn't tell Adam to turn around and take her home. Hanging those drapes now seemed an irrelevant task. But somehow the words never got said. When he pulled up in front of his apartment building he came around to let Francy out and then opened his trunk and hefted the heavy plastic bag full of sewn fabric. With it slung over one broad shoulder he followed her up the walk. They said very little, but the air between them seemed peppered with unspoken questions.

As Adam slid a key into his lock, Francy examined him covertly, vividly aware of his lean height, the taut line of his hips and the flexed strength in his arms. His wrists were dusted with golden hair that she found herself wanting to reach out and touch. As she brushed past him she felt the tiny hairs on her own body lift until each seemed to be standing rigid.

When she'd told Teresa that Adam hadn't been pushy during their few dates, she'd been telling the truth. He'd treated her with a kind of courtly solicitude that for Francy was a new and rather exhilarating experience. But he had kissed her, kissed her in many different ways. There had been brief, friendly pecks while they laughed at some shared joke, and tender caresses when they'd stolen a moment to lean into each other's warmth as they had the night of the moonlit cruise. Then there had been the long, hot kisses, the kind they'd shared in his car just before he said good-night. Those had been the clinchers. Each date, she'd told herself, would be their last. She would be sensible and call this nonsense off. Where could it lead, but to trouble? Then all Adam had had to do was kiss her, and she'd forget her resolution and agree to a next time. Surely just one more time couldn't hurt.

Inside the door Adam's apartment was cool and dark. "Can I get you a drink?" he queried.

"No, I'm still sloshing from all that beer at the bull roast." She walked to the couch where he'd laid the curtains and fingered the thin plastic guarding them. "Maybe I should get started on these."

"There's no rush."

"Don't you want to see how they look?"

"Not at the moment." He was standing in the center of the room, staring at her, hands clenched by his sides. Her dark gaze locked with the concentrated blue of his, and she was unable to look away or pretend any longer that their conversation was about drapes.

"Did I frighten you back in the car?" he asked gruffly.

"No."

"The last thing I want to do is frighten you."

She felt the corners of her mouth lift. "Adam, I'm twenty-five and I grew up in a tough neighborhood. I know what men generally want from women."

"Do you? I think you make it sound simpler than it really is."

Francy's throat felt so tight that she had difficulty speaking. "You'll have to explain that," she said huskily.

"When I'm with you I want so many different things. Sometimes I just want to look at you, at the way your hair waves around your face and gleams like polished coal in the sunlight. Sometimes I just want to listen to you. You have a beautiful voice, Francy. Your laughter is the sound of happiness."

Francy gazed back at him. Did he mean all this? She'd heard so many fancy lines from men who used them like fishing lures. Was he telling her the truth, she wondered. Then she realized with a blinding stab that he was. This was not a man who lied to women, or to anyone. What he said, he meant. What he seemed, he was. It was as simple and as baffling as that.

"But sometimes," he went on tightly, "just looking at you and hearing you aren't enough. Like now, Francy."

"Now?"

"Like now, when I want you in my arms so badly that I can't think of anything else."

Her voice trembled slightly. "Why are you saying this to me now, Adam?" He was holding himself in check. Every inch of her could sense that. But then so was she. Her own muscles ached with tension.

"Because I want to warn you. Feeling the way I do, it wasn't really fair of me to bring you here. In a minute I'm going to break all my rules about you and come over there and grab you."

"You should have told me we were playing a game," Francy said, and walked toward him.

A moment later they were in each other's arms. Adam hugged Francy to him so tightly that she was lifted off her feet. She didn't care that she had only his strength for support. Her fingers locked behind his neck, and she looked up into his face.

"No game," he whispered fiercely. "I just wanted to give you a chance to get to know me. I didn't want to scare you off. I promised myself I'd go slow."

"You have," she said, and lifted her lips to his.

"Francy, I'm crazy about you," he muttered and then kissed her so long and so hard that she felt dizzy. But it was an exciting dizziness. Passionately Adam's mouth moved on hers. As his sensuous kiss deepened, her head was flung back while blood raced and pounded in her ears. With one hand, he cupped her bottom, pressing her body tightly to his. The contact was so electrifying that Francy gasped aloud. Adam seemed to be giving off sparks which sent tongues of flame churning down her bloodstream.

"My God, I want to make love to you," he growled, loosening his hold so her feet touched the floor once more.

"I know."

"How could you not know? It's pretty obvious, isn't it?" He laughed, but there was little humor in the sound. He cupped her face between his hands. "Francy, how can I say this? I want to show you how I feel. Will you let me? Will you trust me?"

He gazed down at her with such blinding desire lighting his eyes that she sagged against him. "It's not that I don't trust you. I do. It's just..." But she could say no more. Her weak attempt at sanity died on her lips and all she could muster was a breathless, "Yes."

"Say it again."

"Yes, Adam. Yes."

He scooped her up into his arms and carried her toward the bedroom. As he strode across the floor, Francy stared up at the bottom of his chin, thinking that she'd never seen his bedroom before and that this was madness. But she didn't tell him to put her down. She simply wasn't capable of that.

When he lowered her onto the bed in his shadowy, simply furnished room, she gazed up at him helplessly. She was afraid of what she was about to do, and yet she wanted him desperately. She simply hadn't the strength to leave this man now, not when she'd been dreaming about this, not when her body ached for his. Abandoning her last reserve, Francy held out her arms.

Immediately Adam came to her, kissing her feverishly as his long, hard torso covered her small, yielding one. Then, while his tongue mingled with hers, she felt his hands on her breasts, kneading and possessing their softness.

She wanted more. She wanted him to open her blouse and take her breasts into his mouth. Wordlessly she arched her back, and then sighed with pleasure as she felt his hands at the buttons. The slide of cloth and then cool air brushed over her bared nipples.

"You're so beautiful, so sweet," Adam murmured. He was staring down at her breasts, the burning blue of his eyes so intense that it seemed almost radiant. "I want you in my mouth. I want to taste you."

"Yes." She laced her fingers in his hair and drew his head down to her. Then, closing her eyes, she arched back, luxuriating in the wet, warm sensation of their intimacy. The aching pleasure went on and on. Yet it was only the beginning.

Tenderly Adam undressed her. Running his hands over her waist, belly, hips and legs as though he were a sculptor, he dropped kisses and whispered words of admiration. "So little, so perfect. You're wonderful, Francy. You're a miracle."

"Take your clothes off, too," she urged. "I want to see you."

His eyes shone. "Do you?"

"You know that I do."

Chuckling, he lifted his shirt over his head and then stripped off his slacks. While he removed his clothing, Francy watched wide-eyed. She took in the dark gold hair on his chest that ringed his nipples and then dipped toward his flat belly. He had the long-limbed, rangy build of a swimmer or a basketball player. There was no softness, only clearly defined muscle over cleanly sculpted bone and sinew. On his legs she could see traces of the scars that lingered from his train accident. The thought brought a faint frown to her eyes. But it was soon gone when he lowered himself to the bed and took her back into his arms.

While the afternoon sun slid behind cloud, and the cool evening shadows gathered around them, they kissed and caressed, stroked and adored. Adam was a tender lover. But when, finally, he'd sheathed himself to protect her and his desire-inflamed body sought and found refuge inside hers, he was tender no longer. He became a demanding, impetuous lover forcing her with him up the breathlessly stepped heights of his rising passion. At last, with a final gasp of mutual discovery, they reached the top of that climb together and slid silkily down the other side.

As Adam's body collapsed against hers, tears stung the backs of Francy's eyes. How would she ever be able to walk away from this man now?

# CHAPTER NINE

CLARKE STOOD GLOWERING over Adam's desk. "Listen, pal, you're a lucky man. If you didn't have a smart secretary with a suspicious eye, you'd be missing a hand."

"You could be right." Both men stared down at the large envelope with the telltale wire sticking from its flap. "This is my first letter bomb. I thought it only happened in spy novels."

"Apparently not." Clarke picked up the ragged looking bundle, which had already been examined and defused by the bomb squad. "They said whoever did it was an amateur. At least you're not up against a professional hit man."

"No, just some crazy who's not too good at reading how-to bomb manuals."

"A crazy who's really got it in for you and who could eventually get his act together. I mean, those death threats you've been receiving are pretty hair-raising. And now this letter-bomb thing...." Clarke shook his head. "What are you going to do about this?"

Adam grimaced. "What can I do? I've notified the police, and I'm keeping an eye out. If the creep ever comes out of the bushes, I'll nab him. In the meantime, I can't spend my life looking over my shoulder. There's just too much to get done." Pointedly he opened a folder and began to peruse it.

But his boyhood friend and colleague wasn't ready to drop the subject. "Does Francy know that someone's out for your hide?"

"No," Adam replied roughly, "and I don't want you telling her. She's not to be worried about this nonsense."

Thoughtfully Clarke studied the top of his friend's head. "I like her. She's a real peach. Those eyes are something. And what a great laugh. She really puts her heart into it."

"Yes." Adam's expression softened, and he looked up, a smile beginning to form on his lips. "She's a special lady."

"Not your usual type."

"What do you mean by that?"

"I think you know what I mean. Has your mother met her yet?"

"Not yet." Unconsciously Adam began to twirl the point of his pencil between his thumb and forefinger.

"Should be interesting when she does." With a brief salute, Clarke turned to stroll out of Adam's office. As Adam watched his friend depart, a frown settled on his face. Clarke had always had a knack for ferreting out touchy issues. Lately Patricia had been at her son for an introduction to his new friend.

"I'd like to meet this young lady, Adam. Why don't you bring her around? Are you ashamed of her?"

Adam's feelings toward Francy had nothing to do with shame. But he wasn't ready to show her to his mother, either. That wasn't because he was afraid of Patricia's opinion. Quite the opposite. He was afraid of what Francy's reaction might be to his mother. When Patricia Pearce chose to assume her lady-of-the-manor airs she could be an intimidating experience. What if

Francy took one look and decided to run the opposite way? He still felt so uncertain of her. Even though they had become lovers, it was a tenuous relationship. No, Adam decided, he wasn't yet ready to bring Francy home to mother. First he wanted to bring her home to himself.

"IT'S BEEN TWO WEEKS since the bull roast," Francy mused.

"Yes, and this is only the third time we've made love. It's not enough."

"It isn't?"

"No, it damn well isn't," Adam said with a growl as he pulled her to him.

"Hey, stop that! You're crushing the French bread!"

They were lying in Adam's bed, a bottle of wine and a plate of food between them. Scented summer air filtered through the window, caressing their damp bodies. Shadows gathered in the corners, stretching out here and there to sculpt a rounded limb or the smooth curve of a bare hip. The bed itself was a study in shades of white, brown and gold. There were the rumpled white sheets on which they lay sprawled and the vase of coin-bright dandelions Adam had playfully picked for Francy in his backyard. They nodded on the bedside table like a bouquet of small dusty suns. Next to the sable of Francy's rich locks, Adam's hair seemed almost as bright as the golden flowers, high noon against velvety midnight.

"I'm hungry for you," he muttered as he planted a heady kiss on her soft lips.

"You can't be. Not after the way we've just spent the afternoon," she responded with a giggle. They had made love with the abandon of children just discovering life's riches and greedy to experience them all. They had gazed and tasted and touched, murmuring into each other's eager ears the inarticulate sounds of passion. Now, however, Francy pushed herself away and turned toward the plate. "Besides, I'm hungry."

."All right, woman, you win. I suppose I can't let you starve. But as far as I'm concerned, you're the most delectable thing on this bed." As Adam reached out to fill her wineglass, his admiring gaze played over the curves of her figure, lingering on the soft thrust of her breasts beneath his shirt, which she'd modestly pulled on to hide her nakedness. "Beautiful," he murmured.

Blushing faintly, Francy popped a grape into her mouth and then busied herself cutting a slice of French bread and spreading it with creamy pepper-seasoned cheese. She shivered slightly as she considered what had just happened between her and the lean man gazing at her so possessively.

The first time she and Adam had made love, she'd gone home and lain in bed feeling alternately wonderful and then deeply irritated with herself. The irritation was a product of fear. *I'm getting in too deep with him,* she'd told herself. *It can't possibly work out.*

For several days after that she'd made excuses not to see him. It hadn't been difficult. Between the evening class she was taking, the demands of her family and everything that had to be done at the shop, she really was ferociously busy.

But Adam had been persistent, and eventually, as always seemed to happen where he was concerned, she'd weakened. This afternoon she'd *really* weakened, she admitted to herself with an ironic little laugh. When Adam had invited her for a picnic, she hadn't been able to resist. Now they were having that picnic in his bed.

But how could she regret the sweet summer lovemaking they'd just shared? It had been glorious.

"You're staring at that grape as if it's a crystal ball. What's going on behind those big dark eyes?" Adam queried. Reclining against the headboard, balancing a half full wineglass in his left hand, he watched her closely.

"I wonder what it would be like if we did have a crystal ball," Francy returned lightly. She twirled the pale grape between her thumb and forefinger. "What if we could look into this and see the future?"

Playfully Adam reached out and took the tiny green orb from her fingers. "Let's see what I can do." He put it down on the sheet between them. Then he reached over to grab the lampshade from his bedside lamp and with a ceremonious flourish, popped it on his head. "Now we're ready for action," he declared and turned back to raise his hands melodramatically over the tiny bit of fruit.

"What are you doing?" Francy demanded between fits of laughter. He looked so absurd sitting there wearing nothing but a fringed lampshade.

"Your wish is my command. I'm going to try and peer into the future. Since I'm inexperienced at this, I'll start small. Let's see if the grape will tell me what's going to happen in a few hours." He fluttered his fingers. "Tell me, oh grape, will I be sleeping alone again tonight? Or, perchance, will I have a beautiful black-haired witch in my arms—one who'll stay to have breakfast with me in the morning instead of disappearing with her pumpkins at midnight?" Under his eyebrows, Adam shot Francy an inquiring look.

She batted lightly at his shoulder. "You know I can't stay all night with you."

"Why not?"

"Oh, for heaven's sake, Adam, we've already gone over this. You know why not. I live at home with my mother and sister. I can't do exactly as I please. Mama would have a fit if I traipsed in some morning after staying out all night with a strange man."

"Hey," Adam corrected, removing the lampshade and suddenly looking far less playful, "I'm not a strange man. I'm Adam, the guy who's made it pretty plain that he's crazy about you."

Francy's gaze skittered away from his. Crazy about her? What did that mean, she wondered. It was obvious that he liked to make love to her. Would he be crazy about those aspects of herself that she'd deliberately kept hidden from him? Francy was pretty sure she knew the answer to that one, and it was a resounding no.

"This isn't the last century and we're not kids, Francy," Adam was going on. "You're twenty-five, a grown woman. Surely your mother will understand that an adult relationship involves more than dates and good-night kisses."

"I don't think so." Francy knew that as far as her mother was concerned, an adult relationship meant marriage and children. But she had no intention of raising that subject with Adam. Marriage was the last thing she wanted to discuss with him. Theirs was strictly a crazy fling.

Looking discontented, he stared at the ceiling. "I'm going to be lonely for you tonight. I want to see you lying next to me in the moonlight, and I'd like to wake up next to you."

Francy didn't know what to say. What he'd just described sounded pretty good to her, too. She glanced down at the grape, which still lay between them. "Now it's my turn."

"What?"

"You've had a go at telling the future. Now it's my turn. Hand over that lampshade."

Amused, Adam picked up the fringed construction and gently crowned Francy's luxuriant waves with the unconventional headgear. "Are you going to have a second look at tonight?"

"No, I'm a little more adventurous." She poked her tongue into the corner of her cheek. "I'm going to try for ten years from now."

"Ten years? You are ambitious." Adam looked suitably impressed.

With an air of concentration, Francy leaned over the grape. While her hands hovered, weaving intricate dancelike patterns over the tiny orb, she chanted, "Reveal the future to me, oh grape! Reveal! Reveal!"

Adam glanced from Francy to the grape. "Is anything happening? I don't see it clouding up."

"Yes, you of little faith, something is happening."

"I knew you were a witch. What do you see?"

"The clouds are parting."

"No kidding? I'm awestruck."

"That's not all. The mist is being blown away, and I see a crowd."

"What sort of crowd?"

"A happy, cheering crowd. A noisy, sweaty crowd. They're waving flags, eating fried chicken and holding up babies to be kissed. And they're all screaming one thing."

"What's that?"

"Adam Pearce for president."

Leaning back against the headboard, Adam laughed loudly. "I knew I shouldn't have told you about this campaign I may be getting myself into. Now that you know I have political aspirations, you're never going to stop teasing me, are you?"

Through the white fringe drooping over her nose, Francy studied Adam's relaxed countenance. "Have you always wanted to get into politics?"

"What do you mean?" He finished off the last of his wine and reached to tear off a hunk of bread.

"I mean running for office is something that would never even enter my head. When did it get into yours, and why?"

Looking thoughtful, Adam ate a rolled-up slice of pastrami and then with precise, efficient movements began to spread cheese on his bread. "My family is different from yours."

"I think I've figured that much out."

Ignoring her dry tone, he went on, "The Pearces have lived in Howard County for over a century. They've always taken a proprietary interest in the area. My great-grandfather was a judge, and my father served on the county council. So political involvement on that level comes naturally to me."

"But it's more than that with you, isn't it?" Francy queried. "From what I've been able to pick up, you have kind of a sense of mission. I mean, you're no ordinary prosecutor. The way people talk about you, they make you sound like a one-man SWAT team." She folded her legs beneath her and clasped her knees. Suddenly she was intensely curious to hear his response.

"You've been paying too much attention to Clarke Burdette."

"I like Clarke. Besides, he's known you longer than almost anyone. Naturally I'm interested in the stories he tells about you."

Adam shook his head. "All right then, purely in self-defense, I'll tell you one of my own stories. Maybe it will make you understand a little better how I feel about things." He locked his hands over his flat stomach, and regarded her thoughtfully. "I remember once you talked to me about your father, and I told you a little about mine."

"Yes, you said you never knew him very well, and that he was a remote person."

"Yes, I think William M. Pearce was a throwback to the last century, a sort of Edwardian gentleman. He was fifty when I was born, so he never played ball with me or took me to the circus. I don't think I ever saw him in his shirt sleeves. The way I remember him he was always dressed in a pin-striped suit and carrying a briefcase."

Francy felt a twinge of sympathy for the little boy who had been so cut off from his father. "I'm sorry," she said sympathetically. "That must have been rough."

But Adam only laughed at her. "No, it wasn't really. Just because he didn't play ball with me doesn't mean he didn't love me. Though he never said so, I think I always knew that he did. And I admired him. I was sorry he was away from home so much, but somehow I was always certain that whatever he was doing was important and needed to get done."

"You must have been an unusually generous little boy."

Adam shrugged. "I wouldn't know about that. Pampered only children don't get much call to be generous."

"Is that how you thought of yourself? Pampered?"

"When the maid took me home to visit her family, I realized that the way the Pearces lived wasn't the usual."

"How did that make you feel?"

Adam gazed out the window. "Guilty."

"Guilty?"

"It isn't right that a few should have so much and others so very little. I'm proud of my home and my heritage, but at the same time..."

As his voice drifted off, Francy cocked her head. It had never occurred to her before that Adam felt guilty about the abundance fate, Mother Nature and the world had heaped on him. Suddenly a maverick thought popped into her head. Was that the basis of his attraction to her? Was he trying to atone by hooking himself up with someone so far out of his class? But the notion was so painful that Francy couldn't bear to entertain it for more than a few seconds.

"We're getting away from the story I wanted to tell," Adam said. "We were talking about my father."

"Yes."

"When I was twelve, he died. Among the papers he left was a letter to me, a sort of guide to life."

At Francy's expression, Adam smiled. "I know, it's just the sort of thing a gentleman from a bygone era would do, isn't it? Instead of talking to his son about life, he bequeaths him a letter. I can just picture my father writing that letter, too. He would have been alone in his study late at night, smoking his pipe." Adam's smile shifted, became bittersweet. "Anyway, I was touched by what he wrote and that he'd taken the time to write it for me. Let me see if I can describe it to you."

"Please."

"It started out with a conventional greeting, but then it got right down to the matter at hand, the guide-to-life part. He said that he believed there were two goals in life—personal happiness and making the world a better place to live in."

"That sounds reasonable."

"My father was nothing if not reasonable. He went on to explain that, in his view, the first goal cannot be obtained by seeking it directly. It has to be obtained through the second."

"You mean he thought a person could only be happy through making the world a better place?"

"Exactly. Oh, sure, immediate happiness can come from things like a good dinner, a good game of tennis, a night out on the town. But a life devoted to pursuits like that would become boring."

As Francy studied Adam's face, her dark eyes glowed. "And that's why you're not just a rich playboy, why you've worked so hard to get where you are and why you're thinking about going into politics? You're pursuing that second goal your father wrote you about?"

Adam looked slightly sheepish. "Now that I've put it into words, it sounds silly and pompous, doesn't it? Adam Pearce trying to make the world a better place—sounds like a slogan for some lousy television commercial." Reddening, he tightened his arms around his knees.

"Oh, no, it doesn't!" Francy launched herself at him, throwing her arms around his neck and hugging his stiff body to her breast. "It sounds wonderful and noble. And that's exactly what you are, Adam Pearce. You're wonderful and noble and handsome and good. You're unbelievable!"

Enthusiastically she began to rain kisses on his forehead and cheeks. Laughing, he responded with de-
light, throwing his strong arms around her and hugging
her soft, curvaceous form to his. For several minutes
they rolled back and forth on the bed, playfully hugging and kissing. But then the affectionate rough-and-
tumble game turned to ardor.

"Oh, Francy," Adam murmured, his blue eyes simmering into hot cerulean pools, "you've just thrown my
pursuit-of-happiness theory into a cocked hat. When
I'm with you, I don't want to make the world a better
place. I only want you." As he kissed her, his hand
stroked the satiny round of her hip.

Francy arched toward him, gasping with quick, sharp
pleasure as he unbuttoned her shirt and then slid down
her body and lowered his head to her swelling breasts.
In his hands she felt weak, willing and, strangely, utterly safe. Later, she knew, that feeling of thrilling security would evaporate. But now, with Adam's fingers
and lips coaxing her every sense into jolting, electrifying life, she had no choice but to give herself up to him
completely.

Sculpted by mauve shadows, they lay entwined. Oblivious to the twilight deepening around them, they
kissed and caressed, sighed and murmured. Pleasure,
like a silken cloud, enfolded them and as they lay in
each other's arms the world beyond shrank to nothing-
ness.

But at last, utterly sated, Francy opened her eyes and
looked out Adam's bedroom window. Stars pricked the
languorous night sky.

"It's getting late," she murmured. "I have to go."

"Don't say that." He clasped her tighter.

"I have to." She chuckled. "I hate to think what's happened to the remains of our picnic."

"I suspect I have a few bread crumbs in my sheets," he agreed.

"What will your cleaning lady say?"

"I don't care what she says."

"But I do. Besides, now that you're thinking of running for public office, you'd better watch your reputation. What if she sells a story to the newspapers? I can just see the headlines. 'Candidate's private life one long orgy. Likes to mix food and sex in bed.'"

Adam sighed. "I'll clean up before she gets here tomorrow."

Francy tried to loosen his grip on her so that she could struggle into a sitting position. "I'll help you do it right now before I leave."

But Adam was not to be dislodged. "Don't leave," he said deeply.

Through the gloom, they stared into each other's eyes, an unspoken battle of wills between them. "Adam, I have to. I can't live like your other lady friends. I'm not Barbara Kains. I don't have my own penthouse apartment."

Releasing her, he sat up and raked an impatient hand through his thick hair. "Why are you bringing Barbara's name up now? What's she got to do with us? You know I haven't seen her since I met you."

"I don't know why I mentioned her." Suddenly chilled, Francy pushed herself up against the headboard and peered around the dark room for the clothes that had wound up in piles on the floor hours earlier. "I guess I keep thinking about her because she seems so much more like your type. I keep wondering why I'm here with you and she's not."

"It's you I want. Not Barbara, you."

"So you say, but I just can't understand it. We're so different. We come from such different worlds." Avoiding his eyes, Francy got out of bed and started feeling around the floor for her clothes. When she located her underwear, she pulled on her panties and hastily snapped her bra.

From the bed, Adam sat watching her. Then, with a look of resignation, he reached for his own jeans and shirt. "We still have a lot of getting to know each other to do, don't we?"

She glanced over her shoulder at him. "This afternoon was pretty chummy."

"That's not the kind I mean. Between you and me that kind comes naturally. The rest is like pulling teeth. When can you see me again?"

Francy tugged her pink sundress over her head and stepped into her sandals. "I don't know. Next week is going to be very busy. There's a lot to do in the store."

"I have Tuesday night free."

"But I don't."

Adam looked distinctly disgruntled. "Why are you always busy Tuesday and Thursday nights? Your store closes at five, doesn't it?"

"Yes, but there are other things in my life besides the store. I'm still going out on calls to do measuring."

"Every Tuesday and Thursday night?"

Francy switched on the overhead light and surveyed the ruined bed. "Squashed grapes, crumbled bread—nice!" she grumbled.

Adam stood eyeing her, a frown on his face. "Forget the bed."

"I'm not going to forget it."

She began to tug the sheets off. But Adam reached out and stayed her hand. "You didn't answer my question. What do you do Tuesday and Thursday nights?"

A spurt of resentment stiffened Francy's spine, and she straightened. Why did he think he had the right to pry into her life? She didn't pry into his. Or did she? Suddenly she realized that that was just what she had been doing—asking him questions, trying to get some insight into what made him tick. And he'd done his best to be open with her.

"I go to a class," she told him.

He looked interested. "Oh? What type of class?"

"A literature class." That was all she intended to tell him.

"I didn't know you were continuing your education. That's good." He appeared genuinely pleased.

"Thanks."

"I don't understand why a bright person like you would drop out of school in the first place."

"It's a long story."

"I have time to listen."

"Adam, not tonight. Now, can we get back to straightening up this mess?" She pointed at the tangled sheets.

His expression darkened. "No, no, we can't." Taking her hand, he led her out of the bedroom and into the kitchen where he sat her down at the table. "Francy, I need to talk to you."

"About what?"

"About us." He quickly finished snapping his jeans and buttoning his shirt as he spoke. "I mean, we can't go on snatching a few hours every other week. We have to spend some quality time together. If you can't do it here, so close to your family, then let's do it someplace else."

Francy was confused. "I don't know what you're talking about."

"I'm talking about a vacation. You know, going away someplace together and just relaxing and having fun. I mean, you know what a vacation is, don't you? You've taken them before."

"I've gone to Ocean City a couple of times."

He looked amazed. "Is that all?"

"Vacations are expensive, Adam. Not everyone can afford them. I certainly can't. Right now, with the store and all, I'm pushed to the very edge."

"Well, if anyone needs a getaway right now, it's you. I have a proposition. Ben Catlett has agreed to manage my campaign. He likes to take his boat to Bermuda every summer, and he's there with it right now. The first week in July I'm flying out for a few days to do some strategy planning with him."

"Sounds nice. Bermuda is a great place, I hear."

"It's a terrific place, a little paradise on earth. Come with me, Francy."

"What?" Her jaw dropped.

"We can be together there, do some of that getting to know each other that we need."

"But you'll be busy with this Mr. Catlett."

"I'll have plenty of free time, and we'll have our own place. Say yes, Francy. I promise you won't regret it."

"Adam, I can't afford—"

"Don't talk to me about money," he cut her off roughly. "I want to take you, Francy. Please say yes."

Francy reached for her purse and stood up. "I don't know," she mumbled. "I'm so busy with the store."

"It'll only be a few days."

"What would my mother say?"

"I'll talk to her, if you want."

"Oh, no!" Francy could just imagine how that conversation would proceed. With Adam at her heels, she began to walk toward the living room. "I need to go. Will you take me home now?"

He grabbed his keys off the mantel. "Of course."

Francy fled out the door and down the walk toward his car. But it was no refuge. Once he slid behind the wheel she became his captive audience. All the way back to Little Italy he argued the reasons she should go away with him.

The man wasn't a lawyer for nothing, Francy reflected. One by one he crushed all her objections, making them seem foolish. When they finally parted, she was feeling doubtful and beleaguered.

However, Adam's mood was jubilant as he pulled away from the brick row house where he'd dropped Francy off. He was sure she would come with him. And once they were alone together for a few days, they would get things straight. Bermuda was heaven, an ideal setting in which to woo and win the reluctant dusky-haired goddess he'd set his heart on.

Whistling between his teeth, he accelerated through a green light and cruised down the semideserted streets of Baltimore. Back in Catonsville, he parked the car and headed into his apartment.

Without her, the place had a deserted air. Still, there was plenty to show that she'd been around. Take the transformed living room. With its fresh coat of paint and wallpaper and new drapes and slipcovers, it was a place where Adam really enjoyed being—all the more so because Francy was responsible for the change.

"Worth every penny," he murmured as he touched the nubby texture of the grass cloth wallpaper. He smiled, thinking of how Francy's pert little bottom had looked as she'd stood on a chair hanging it. Everything about her was cute, even her Italian temper. When he was with her he felt complete, as if he'd found the other half of his true self.

Just then the phone rang. Startled, Adam swiveled on his heel. He was used to getting calls late at night, of course. Mostly they were from the police and they were bad news. Had something happened in the county that he needed to know about before the papers got hold of it, he wondered.

"Pearce here," he said after he'd lifted the receiver.

There was a pause, which made him stiffen slightly. Then a stumbling voice whispered, "Mr. Pearce?"

"Yes?"

"It's J.D., Mr. Pearce. Hope I'm not bothering you or nothing."

Adam relaxed. "J.D., why are you calling me so late? You aren't in any kind of trouble, are you?"

"Well, sort of, maybe."

Adam began to massage the spot between his eyebrows. J.D. Pike was a mentally slow custodial worker who'd adopted Adam as his own personal Good Samaritan. Two years earlier J.D. had almost been convicted of a liquor-store robbery. If it hadn't been for Adam, who'd been convinced that the thirty-year-old retarded man had been framed and who'd ferreted out evidence to convict the real culprits, J.D. might have spent years in prison. So impressed had J.D. been by Adam's good offices that he'd gone on calling Adam whenever he needed help. This could include anything from a broken washing machine to a spat with a neighbor.

"Why don't you tell the guy to get lost?" Clarke had queried after Adam had spent one particularly trying afternoon straightening J.D. out.

"I don't know," Adam had replied. "He hasn't got many friends. And he can't read well enough to look for help in a phone book. The poor guy is so pathetic, I can't seem to say no to him."

Adam didn't have it in his heart to say no this time, either. "What's the trouble, J.D.?"

"Well, I'm sorta stuck out here in this bar, see. Some guys drove me out, to have some fun, they said. Then they went away, and I ain't got no money to pay the check."

Under his breath Adam muttered a mild curse. "Okay, what's the name of the place?"

"I can't read the sign. You know I always had trouble with my letters, Mr. Pearce." J.D. sounded abject and ashamed.

"Ask the waitress."

"Oh, okay." There was a brief pause and then J.D. returned to the line. "Roadview Inn."

"Yes, I know where it is. Just sit tight, J.D., and I'll come out and take care of it."

"Oh thanks, Mr. Pearce." J.D.'s voice was flooded with relief. "You're a great guy, you know that?"

"That's okay, J.D. Just wait. I'll be there in twenty minutes and settle that bill for you." After he hung up, Adam grabbed his car keys and hurried out the door.

An hour and a half later, he pulled up again in front of his house. He had been tired before; now he was exhausted. *Clarke better not hear about this,* he thought as he climbed out of the car and mounted the steps to his apartment. *If he finds out he'll be telling me what a sucker I am for the next two weeks.* Still, Adam didn't regret helping poor J.D. It was a cruel thing those rowdies had done to him. They had carted him out to the inn, ordered themselves up a regular Roman banquet, and then, laughing up their sleeves, departed leaving him holding the bill. Why, the poor guy couldn't even read the menu much less order all the food that Adam had wound up paying for.

*I need to find some way to protect him from this sort of thing,* he thought. Mulling over several ideas, he went to the refrigerator for a beer. He was just pulling the tab on a can when once again the harsh ring of the phone disturbed the quiet of his apartment.

"Now what?" he asked himself as he lifted the receiver. He'd driven J.D. home. Surely he was okay. Was there some other problem in the county that he had to take care of tonight?

He put the telephone to his ear and listened. But instead of the crisp voice of a worried police officer, he was greeted by a long silence and then a sneering laugh.

"Who is this?" Adam demanded.

But the laughter just went on and on, echoing hollowly down the line.

Adam scowled at the receiver. He was about to slam it back down when the crazy laughter stopped abruptly. "Time is running out, Pearce," a menacing voice whispered. "It won't be long now."

# CHAPTER TEN

"HE ASKED YOU TO GO WITH HIM to Bermuda?" Teresa dropped the account book she'd been going over.

"Yeah."

"What did you say?"

Francy pretended to straighten a panel of rich velvet fabric samples. "I said I'd think about it."

"Mama will pop her cork."

"She keeps telling me how much she likes him."

"She doesn't like him that much," Teresa replied darkly. "She doesn't like any man that much. She's going to ask him to give all her spaghetti sauce back and then have a fit and fall in it."

"I know." Francy plopped down on a small upholstered stool, her shoulders drooping. Nervously she smoothed a pleat on her white cotton skirt. It was close to three o'clock, a slow time, and, except for the two Rasera sisters, the shop was deserted.

"I feel so confused. Tell me what you think I should do." Francy cast an unhappy look at Teresa.

The other young woman snorted. "You're asking my advice? Have you forgotten that I'm the girl who married Mr. Wrong and made a big mess of her life?"

"You've got four beautiful children."

"Yes, but not much else." Teresa pulled out a small wooden chair and perched on it. Seven pounds lighter than she'd been a month earlier and dressed in a crisp black and white cotton print dress, she looked neat and attractive. Her hair had been cut short to frame her full face and lately she'd been experimenting with makeup that flattered her olive coloring.

"You've got your family and the shop," Francy pointed out.

"Yes," Teresa admitted. "Actually I do feel better about things lately. The shop is doing pretty well. If we hang in there, it'll make it, don't you think?"

"I don't know. It'll be another couple months before we break even. But if the orders keep coming in..."

Teresa's voice was warm. "They're going to, thanks to you. You've been working like a dog. Maybe you do need a vacation." She eyed her sister thoughtfully. "They say Bermuda is a pretty great place. People like us don't get to fly off to spots like that very often."

"Actually we never get to fly off to spots like that," Francy retorted with a laugh. "When was the last time we were able to afford a vacation? I can't even remember. Besides, if I took off for three days, who would mind New Beginnings?"

"I would. If anything stops you, it shouldn't be the shop."

"Then what should it be, besides Mama?" Francy queried plaintively.

For a full minute, Teresa was silent, her gaze fixed on her younger sister's worried countenance. "I have a feeling that things between you and Adam Pearce have gone a lot further than you're telling me. They have, haven't they? Just how serious are you about this man?"

Francy covered her face with her hands. "Oh, Teresa, I'm making a fool of myself. I think I'm falling in love with him."

"Are you crying?" Teresa demanded. Frowning, she leaned forward and tapped Francy on the knee.

"No." Francy lifted her head. Her eyes were red, but still dry.

"Why are you so upset? He likes you, doesn't he? He's made that pretty plain. And Bermuda is expensive. He wouldn't invite you to go with him if he didn't think a lot of you."

"Yes, but . . . we're just not right for each other. It's not going to work out." Francy put her hand over her heart. "I can feel it here."

Teresa quirked a shrewd eyebrow. "Have you told him about the reading yet?"

"No."

"You're going to have to do that, you know. You can't go on deceiving him."

"I know, I know. But not yet."

Teresa sighed with exasperation. "Look, you asked for my advice. I'm going to give it to you. Obviously you're hung up on this guy. When a woman feels like that, she can't just turn her back and say forget it. I mean, maybe it would be smarter, but we're just not that way inclined. Believe me, I know. No matter what, where her heart is concerned a woman has to play it out to the bitter end."

Francy nodded. In her own heart she knew that her sister was right.

"You said Adam thinks you need to spend some uninterrupted time together," Teresa continued. "I think he's got something there. The two of you have a lot of things to get straight, and it looks to me as if you're not going to do it the way things are. Go away with him. Have a great time. And, for God's sake, tell him about the reading!"

Francy clasped her hands. "What about Mama?"

"Yeah, well, that's not going to be too pleasant," Teresa agreed. "She'll probably say some awful things and be mad for a couple of weeks. But she'll get over it. I'll talk her around while you're gone."

For a moment Francy sat frozen with indecision. Then she reached across and squeezed Teresa's hand. "Thanks."

"Any time. Just remember, listen to me at your own peril. I screwed up my life by taking my own advice."

"You're older and wiser now."

"I'm a lot older, that's for sure." Grimacing, Teresa got to her feet. "Which reminds me, the kids are going to be stopping by from school any minute now. So get ready for crazy time."

"I thought you said that Gus was closing up his shop early so that he could take you all down to the Polish festival?"

"That's right." Teresa's smile was suddenly gay. "The kids have really been looking forward to it. They like Gus because he buys them all the food they want. Tonight they'll all be sick on Polish sausage." She shot Francy a questioning look. "It's okay, isn't it? I mean, you don't mind handling things by yourself until closing time?"

"Of course not!" Francy got to her feet and straightened her skirt. "Not that many people come in after four, anyway."

Just then the bell at the door rang and Jerry's small dark head appeared in the entry. "Hey, Ma, Mike and Jenny are havin' a fight."

"What? Those devils! I warned them!" Scowling, Teresa rushed outside to tend to her brood.

Francy poked her head out the door, saw that the brother and sister squabble was minor and returned to her work. Not long after that, Gus and Teresa left with the children in hand and Francy was on her own.

She enjoyed the sudden quiet. It gave her a chance to sort through some of the work she'd managed to get done over the weekend and figure out what else she needed to do to catch up on her orders. Teresa had been a big help with that. She'd never taken to making slip-covers or doing upholstery, but she could sew drapes. So far most of the orders that came in were for drapery.

"Somehow I need to convince people of the charm and durability of slipcovers," Francy muttered to herself. What would it take, she wondered. Advertising? But advertising was so expensive. Still, if that was what it took...

Francy paused over a fabric remnant that had been left over from Adam's order. As her fingers explored the texture of the nubby material, all thought of business decisions evaporated from her head. She remembered the feel of Adam, his mouth against hers, their bodies meshed. His skin was satiny, his toughened palms like warm suede. A wave of heat washed up her neck, and she put a hand to her forehead. "Teresa is right," she acknowledged aloud. "It's too late to pretend that I can back away. I have to see this thing through."

The bell on the shop door startled her so that she spun around, an alarmed expression on her piquant face.

"Hey, I didn't mean to scare you."

As she gazed at the thin young man who stood hovering uncertainly in the entry, Francy's mouth opened in a round O of astonishment.

"Francy? Remember me?"

"Jimmy? Jimmy Alonzo?"

His generous mouth quirked into a lopsided grin. "So you haven't forgotten your old partner in crime, huh?"

"Of course I haven't forgotten," Francy cried. Opening her arms wide, she flew across the room to give her unexpected visitor a joyful hug. "What are you doing here, for heaven's sake? It's been years!"

ADAM TIGHTENED Francy's seat belt. "There's nothing to be afraid of."

"Tell that to me after the plane comes down again, and I'm back on dry land."

He shook his head. "I can't believe you've never flown before. You amaze me."

"That's me, the amazing Francy!" She did her best to make it sound like a joke, but she wasn't so sure that it was funny. She didn't need Adam underlining how different their two lives really were. For him hopping a plane to some distant point was an everyday thing. For her it was a first—and a pretty momentous experience.

Francy peered out the airplane's window. Despite her initial and continuing doubts about taking this trip with Adam, she couldn't help but be excited.

"I wish you'd let me come in and talk to your mother about our trip," Adam said. "The look she gave me as we drove off would have made a lesser man wither up and die."

"Listen, if you'd gotten out of your car, she would have thrown her spaghetti pot at your head." Francy frowned. Teresa's predictions about Mama's reaction to this vacation with Adam had been all too accurate.

Adam looked concerned. "I'm sorry if I made trouble between you and your mother. I really didn't think she'd take it so badly."

"That just goes to show what you know about Italian mothers. Anyway, let's not talk about Mama. She'll have calmed down by the time I get back. And she's not going to toss me out of the house. I'm supporting her."

"Ladies and gentlemen," a voice on the loudspeaker said. "A flight attendant will run through some of the safety precautions with you. If you'll look above your head, you'll find an oxygen mask. In the unlikely event of a loss of cabin pressure..."

"An oxygen mask," Francy gasped. She grabbed at the card of safety directions, scowling hard at the pictures as she tried to memorize what the flight attendant said.

"There's nothing to worry about," Adam whispered, amused.

"That's probably what Amelia Earhart said," Francy snapped.

Despite Adam's assurances, she was so nervous as the plane finally took off that her stomach did flip-flops. When the jet was airborne, she heaved a sigh of relief. Then she looked out the window again, amazed at the landscape of fleecy clouds through which they seemed to be sailing. As they flew on, they left the land behind and headed out to sea. Far below them patches of blue ocean glittered in the morning sun.

"What would happen if a motor conked out and we were dumped in the middle of the Atlantic?" Francy queried.

"Not to worry," Adam replied with dry humor. "The stewardess is bringing us our shark repellant now."

Chuckling at his joke, Francy accepted the plastic tray containing the airline's idea of breakfast. But she was too excited to eat much of her lukewarm sausage and reconstituted eggs. After a desultory effort, she pushed the food aside and turned her attention back to the window. Now there was nothing to be seen but sky and a bed of cotton-ball clouds. It was incredible to think that she and Adam were flying east into the sun, leaving the real world of their two separate lives far behind.

"I like your outfit," Adam commented warmly.

Francy turned to find him studying her, admiration clearly etched on his strong, regular features.

"Thanks. I made it myself."

"You look as if you just stepped out of a fashion magazine."

"I'm too short to be a model." Nevertheless, Francy was pleased by the compliment. Once the decision to accept this trip with her lover had been made, she'd somehow found the time to buy a stylish garment bag and sew herself a new wardrobe to pack inside it. Wherever he took her, she wanted to look as if she belonged at his side, so she'd been at pains to select quality fabrics and fashionable designs. The suit she was wearing now was of pearl gray linen. Its short, straight skirt and loose, three-quarter-length boxy jacket flattered her petite figure. And the deep pink tunic-style blouse set off her dark coloring. Francy recalled how she'd spent two entire evenings the week before hunched over her sewing machine stitching the ensemble together. It hadn't been an easy job, not with Mama hovering in the doorway making dire pronouncements.

"How is this man ever going to respect you if you go away with him like some painted lady? You're making a big mistake, Francy!"

"Maybe," she'd replied grimly, "but it's my mistake. I'm the one who's going to have to live with it."

"He's not serious about you, Francy. He's just making a fool of you."

"If anyone's making a fool of me, it's me. But I figure I ought to get some good memories out of it. Don't ruin the whole thing for me, Ma. Let me enjoy as much of this as I can."

Now, remembering that conversation, Francy studied Adam's clear blue eyes. "Do you respect me?" she heard herself ask.

"What?" Adam looked thunderstruck. Then he started to laugh. "Francy, I respect you about as much as anybody I've ever met. And I also adore you."

*But I'm beginning to love you,* she suddenly thought. *Oh dear, what am I going to do?*

Through the last hour of the flight thick clouds hugged the plane like mashed potatoes. Then, as if by magic, the cloud cover suddenly dispersed. The airplane dipped low and Francy saw land below them.

"That's it, that's Bermuda," Adam told her.

Like a giant's gold and green fishhook, it floated in an azure-tourmaline-emerald sea, its beaches washed by long undulating lines of gentle froth.

"It's gorgeous," Francy breathed.

"It is beautiful." Adam took her hand. "We're going to have a good time. You'll see."

An hour later as their taxi cruised through winding narrow roads fenced with limestone walls and tall pink flowered hedges, she believed his prediction.

"This place is unreal," she said, gazing up at the hillsides flashing past. They were studded with pastel houses and giant red poinciana. "What's that sweet scent in the air?"

"The oleander," Adam told her.

Instead of a big hotel, Adam had chosen a cottage colony for them to stay in. It was a lovely secluded place with manicured grounds and a private beach a stone's throw from their quarters. Their cottage, which boasted a private front porch, was spacious and airy. Inside were two double beds. As Adam threw Francy's garment bag down on one of them and tossed his own on the other, she wondered for a fleeting moment or two whether he intended for them to sleep in separate beds.

But he soon clarified that point by seizing her in his arms and kissing her ardently. "I've been dreaming about being alone with you for so long. I can't wait until tonight to make love to you."

"Neither can I," she told him breathlessly.

Adam was still a wonder to her. All during the plane trip she'd been blazingly conscious of him, his long muscular legs so close to hers, his strong, capable hands resting on his knee or folded over his chest as he relaxed in his seat. She'd wanted to reach out and touch the fine gold hairs that glinted on his wrist. More than once, when he shifted or crossed his legs, her eye had been drawn to the hard contour of his thigh. With a tactile memory that was almost painfully vivid, she had recalled how it had felt pressed hard and urgent against hers. The fresh smell of his hair, the masculine texture of his skin—all these things came back to her in such intense and potent clarity that they seemed a part of her own chemistry.

Now, as he took her in his arms, she melted against him. With an eager abandon that would have shocked her a few weeks earlier, she offered first her lips and then her willing body.

"Oh God, you're exactly what I need, Francy," he whispered hoarsely. With one hand, he reached out and swept his luggage off the mattress, seemingly oblivious of the clatter it made as it fell to the floor. Then, with taut, shaking fingers, he undressed her and himself and carried her to bed. "When we're together like this, I don't need any other paradise," he murmured. His mouth moved against her tautly arched throat. "All I need is you."

"Yes, yes," she answered and clung to him.

AN HOUR LATER, Francy whispered teasingly, "Are we going to spend our entire Bermuda vacation in this room?"

Adam stretched his lean length and then drew her closer to his side so that he could drop a lingering kiss on her forehead. "It would be okay with me."

"Well, not with me. I want to see some of this island heaven."

He smiled into her eyes. "I'm looking at heaven right now. But you're right, we should get out on the beach and take a swim. I want to watch your face when you spot your first tropical fish."

After Adam phoned Ben Catlett to set up a schedule of meetings, they unpacked their bags. As Adam watched Francy shake out a high-cut black maillot, he said, "I'm going to rent snorkeling equipment for us."

"Snorkeling! But Adam, I can't swim very well. I mean, I can dog-paddle across the pool at the Y, and that's about it."

"Swimming in this water is practically effortless," he told her. "It's so saline that it's super buoyant. And there's nothing to snorkeling. I'll teach you."

Francy had her doubts, but Adam was determined. Clad in royal blue trunks, he led her out of the cottage and into the tropical turquoise waters that washed up gently against the coral pink beach. There, around a picturesque outcropping of volcanic rock, he showed her another world.

"I can't believe the fish," Francy cried as she stared into the clear aqua depths. "What are the yellow and black striped ones?"

"Sergeant majors," Adam told her. "And the black ones are angels. See that big guy with the yellow markings hovering around your ankles? He's a blue angel."

Francy put her mask on so that she could get a better look. When she came up again, she said, "He's beautiful. But what does he want? Why does he keep hanging around me that way?"

"Probably hungry," Adam told her with a wicked grin. When she squealed and started struggling back toward the shore, he seized her in his arms, pulled her underwater and kissed her. When they came back up for air, he growled, "Hungry like me. But for the next three days, I'm the one who's going to nibble on your toes. Not the fish!"

Three perfect days—that's how it was. Three glorious, sunny days of ideal weather and fabulously memorable moments. Though Adam had daily breakfast meetings with Ben Catlett to discuss his political future, his afternoons were free. He and Francy made the most of those golden afternoons. They rented a motorbike and toured the island, Francy on the rear clinging to Adam's narrow waist in a state of terror mixed with high glee.

When they came back they ate at their hotel's quiet restaurant. Francy had been afraid that ordering food from a menu she couldn't read would be a major hurdle. But as it turned out, even that went relatively smoothly. Since their waiter always told them the specials of the day, she was able to order without a fuss.

For lunch most afternoons they picnicked on the island's glorious public beaches. Francy oohed and ahed at the unreal beauty of Jobson Cove and Stonehole Bay, a jewel of a swimming hole protected by lunar-like walls of volcanic rock.

"I guess I never really believed that spots like this existed," she exclaimed, her eyes rounding into huge dark mirrors as she gazed at the natural loveliness around her. "It's good for my soul to know that they do."

Adam put his arm around her. "I've been here before, but it wasn't as beautiful then as it is now."

She looked at him quizzically. "You mean it's changed?"

He dropped a salty kiss on her lips. "No, the only difference is that I'm seeing it with you. But that makes all the difference, Francy, all the difference."

One evening they took a midnight cruise out of Hamilton Harbour. After they boarded the glass-bottom boat and found seats on the upper deck, it putted gently out to open water, leaving the hustle and bustle of the busy cruise ship harbor behind. A carpet of brilliant stars pricked the velvet sky above, their formations so clear that Tom, their loquacious guide, could point his flashlight at the various constellations and everyone could easily see the figures he described.

"More than two thousand years ago," he began his lecture, "the Greeks imagined they saw various figures in the sky and named them for their legendary characters." He directed the beam of his flash. "Ahead of us is Cassiopeia, the proud queen of the Perseus legend. To your right is Ursa Minor, or the Little Dipper. Ursa Major, or the Big Dipper, is nearby."

When the lecture was finally over and the boat's motors cut off over a reef so that the passengers could go below to look at fish through the floodlit glass bottom, Francy and Adam stayed on the upper deck. Awestruck, Francy leaned her head against Adam's broad shoulder and stared up at the spectacle of the night sky.

"In Baltimore there's so much light that you really don't see many stars," she whispered. "I never dreamed a sky could be like this."

Adam stroked the silky mass of her hair. "There are so many things I'd like to show you, so many places."

Moved by the beauty of the night and the piercing closeness she felt to Adam, Francy sensed tears burning at the back of her eyes. If only life were simple, if only she and Adam could always be like they were at this moment.

On the taxi ride back to their cottage, Francy told herself that she couldn't go on deceiving him. She had to find the courage to be honest and tell him the truth about herself and her inability to read. But what if he despised her? What if he looked at her with pity? How would she bear it?

When the driver dropped them off, they strolled along the grassy path that led to their quarters.

"Tired?" Adam queried.

"No."

"I left an unopened bottle of wine in the sink," he volunteered. "We can crack it out on the porch and watch the moon on the water for a while. What do you say?"

"That sounds good." Francy steeled herself. It was almost as if the fates had heard her resolution and were now giving her the perfect opportunity to make good on it. Tonight she would tell her lover about the reading.

A few minutes later they sat side by side, comfortably ensconced on white lounge chairs. From their vantage point on a hill overlooking the ocean, the starlit view of the water swirling in over the sand was breathtaking. A gentle breeze fanned their cheeks and carried the lulling music of the rushing waves.

"Makes you think about life," Adam said.

Francy had been so caught up with her own dilemma that his low voice startled her. "What do you mean?"

"Oh, a lot of things. During these meetings with Catlett I get asked a lot of questions, and not just about my political ambitions. There are times in your life when you have to take stock, when you have to decide what it is you really value, what you think is important. And you have to decide what you want."

In the darkness, his strong profile was a pale outline. Francy gazed at it anxiously. "What do you want?"

He reached out for the wine bottle at his side, wedged it between his knees and began working to pull the cork. "I've told you I'd like to make the world a better place."

"Yes, that's why you're going into politics. But politics isn't going to be your whole life, is it? What do you want for yourself, personally?"

There was a little pop as the cork came out. Smiling lazily, Adam poured wine into two glasses. "Oh," he said as he handed Francy one of them, "the usual things." He gazed into her eyes. "I want a wife, a family, a home."

Suddenly Francy didn't know where to look. Hot blood flooded into her face, and she stared down into her glass. "You want kids?"

"Yes, lots of them." She heard the creak of his chair as he settled back into it. "I know how it is to be an only child, so I'd like a different kind of family than I had. I'd like my kids to have half a dozen brothers and sisters." There was a smile in his voice. "I can just picture this brood. Some will be blue-eyed like me, I suppose. But others will be dark like their mother. I'll have to work hard not to make the brunettes into my favorites—especially if they have black curly hair and big brown eyes. I'm a chump for that combination."

Francy almost choked. "Sounds as if you have their mom all picked out."

"Maybe I do," Adam said. "Maybe if you ask, I might tell you who the lady I have in mind is. Anyhow, I know just what kind of kids she and I would have together."

"What kind?" Francy queried in a strangled voice.

"Great ones! Top of the line! We Pearces are very family-proud, you know. Well, these kids would be good-looking, athletic and smart as they come. In fact," he added, shooting her a teasing look, "if I don't want to be bankrupted by these future geniuses, I'd better start saving up now for their Harvard educations. Don't you think?"

"They're all going to Harvard?"

"Of course. All the Pearces go to Harvard. It's a family tradition." As he waited for Francy's response, his teasing grin widened.

But instead of replying, Francy looked away. She gripped her wineglass so tightly that the pale liquid inside it trembled. She knew that she'd just received the introduction to a marriage proposal and that if she made the proper response, Adam might even follow it up with the real thing.

But how could she? If she were the mother of Adam Pearce's kids, they wouldn't be going to Harvard. No, since dyslexia was an inherited trait in her family, the chances were very good that they'd be in remedial reading classes. While other children delved into the classics, they'd still be struggling to make sense of a sentence. How would the Pearces with all their family pride like that? Not much, she guessed.

"Well, now that I know what you want," she said, "how about letting me tell you what I want."

"I'd like to hear it." There was an eager, expectant note in Adam's voice.

"I want my shop to succeed. And then I want to expand it and open another. I want to be a big success in business, a millionaire career woman."

Francy didn't need to look at Adam. She knew he was staring at her as if she'd slapped him.

## *CHAPTER ELEVEN*

"THE STEAK WAS DELICIOUS, Mr. Catlett." Francy put down her fork and smiled across the large mahogany table.

"Glad you liked it," Ben Catlett returned expansively. "Doctor says I'm supposed to watch my cholesterol. But I'm not ready to trade in my T-bone and baked potato for broiled chicken yet."

While Adam and Ben chuckled over this, Francy sipped her Perrier and looked around the stateroom of the luxurious cabin cruiser where Ben Catlett lived. The *Primary* was so roomy and, with its teak paneling, brass fittings and cushiony furniture, so comfortable, that it hardly seemed like a boat at all. Only the occasional swell of the water and the twinkling lights of St. George's picturesque harbor just outside the windows gave it away. As Francy gazed out at those beckoning lights she felt as if she'd stepped into another life.

During this trip with Adam she *had* stepped into another world, she reminded herself. Was this environment where people lived on yachts, dined regularly in fancy restaurants and traveled anywhere they pleased on a whim one that she could fit into, she asked herself. Tonight hadn't made her any more positive about the answer to that question. This was Francy's last evening in Bermuda. When Adam had asked her to spend it having dinner with his political adviser, she resisted the idea. But Adam had made it sound as if this dinner party was important to him, so she'd finally accepted.

She'd expected to be uncomfortable with Adam's new mentor. After all, she wasn't really comfortable about being here in Bermuda as Adam's guest in the first place. How could she be when her mother's parting words kept echoing in her ears—"You'll be sorry!"

But she hadn't been prepared for the degree of uneasiness she'd experienced this evening on Ben Catlett's luxurious yacht. Not that he wasn't polite. His manners were faultless. It was just that whenever she glanced into those shrewd gray eyes, she knew she was being assessed—weighed and balanced on some invisible but very real scale. She couldn't get over the feeling that the man could see right through her—that he knew her guilty secret and had already judged her unworthy of Adam.

In defiant reaction, she'd forced herself to behave as naturally with him as she possibly could. She'd treated him as if he were no different than Gus Venturo or the other older neighborhood men she'd grown up with in Little Italy. She'd joked and laughed and refused to behave like anyone other than herself. Now she wondered if she'd done the right thing. Had she embarrassed Adam?

Worriedly she looked at him. His burnished head was bent close to the older man's grizzled one while they talked earnestly about party politics. Some of the names they mentioned she recognized. But most of their conversation might as well have been in a foreign language. Francy knew about the politics in her neighborhood, of course. And she watched the news on television. But if you couldn't read a newspaper, it was hard to keep track of the goings-on in the city in any depth. Suddenly she felt the need to escape.

On the pretext of visiting the bathroom, she left the cabin and went outside onto the deck. "You'll find guest heads below deck," Ben Catlett told her. "There's one for ladies and one for men."

It was another perfect night. The stars were out in force again, spraying the velvet sky with glitter. For several minutes Francy leaned against the railing, breathing in the ocean air and watching the gentle swell of the moon-streaked water. Unconsciously she fingered the fabric of her sheer white cotton dress. She had copied it from a picture of an Yves Saint Laurent design that she'd seen in a fashion magazine, and now she was very glad. Its distinctive one-shoulder silhouette and subtle allure had helped her get through the evening.

Sighing, Francy took another breath of the cool night breeze. Then, realizing that it might be a good idea if she visited the bathroom after all, she turned to her right and headed for a stairway. At the foot of it she stepped into a narrow, dimly lit corridor. This brought her to two doors with signs on them.

Francy could easily recognize a sign that said Ladies. But neither of these remotely resembled that. With a frown, she peered at them. Under her breath, she read out the letters. "Inboard" was printed on one brass plaque. "Outboard" appeared on the other. Those couldn't be the bathrooms, could they? Francy turned away and proceeded down the corridor. But she didn't come to any more doors with signs on them. When she reached the end, she stood scratching her head and wondering what to do next.

"Can I help you, miss?"

It was the white-jacketed waiter who had served their meal. He was standing just behind her carrying cups and a coffeepot on a silver tray.

Acutely embarrassed by the absurdity of her situation, Francy said lamely, "I was just looking for the ladies' room."

He pointed toward the stairs. "It's just down at the end there."

"I didn't see it."

Francy had no doubt that he was surprised by her obtuseness, but he was too well-trained to be obvious about it.

"If you'll just follow me, I'll show you," he told her courteously.

Feeling about as competent as a kindergartner on her first day at school, Francy did as he bade. A moment later he paused in front of the door with the sign that read Inboard. Francy stared at it. What in the world did it say? She had tried to apply the lessons she was learning in her reading class and sound it out. But when she had done that she hadn't come up with anything that seemed the least bit familiar.

"Some people do find the signs confusing," the man told her kindly. "Oh, and miss, marine heads can be tricky. Please read the instructions carefully."

"I will," Francy told him and then hastily opened the door and closed it behind her. What kind of people besides herself found the signs confusing, she wondered. The ones with below-normal IQs? Inside the compact cubicle she stared down at the toilet. It certainly looked different from what she was used to. There was some kind of pump attached and on the wall above it a framed sheet of paper with a long list of printed instructions had been affixed.

Once again Francy leaned forward and peered at the letters. But it was hopeless. The little black lines and squiggles were inscrutable. *What now?* she asked herself.

Well, she could just go ahead, use the thing and hope for the best. But what if it flooded? As she imagined the worst, Francy's cheeks turned hot. Regretting the large glass of Perrier she'd just tossed down, she turned away and stared at herself in the small oval mirror above the washbowl. "How much longer are we going to be here?" she muttered. "If I don't have any coffee or after-dinner drinks, can I make it through the rest of the evening?" Francy put a hand to her temple. A headache was already beginning to throb. Was there anyone else in the world who faced the problems that had bedeviled her all her life, she wondered. What was she doing here? How could she hope to fit into a world where she was so out of her element?

"THAT'S A VERY PRETTY YOUNG LADY you have with you," Ben Catlett said as he opened an engraved silver box and offered Adam a cigar.

"I think so." Adam refused the cigar, but accepted a glass of brandy.

"I have to admit that she's not what I expected."

Adam cocked his head. "Oh?" He wasn't sure why he had wanted Francy to meet Catlett. Certainly, it had not been because he desired the older man's approval. Rather, it had been out of a need to make some sort of public declaration. Last night when he had indirectly brought up the subject of marriage, she had rebuffed him. He was still smarting from that rejection. But it didn't change how he felt toward her. Every day he spent in Francy's company and every night he took her into his arms made him more certain. She was the woman for him, and the time had come to let the world in on that fact. Warily he gazed at Catlett, wondering what he intended to say.

"Usually men with your background get hooked up with a particular type of woman."

"What type is that?"

"Oh, someone like themselves who's gone to the right schools and was brought up knowing how to pour tea. But your Francy doesn't come from that sort of world, does she?"

"She was born in Little Italy and still lives there with her family."

Catlett pushed his chair back and crossed his legs at the ankle while he lit his cigar. "I'm curious. Did she graduate from the University of Maryland?"

"No." Adam hesitated. "As a matter of fact, she never finished high school."

"Oh?" Catlett raised an eyebrow. "Why is that?"

"I don't know." Adam made his voice neutral, but he couldn't hide from himself that he was bothered by Francy's lack of formal education. She was so bright, so obviously intelligent. And she was well-read, too. Several times he had gotten into discussions about literature with her and had been really impressed by her knowledge and insight. She certainly knew her Shakespeare backward and forward. She could even quote the bard at length and with great feeling. Why had someone with that kind of alert, curious mind dropped out of high school?

From the beginning he had been plagued by the paradox of it. Yet, whenever he'd tried to question her about her schooling, she'd put him off. It was as if there were parts of her life that were off-limits to him. And that hurt—especially when he was beginning to want to share everything with her.

"Well, you'd never know that she hasn't got a diploma from talking to her," Catlett was saying. "She's obviously as smart as anyone with such a pretty face and figure has a right to be. Just how serious are you about this girl, Pearce?"

Adam's blue gaze hardened slightly. "Why do you ask?"

"I wouldn't if we were just here for a friendly dinner party. In that case I would be well aware that it was none of my business. But you've told me that you want me to handle your campaign. And in the last three days I believe you've made a pretty strong commitment to a future that's going to turn your way of living inside out. You're savvy enough to know that your private life is going to become public knowledge. So, I'm afraid that does make it my business." Catlett looked down the length of his cigar. "I don't know how to phrase it delicately. Do you intend to make this young lady part of the future we've been discussing?"

"And if I do?"

Catlett's answer was as direct as Adam's question. "Then I need to know about it."

For several seconds the two men's gazes held. Then, as if acknowledging the reasonableness of Catlett's request, Adam nodded. "All right, I'm in love with Francy. I'd like to marry her. But so far she hasn't indicated that she's willing."

"Have you asked her yet?"

"No. But I intend to soon. And when the time comes, all I can do is pray that she'll say yes."

Catlett smiled faintly. "She will."

"How can you be so sure?"

"Because I've seen the expression in her eyes whenever she looks at you and because you're not the kind of man that women turn down. When the time comes, she'll agree." Catlett took a leisurely puff of his cigar and then blew out the smoke in a thin gray plume. "The question is whether or not, with the future you're beginning to plan for yourself, she'll make you the right kind of wife."

Adam stiffened. "That's not an issue in my mind."

"No, of course it isn't. You're in love. You didn't need to tell me, actually. The signs are unmistakable. You're besotted with this girl. Men who are in that unbalanced state of mind are in no condition to think logically. I, however, am not in love. I am able to look at the two of you together very clearly. And since it's part of my job to reason for you, I'll tell you what I think."

Adam's fingers tightened around his brandy glass. In the artificial light, his eyes were a cool, intense blue. "Go right ahead. But it won't make the slightest difference to my feelings for Francy."

"I think for the purpose of winning an election, the two of you will make an ideal couple."

Adam's brow lifted.

"Pearce, one of the things that has concerned me about you as a candidate for our party is your background. You're so obviously a class act, if you will, that the ordinary joe may have trouble relating to you. It's not that you're standoffish, it's just that you don't project that folksy, salt-of-the-earth quality that makes it easy for the average person to identify with."

"I'm running for office because I want to do something for the people of Maryland, not win a popularity contest."

"But an election is a popularity contest. You know that as well as I do. Now, to my mind, this young lady of yours may be the answer to a prayer. She's the perfect foil for you, and not just in looks. You're the white knight, pure in heart, if a little remote. But she's pretty, cuddly, warmhearted, down-to-earth and was born in a Baltimore row house, right?"

Adam nodded.

"She's even ethnic. What more could you ask? If you're smart, Pearce, you'll get a ring on this gal's finger pronto. The sooner you can show her off to the voters, the better."

Just outside the stateroom door Francy stood with her hand frozen on the knob. She couldn't believe what she'd just heard. Was Ben Catlett recommending that Adam marry her because she'd be good for his political image? A sick feeling clogged her throat. After the trouble she'd had with even finding much less using the man's bathroom, this was more than she could handle.

Resolutely she pushed open the door. Both men looked up at her, their expressions startled and, if she wasn't imagining things, a little guilty.

"Hello, there," Catlett said heartily. "How are you doing?"

"Not too well," Francy answered tightly.

Adam eyed her with concern. "You do look a little pale. Aren't you feeling well?"

"No, I'm not," Francy replied. "As a matter of fact, I've got a terrible headache. I'm sorry to break up the party, but would you mind taking me back, Adam?"

"YOU LOOK BETTER THIS MORNING. How'd you sleep?"

"I slept fine," Francy lied. As she climbed out of bed and then stretched, she reflected that she'd had a rotten eight hours' sleep. Using her headache as an excuse, she'd spent the night in the cottage's hitherto unused extra double bed. Lying there alone, listening to Adam's regular breathing on the other side of the room and asking herself a million painful questions hadn't exactly speeded her into dreamland. She doubted that she'd gotten more than a couple hours of real rest.

She wasn't sure why she was so disturbed by the conversation between Adam and Ben Catlett that she'd listened in on. After all, she'd only overheard Catlett say that her grass-roots background would be good for Adam's image. It wasn't as if Adam had told the man that was why he'd pursued her in the first place—because she might bring him a few extra votes. Such a notion was utterly preposterous. Yet at the moment Francy was feeling so confused and unsure of herself that anything could push her off the emotional tightrope she walked.

During her nighttime hours of self-doubt and questioning, though, she'd realized how unfair she was being to Adam. What Ben Catlett had said wasn't Adam's fault. On their last night together in paradise they should have been lying in each other's arms, not sleeping apart. They might never have a chance to be together like this again. *Why can't I snatch at happiness when it comes my way,* Francy wondered. *Why do I have to put it under a magnifying glass until I find something wrong with it?*

"You certainly look fine," Adam said, his gaze drifting over the white satin nightshirt that clung to her curves. "I'm glad. I was worried about you last night." He sat up in bed, the blanket over his narrow waist, but his upper torso was bare. Trying not to look at his broad tanned chest with its dusting of dark gold hair, Francy padded across the room, pulled her garment bag out of the closet and spread it on her bed.

"Do you have to start packing now?" he queried.

"My plane takes off at eleven, remember?"

"How could I forget. I don't suppose there's any way I could persuade you to stay over another couple of days and go home with me on Saturday?"

Francy shook her head. "We already talked about that. I have to get back to the shop. I feel guilty about leaving it so long, as it is." She spread her white dress out lengthwise in the garment bag and then made herself look very busy stuffing her underwear into the empty spaces around it.

"Francy, stop that and come here," Adam said in a low voice that seemed to vibrate down the length of her backbone.

Slowly she turned. He was watching her, his blue eyes a shade darker, his lean features set in a hungry expression that she recognized because she knew it mirrored her own.

"I missed you last night," he murmured. "I'm going to miss you when you're gone. Forget the packing for a little while, Francy."

Wordlessly she went over to him and sat down on the edge of the bed. For what seemed a long time they gazed into each other's eyes, reading myriad messages that couldn't yet be put into words. Then, slowly, their heads inclined toward each other and their lips met. With a sigh of pleasure, Francy's arms went around Adam's strong neck, and she let herself sink into the rising excitement of his embrace. A moment later, everything but the strength of his arms and the singing feeling in her blood was forgotten. "Oh, Adam," she whispered huskily.

"Francy, God, but I want you! You can't possibly know!"

"No? Then why don't you show me?"

"I will my beautiful, Francy. I will."

SATISFYING AS THE RELEASE of their lovemaking was that morning, it eventually had to end. While Adam showered, Francy finished her packing. Then they dressed and went to breakfast together. Neither of them ate much of the cholesterol-rich British breakfast their hotel provided, and as they drank their second cup of coffee their conversation was desultory.

"There's no need for you to go to the airport with me," Francy pointed out.

"Of course I'll go with you. I've already ordered a cab. It will be here at ten." He checked his watch. "That gives us twenty minutes to get back to the room and look under the bed to make sure you haven't forgotten anything."

Francy smiled, but she really felt like crying. Intuition told her that when she flew back to Baltimore, the fragile, rainbow-colored bubble she and Adam had thrown up around themselves was going to burst.

Arm in arm they strolled down the neat, white stone path that led to their cottage. "I wish I had time to take one last swim," Francy said, shooting a regretful glance at the turquoise water lapping against the sandy beach.

"You would if you'd only stay another day. That plane reservation can still be changed."

"Adam—"

"I know, I know. Duty calls."

They rounded the corner of their cottage and stopped dead. A woman in a peach silk dress was sitting on the porch observing them alertly.

"Mother!" Adam exclaimed in astonishment. "What are you doing here?"

"Waiting for you, what else?" She turned her attention to Francy. "Is this the young lady I've been hearing so much about?"

"This is Francesca Rasera," Adam replied stiffly.

"Delighted to meet you, I'm sure. As you've already guessed, I'm Patricia Pearce, Adam's mother."

For several seconds Francy stood frozen, gazing up at the woman who'd just introduced herself. Patricia was not what Francy had imagined when she had tried to picture Adam's only living parent. In her mind's eye she'd seen an older woman with gray curls. Patricia wasn't like that at all. With her golden hair, faultless makeup, designer dress and elegant manner, she was a more mature version of Barbara Kains. And she had exactly the same effect on Francy. She made her want to check her fingernails to see if there might be dirt under them.

Thanking her lucky stars that she was wearing her travel suit, which she knew looked good on her, Francy managed a polite smile. "How do you do, Mrs. Pearce. I'm pleased to meet you, too." Which was far from being the truth. Staying alone with Adam in a hotel room—these were anything but the circumstances under which she wished to be presented to his mother.

Sensing the tension between the two women, Adam looked from Patricia to Francy and then back again. His brows drew together and he said, "Mother, I'm afraid this really isn't a good time for a surprise visit.

Francy has a plane to catch, and I was just about to go with her to the airport.''

"Oh, no!" Francy exclaimed. "There's no need for you to come with me. I'll take that taxi by myself." Withdrawing her key from a pocket, she hurried up the steps and stuck it in the lock. But as she turned the knob, a vision of the rumpled bed in which she and Adam had made love earlier that morning popped into her mind.

Turning, she gave Adam a sharp look and said, "Would you mind entertaining your mother out here while I finish packing? I won't be more than a few minutes." From the edge of her eye she caught the expression on Patricia's face. Though her mouth was set into a polite smile, there was a tightness at the corners, and Francy knew that the older woman was having no trouble guessing why she wasn't being invited in.

Struggling with a hot wave of embarrassment mixed with anger at finding herself in such an awkward situation, Francy didn't wait for Adam's answer. Instead, she stepped briskly inside, shut the door behind her and began to fly around the room straightening it up. After she'd made the bed and dropped Adam's scattered underwear back into the drawer, she scanned the bathroom, closets and bureau for any of her own things that might still remain. Within just a few minutes she was zipping up her bulging garment bag and snapping it closed. Then she hefted the bag and began dragging it across the floor toward the door.

Outside, Adam and Patricia sat regarding each other. Patricia's expression was cool and bland, Adam's was distinctly annoyed. "Mother, just why are you here? And at this hour? You never told me that you intended to show up in Bermuda."

"I hadn't planned to, but I changed my mind. And why shouldn't I come see my son at ten o'clock in the morning? You never mentioned that you would be entertaining a guest." Lifting one delicately arched eyebrow, she slanted him a derisive look.

Adam was about to retort when the door opened and Francy appeared, tugging her garment bag behind her. Quickly he stood up and reached for the luggage. "Let me take that, for heaven's sake. It's too heavy for you."

"No, it's not!" Francy declared, a shade of defiance in her voice. "I'm perfectly capable of handling it myself. You just stay here with your mother while I go on up to the lobby and wait for that taxi."

"I'm not going to let you carry this thing up to the main building by yourself," Adam snapped. The whole situation was beginning to fray his temper.

"You do that, dear. I'll just wait here for you," Patricia said smoothly. "Don't worry about me. I'll be fine." She glanced at Francy and added sweetly, "It was so nice to meet you. Have a good trip."

"Thank you," Francy managed.

"I'm sorry about this," Adam said a few minutes later as they made their way up the hill toward the large pale green building with its steeply pitched, terraced white roof. "I had no idea she was going to show up like that."

"Your mother keeps pretty close tabs on you, doesn't she?"

"She tries," Adam admitted through clenched teeth.

"Is that why you've never married? Has she disapproved of all the women you've brought home?"

He shot her a narrow look. "No, just the opposite, in fact. She's been shoving eligible women at me for at least a decade. It may be one of the reasons I'm still a bachelor.''

"One of the reasons?"

"Another one is that until recently I hadn't met the right woman.''

Francy swallowed. "I can just imagine what she thinks of me.''

"No, you can't. For God's sake, Francy, I know you're embarrassed, but there's no reason to get hysterical.''

"I'm not hysterical.''

"We're adults,'' Adam pressed on doggedly. "And we're not living in the last century. My mother is aware of that.''

"Oh, look, there's my taxi!'' Francy exclaimed. There never was a more welcome sight. She began to hurry toward the front door, her heels clicking a rapid tattoo on the pavement.


TEN MINUTES LATER Adam stalked back down the path. When he once again rounded the corner of his cottage Patricia was still on the porch, smiling serenely out at the lapping water and rocking gently.

"All right,'' Adam demanded, "what's this all about? Why are you here?''

"I told you. I'm here to see you and hear about your progress with Ben Catlett.''

"That's the only reason you came?'' Adam queried suspiciously.

"Well, I thought I'd do a spot of vacationing. Don't you want to know where I'm staying?''

"Where?''

"Club Med,'' she told him with satisfaction.

"Club Med?'' Adam was surprised.

"It's the ideal place for a woman traveling alone—free-flowing wine, entertainment, lots of interesting people. And so Gallic! Last night I met a fascinating Frenchman. It's time I got out more, don't you think? After all, I'm still a fairly attractive woman. Speaking of which—" Patricia shot a meaningful glance at the cottage door "—I do hope I didn't embarrass your pretty little friend."

Adam tugged at his collar. "Of course you embarrassed her. What I'd like to know is whether or not it was deliberate."

Patricia's eyes rounded innocently. "Adam, dear, how was I to know that she was with you? You never said a word. I thought that this was just a business trip."

He met his mother's look levelly. "Francy and I needed some time to ourselves."

Patricia waved a manicured hand that took in the cloudless blue sky, palm trees and sparkling ocean. "Well, you certainly had it here. That's quite a figure she's got. I imagine she's very fetching in a bikini."

"Francy doesn't wear a bikini."

"What a pity. She's obviously Italian. Is she the girl you told me about who makes slipcovers?"

"Yes."

Mother and son regarded each other warily. "Adam, you can't really be serious about her."

"I'm very serious about her. I'm in love with her."

Patricia's nostrils flared. "Why couldn't you have fallen in love with Barbara?"

"I tried, but it just didn't work. It's Francy I want."

"Are you actually thinking of asking her to marry you?"

"Yes, I am."

Patricia lowered her lashes, shielding the expression in her eyes. "Have you considered what this will mean to your future? The two of you coming from such different backgrounds—it's bound to create problems."

"I don't give a damn about any of that. I love her, and I want her to be my wife."

Patricia's fingers curled tightly around the arm of her chair. "What about your campaign?"

"What about it?"

"Have you introduced Francy to Ben Catlett?"

"Yes, I have. He liked her, as a matter of fact."

Again Patricia drew a deep breath. Then she lifted her hands and pressed her palms together. "I can't help feeling a little hurt that you introduced her to Ben while you were still keeping her a secret from me."

"Frankly I was afraid you would intimidate her."

"I don't go around intimidating people."

Adam laughed at that. Sobering, he said, "I don't want to keep her a secret anymore. I'm proud of her, and I want everyone to know how I feel about her."

"Then you'd better bring her to Spruce Valley and let her see your real home, don't you think?" Patricia challenged.

"All right. I'll do that."

"When?"

"When?" Adam glanced out at the ocean, his eyes taking on the same startling turquoise sheen. "As soon as I get back, and as soon as she'll agree to it."

## CHAPTER TWELVE

TERESA SHOT HER SISTER a sideways glance. "Are you really back in Baltimore, Francy?"

"Of course I'm back. What are you talking about?" Francy was bent over the cutting table, measuring out cloth.

"Well, it's hard to tell. Yesterday, after you got in from the airport, you didn't say more than three sentences. And today you've been about as chatty as Jerry's turtle."

Francy took some pins out of her mouth. "Yesterday I was tired and Mama wasn't talking to me no matter what I said, and today I've got a pile of work to catch up on."

Teresa's arms went out at angles as she clapped her hands onto her generous hips. "Well, are you going to tell me about it, or aren't you? How was Bermuda?"

"It was very beautiful. Exactly like the postcards, as a matter of fact."

"Come on, you know what I'm asking. How did things go with Adam? Did you tell him about the reading?"

"No, I didn't."

There was a brief, disapproving silence. "You're going to have to. Honestly, it really sounds to me like the guy is serious about you. I mean, I know he called you long distance last night just to talk."

Francy stared down at the scissors in her hand. "Yes, but it's not going to work."

"Where have I heard that before?" Teresa rolled her eyes. "Now what's wrong?"

"He wants a bunch of kids."

"What's so bad about that? Must mean he's thinking marriage."

Francy threw down her scissors. "He wants a bunch of super-smart kids who can all go to Harvard."

"So, our brother went to Harvard, on a scholarship, yet."

"I'm nothing like Paul. You know what kind of children I'm probably going to have."

"Kids like my Jerry, maybe. Is that so bad?" Teresa sounded affronted.

Francy's pained expression softened. "No, of course it's not. How's Jer doing? I didn't get a chance to talk to him last night."

"That's because you didn't talk to any of us. You locked yourself in your room, and when you came down to dinner you were about as good company as a zombie. Of course I have to admit," Teresa added, "that Mama wasn't much better." She sighed. "For your information, Jerry's fine. Sometimes he comes home from school feeling pretty discouraged, but his teacher says he's hanging in there."

Francy nodded. "I know what he's going through, poor kid. At least he's young. When you're my age sounding out those words is about as easy as pushing a rock uphill."

"Isn't it getting any better?" Teresa asked sympathetically.

"A little. I can usually figure out short, simple words, sometimes even whole sentences. But a page of text—" Francy shook her head.

"It'll come. Just keep at it." Teresa dug a crumpled square of paper out of her pocket. "If you can sound out simple words, can you tell me who this guy is? He must have called asking for you half a dozen times."

Francy accepted the paper, smoothed it out and stared down at the large block-printed letters. "J-i-m. Jim? A-l-o-n-z-o. Ala... Ala... Oh, of course, it must have been Jimmy Alonzo."

"Just who is Jimmy Alonzo?"

Francy laughed. "He was my pal back in high school. You must remember the skinny kid who used to carry my books. Well, he's moved back into this area and is teaching philosophy at the community college."

"Philosophy? He must be smart."

"Oh, yes. Jimmy was the smartest kid in class. Why he picked me to be friends with, I'll never know. To be honest, he's the one who made it possible for me to stay in school as long as I did. He used to write my papers for me, let me copy off his tests. He was the only one who knew my secret."

A light seemed to flash behind Teresa's eyes. "Oh, sure, I remember him now. He used to follow you around like a toy on a string. Honestly, Francy, don't you know why he did your homework for you? He was crazy about you."

Francy made a denying motion with her hand. "It was never like that between us. We were just good friends."

"That's because he was a skinny little twerp, and you weren't interested. Does he look any better now?"

"Yes, he does, as a matter of fact." She chuckled. "He's sort of cute now. But it's still strictly a friendship thing."

"Oh, yeah? Then how come he's been calling you every day?"

Francy shrugged. "Probably to set up an appointment. When I told him about my reading class, he offered to give me some private tutoring, and I took him up on it."

"YOU LOOK SPECTACULAR in that red and white sundress," Adam said as he downshifted.

"Thanks." Francy smoothed the printed cotton skirt over her knee and looked out the car window. "You did say that this dinner party was going to be informal."

"It's just a barbecue. What you're wearing is exactly right."

Out of the corner of his eye Adam shot Francy a worried look. The day of his return from Bermuda Patricia had called to propose this dinner party. He'd agreed to it only on condition that she not overwhelm Francy with one of her eight-course ordeals in Spruce Valley's very large and very formal dining room. Even so, he'd had a hard time convincing Francy that she should come. And now he was worried about her reaction when she saw Spruce Valley. Pulling up to her row house to pick her up just now, he couldn't help but be aware of the contrast between the two places. What would Francy think when she saw the sprawling estate where he'd been born? Would it send her into another one of her tailspins about the vast gulf between them? He hoped not.

"Do you realize," he said conversationally, "it's been a week since I got back from Bermuda, and this is the first time I've seen you? Whenever I've called you've been out or too busy to talk for more than a few minutes."

"Well, I have been busy," she answered. "I had a lot of work to catch up on. And Teresa's decided to take a course in accounting, so she can handle our books better. I'm glad she's doing it, but that means I have to spend more time in the store."

"You're taking a class, too, aren't you? You told me that's what you did on Tuesday and Thursday nights."

"Yes," Francy said in an uncommunicative tone.

"A literature course, wasn't it?"

"Yes, but I don't want to talk about it. Let's talk about something else. What have you been doing since you got back?"

Again, Adam shot Francy's shadowed profile a worried glance. All week he'd had the impression that something was bothering her. On the phone she'd seemed edgy, distant. He'd believed her when she'd told him she was too busy to see him. Now he wasn't so sure. Was it really that she was too busy, or was she just trying to shut him out? Why did she have to be so secretive about this class, for instance? What was the big deal with a literature class?

Adam cleared his throat. "It's been a pretty hectic week for me, too." One reason was that he'd laid several traps for the creep who'd trashed his car and kept firing off threatening phone calls and letters. Wednesday night he'd almost caught the guy skulking around in his backyard. But though he'd chased him over several hedges, the intruder had managed to get away. Adam had no intention of telling Francy any of that, of course. Aloud, he said, "I notice you met me in front of your house again. Is your mom still mad at me?"

"Yes, but she's being a little friendlier to me. Today she said good morning."

Adam frowned. "Next time I pick you up, I'd like to come in and talk to her, Francy. I don't want her thinking of me as an evil seducer." He reached out to take Francy's hand. At first it felt stiff and cold. But after a moment or two, her fingers began to relax and curl around his palm.

They drove through Baltimore in silence and then headed down Route 40 into Howard County. At last the black sports car began to roll through wooded countryside. As the cool evening breeze played through her hair, Francy gazed out at the grassy fields and stands of pine and dogwood. The sky was overcast and there was a hint of dampness in the air that suggested rain. But the pearly diffused light only added to the beauty of the pastoral scene, giving it the appearance of a landscape in an English painting.

"It's lovely out here." She withdrew her hand from his. "I can't imagine growing up with all this space."

"Kids get up to a lot of the same things no matter where you put them." He took his foot off the gas pedal and let the car coast down a tree-lined hill. "Francy, you're not really nervous about seeing my mother again, are you?"

"Maybe a little. Who else is going to be at this party?"

"I'm not sure about the guest list. I did ask her to invite Clarke Burdette and his wife. You liked them, didn't you?"

"Yes, I did." Francy smiled.

A few minutes later when Adam swung the Mazda off the road and onto the private lane that led to Spruce

Valley Farm, her smile stiffened slightly. "This is your driveway?"

"Sort of."

"You must have a very large front yard." Swiveling her head to the right, she took in the fenced field with its half dozen grazing horses. The place was very like what she had imagined, but the reality of it carried much more impact. It was one thing to know that Adam was rich; it was another to see just what that meant.

When Adam's ancestral home came into view, Francy's smile was wiped away by a look of amazement. Backlit by the setting sun which shot rays of orange and red light through the purplish-gray cloud cover, the pink stucco mansion with its gingerbread towers looked like something out of a gothic tale. "This is where you were born?"

"Yes," Adam admitted reluctantly. Even to his eyes the place appeared exotic in its sunset frame. He frowned as he scanned the driveway. Several guests had already arrived. The BMW was Clarke's, and he recognized the red Corvette as belonging to Peter Roswell. Pete was a tennis partner of his and had a hell of a backhand, but Adam hadn't suggested that his mother invite the guy to meet Francy. For one thing Pete's wife, Bixie, was so yuppie that she was close to parody. And who did the gunmetal blue Porsche 911 belong to, he wondered.

He pulled up behind it, killed the engine and raked a hand through his hair. He glanced over at Francy. She looked a little nervous, but then anyone would in these circumstances. Maybe he should just stop worrying about her. She was a grown woman, and she had handled herself just fine with Ben Catlett, hadn't she?

"Ready to enter the lion's den?" he heard himself say.

"It's not going to be as bad as that, is it?"

"I hope not."

When they walked around the side of the house, the first thing Adam heard coming from the pool and patio area was the sound of a familiar female voice.

Francy heard it, too. "Barbara Kains is here?" she whispered and stopped short.

"If she is, it wasn't my idea to invite her," Adam growled.

Sure enough, when they turned left and walked through the open gate they spotted Barbara. Wearing a low-cut dotted kelly-green sundress that emphasized her tanned, golden looks, she was standing next to the pool with one hand resting lightly on the arm of an attractive dark-haired man in white slacks and a red knit pullover. The Burdettes were standing a few feet away chatting with Patricia.

Clarke caught sight of Adam and Francy and waved. "Hey, buddy, there you are at last. Your mother wouldn't put the steaks on until you showed up."

Patricia turned and hurried toward them, a welcoming smile on her lips. Adam met it with a fulminating look. Why had she invited Barbara? What was she up to?

Ignoring her son's obvious irritation, Patricia said, "We've been waiting for you. Adam, go and get Francy a nice cool drink, will you, dear?"

With obvious reluctance and a grim expression on his face, Adam strode toward the bar to do as his mother requested.

"Just Perrier or a soft drink for me," Francy called after him. Tonight, her instincts warned, she would need all her wits about her.

"Francesca, don't you look nice. Red is your color," Patricia was saying.

"You look nice, too. Blue is yours. In fact," Francy added, taking in the scene around them with a complimentary wave of her hand, "everything looks wonderful. You have a beautiful home."

That was no exaggeration. Across the way a keyhole-shaped pool was set like a jewel in the flagstone terrace. On the far left colored lights had been strung through the branches of a tall oak. The festive tree sheltered a large grill and banquet table. Candles in glass bowls winked on a smaller table covered in a flowered cloth. Around the edge of the terrace everblooming red roses spilled across a low stone wall.

"We do like to entertain out here on warm summer nights," Patricia said, "but I'm a bit worried." She cast an apprehensive look at the sky. "I do hope it doesn't rain. But just in case, after I've introduced you around, maybe you'd like to get a swim in early? Adam did warn you to bring your bathing suit, didn't he?"

"Yes, it's in my purse." Francy glanced at the half dozen guests. Clarke and Janet had on their suits and had obviously just taken a dip. Maybe she would do the same. Floating in that pool would undoubtedly be a lot easier than trying to carry on a comfortable conversation with Barbara Kains. Thank goodness she'd mentioned to the other woman that she was doing work for Adam, she thought as Patricia led her over for introductions. Otherwise she'd feel even more awkward. But Barbara passed it off with her customary smoothness, greeting Francy as if she were an old pal.

After the introductions had been made and Adam had come back with two tall drinks, Francy excused herself to go and change in the small white bathhouse at the far end of the pool. When she was out of earshot Adam leaned toward his mother and demanded, "Why did you invite Barbara? Just what did you have in mind?"

"Why shouldn't I invite her?" Patricia answered serenely. "She's a friend of mine, and I like her. She's a friend of yours, too, and its time you made amends for treating her so badly. By the way, what do you think of her new beau? Justin Surrey has just taken the position of curator at the Baltimore Museum. Isn't he dishy?"

"I don't tend to think of men in those terms," Adam muttered. He cast a wry look at his mother. Did she think she was going to make him jealous by showing him Barbara's new man? As long as he was sure of Francy, nothing could do that, he thought. If only he really were sure of Francy.

"Think I'll change into my swimsuit and take a dip, too," he said.

"Not until you've talked to Barbara, Adam."

He nodded. "You're right. I'll go say hello now."

Shifting his drink to his other hand, he crossed the patio to the spot where Clarke and Janet and Pete and Bixie were now batting light gossip back and forth with Barbara and her new man.

"You look as if you're still back in the office," Clarke called out as he approached. "Take off that jacket and jump in the pool, man. The water's great."

"I intend to, but first I thought I'd say hello." He slapped Pete on the back, kissed Bixie's cheek and then turned to face Barbara, who was gazing at him with a rather fixed smile on her lips. "Hello there, Barbara."

"Hello there yourself. Long time no see."

"It's been a busy summer. I've had a heavy work load."

"Work load my foot!" Clarke interjected. "Adam's been spending most of his time dodging flying bricks."

"Flying bricks?" Bixie's hazel eyes widened, and Barbara's brow puckered.

"Some psycho has been making our friendly neighborhood prosecutor's life miserable with threats." He turned to Adam. "Officer Nichols told me that your crazy heaved another brick through your window last night."

"Night before last. I almost caught him, actually," Adam replied. He didn't want to talk about the threats, especially not where Francy or his mother could hear. Shooting Clarke a warning look, he changed the subject and asked Pete a tennis question. Then he turned to Justin and extended his hand. "I don't believe I've met your friend, Barbara."

"I'm really glad to meet you," Justin said after Barbara had made the introduction, "and not just because Barb has been singing your praises. I've been impressed by what I've read about you in the newspapers and seen on television, Pearce. Sounds as if you've been doing quite a job in this county. It doesn't surprise me that you've made an enemy or two."

"I hope I've made a few friends as well." Adam looked Justin up and down. He seemed like a nice guy. For Barbara's sake, Adam hoped so. She deserved something better than the hot and cold treatment she'd received from him. "Anyhow," he added, striving for a lighter note, "no one's thrown any bricks at me today, so I think I'll celebrate by following Clarke's example here and chucking this jacket in favor of a bathing suit. Can I talk any of you into joining me for a dip?''

"Not me." Barbara raised a hand. "I spent the afternoon lazing next to my mother's pool. I've had enough chlorine."

"Same here," Bixie chimed in. "And Pete's got a bad ear."

"I was about to say no, too," Justin said, "but maybe I'll change my mind."

Following the direction the other man's eyes had taken, Adam turned and saw that Francy had emerged from the bathhouse. Clad in her black maillot, she was sticking an experimental toe in the water.

"Who's the gorgeous little dark-haired Venus?" Pete queried. "I haven't seen her before. Believe me, I would have remembered."

"Name's Francesca Rasera," Adam supplied a bit stiffly, "and she came with me."

"Then I can certainly see why you're anxious to get into the water," Justin said with a laugh.

"Think I'll take another dip myself," Clarke chimed in. "Take your time getting changed, Adam, old pal. I'll keep Francy entertained for you."

"I'll chaperone," Janet informed her husband sternly.

SEVERAL YARDS AWAY Francy lowered herself into the azure water and sighed with pleasure as its coolness slid over her body. Maybe this wasn't as spectacular as a Bermuda beach, but it was close, she thought. As she dog-paddled across the shallow length of the pool, she gazed around at the posh outdoor setting. It was like a house-and-garden picture from the Sunday supplement. How many times had she studied those photographs and found it hard to believe that such places truly existed? Well, now she was seeing the real thing. And it was Adam's home.

She glanced over at the other end of the pool where he and the rest of the guests stood talking. They, too, looked as if they might be posing for a photograph. Barbara and the redheaded young woman named Bixie were so sleek and well-groomed and beautifully outfitted in their bright sundresses. And the men, too, with their fashionable haircuts and trim tanned physiques, seemed almost like idealizations of the human animal. Certainly Adam was as handsome as any model or movie star.

Suddenly Francy felt as if she were looking at him and his friends from the other side of a wall. *I don't belong here,* a part of her seemed to be saying. *I don't fit in.* Yet, on another level, the stubborn one, she refused to let that thought stay uppermost in her mind. Just as she had when she'd met Ben Catlett, she unconsciously squared her shoulders and firmed her jaw. *I know how real and human Adam is. And as for his friends, they're just people,* she told herself. *They're just good-looking, rich people. They're no better than I am—and even if they are, I'm not going to let them know that I think so.*

"Hey, beautiful, mind if I join you?" Leering good-naturedly, Clarke crossed over and lowered himself into the water. A moment later he was joined by Janet, who straddled the diving board and let her slim legs dangle over the edge.

Francy gave the couple her best smile. "I'm glad to have some company. I was beginning to get lonely."

"Any girl who looks the way you do in a bathing suit needn't worry about loneliness," Clarke told her cheekily.

"Hey, what's wrong with the way I look in a bathing suit?" Janet demanded.

"Nothing, sweetheart," Clarke said as he rolled over and launched into a lazy backstroke. "I'm in seventh heaven, surrounded on all sides by gorgeous women."

Ignoring Clarke, Francy paddled over to the diving board and hung on to the pool's gutter while she talked to Janet. The brown-haired young woman was telling Francy about her two-year-old son when Adam emerged from the changing room wearing bathing trunks. Not long after he hit the water, the other couples gravitated over and settled into chairs so that they could carry on conversations with the aquatic half of the party. While they chatted, Patricia busied herself supervising the meal preparation.

Francy did her best not to seem like the odd man out, but except with Janet, it wasn't easy. The men discussed politics, which was not exactly her specialty. Barbara and Bixie talked about art museums and shopping, with the latter appearing to be the petite redhead's long suit.

"Really, I think I've tried every store in Baltimore. It's so hard to get a well-made evening gown that's different," she complained, "and I'm going to need one for Pete's company dinner."

"I'm still wearing my prom dress to those things," Janet said with a laugh.

Bixie greeted the remark with a horrified look.

"Why don't you have something custom-made?" Barbara suggested. "That's what I always do."

"Yes, but you're single and have loads of free time. It's easy for you to get away to New York."

"Find a local dressmaker." As she spoke, Barbara's eye caught Francy's. "You might even ask Francy here. I can vouch that she's a wonderful seamstress."

"You sew?" Bixie queried, in the same tone of voice she might have used to ask if Francy had an extra leg.

Francy climbed out of the water and reached for a towel. "I have my own drapery business, but I don't do clothing."

"Didn't you make that dress you came in this evening?" questioned Barbara. "It didn't look like something off the rack."

Francy was a little unnerved by the remark. Obviously Barbara had been studying her with a good deal more than a merely casual eye.

"Yes," she admitted, "I make most of my own clothes. But that's just personal. My business is strictly home decorating." Maybe it was false pride, but the last thing she wanted was to be either one of these young women's "little dressmaker." On the lookout for an excuse to get away, she glanced toward the grill. "Mm. Smells as if dinner's almost ready. Maybe I'd better put my clothes on."

"Good idea," Barbara agreed, eyeing Francy's curvy figure.

Later on during dinner Francy managed to hold up her end of the conversation and even told a joke that made everyone laugh. With Adam's arm around the back of her chair and most of the evening's ordeal behind her, she was beginning to relax somewhat. Maybe Adam's mother wasn't so bad after all, she thought. All during dinner Patricia had really been very gracious. Francy knew that she could never be entirely comfortable with women like Bixie and Barbara, but that didn't mean it was impossible to socialize with them. Bixie was even funny, once you got used to her.

"Oh, dear!" Patricia exclaimed, raising a hand to her golden hair. "Was that a drop of water I just felt on my head?"

"'Fraid so," Pete answered. "And I do believe I'm hearing thunder rumble in the distance."

Everybody looked at one another and then reached for their plates and forks. The storm broke just as they'd carried their desserts inside the house.

"Well, at least we got to swim and finish our steak," Adam said as he guided Francy down the center hall and into the living room.

She was too busy looking around to do more than mumble a one-syllable answer. Filled with antiques and decorated with taste and intelligence, the house was just as remarkable inside as it was on the exterior. As she settled down on the cushiony white silk love seat, she gazed around at the room Patricia had called the east parlor. It had pale pink walls set off by a wide decorative border, cleverly draped white lace curtains and a beautiful patterned carpet in the same shades of cream, pale green and pink as the striped fabric on the French chairs. Through the archway there was another room with the same color scheme. On its floor was a custom-made rug in the shape of a harp. A real harp rested to one side along with a baby grand piano, a handsomely worked brass music stand and a collection of stringed and wind instruments. *Must be the music room,* Francy thought.

As if all this pastel splendor were quite the ordinary thing, Adam settled himself cross-legged at her feet and began to fork up the rest of his dessert.

"Well, now, what shall we do to entertain ourselves while the storm rages?" Patricia said after everyone had finished off their chocolate cheesecake and Judy served coffee from a silver urn.

"Why don't we play a game?" Bixie suggested.

"A game?" Patricia looked blank.

"Yes, at the Matsons' last week we learned a really good one, much better than charades. But you need a big old dictionary." She glanced over at a tall bookcase next to the piano on the other side of the archway and then jumped to her feet. "Oh, there's one that looks perfect!"

*What's the dictionary for?* Francy wondered. Nervously she watched the petite young woman pry a fat volume out of the crowded shelf.

"It works like this," Bixie informed the group when she returned to her seat. "The person whose turn it is finds a really strange, obscure word. The other players guess at the definition and write it down on slips of paper. You get the funniest answers. We all laughed and laughed when we played it. It's really a hoot."

Adam shrugged. "Sounds worth a try."

The others, save for Francy, murmured their agreement, and Patricia produced ballpoint pens and slips of paper from a small inlaid desk in the corner. All the while Francy sat stiffly upright on the couch, her hands clenched in her lap and her mind scurrying. How was she going to handle this? What was she going to do?

"I'll start," Bixie said with a bright smile. "Now let me see..." She opened the dictionary and began to flip through its tissue-thin pages.

"We'll probably be here all night while she tries to make up her mind," Pete said. "She can only make snap decisions when she shops."

"Oh, you!" Bixie protested with a busy little wave of her hand. "I've already picked something." She printed out a word in block letters and raised it to her chest so that everyone could see.

"Noctule," Clarke read. "Never heard of it."

"That's just the point," Janet informed him. "We're supposed to guess."

"Now write out your definitions and hand them to me," Bixie instructed. "Then I'll read them out loud and the one who's closest to being right wins the round."

"What if no one guesses?" Barbara wanted to know.

Bixie smirked. "Then I win."

After a few more joking remarks, the guests began to scribble out definitions. Under lowered lashes, Francy watched as Adam's pen moved smoothly over the paper. Though she could see the letters clearly, she had no idea what they said. While her stomach clenched tighter, she put her pen to her own slip of paper and pretended to move it. Noctule, what could that be? Was there any word she knew that she might write down? In her class she had managed to learn to spell a number of simple words. But now they blurred in her mind's eye, letters running into each other as if floating in alphabet soup. What if she wrote something down that turned out to be gibberish?

"Time, everyone!" Bixie cried out merrily. "Pass in your answers."

Swallowing on a bitter taste at the back of her throat, Francy quickly printed out B-I-R-D, folded her piece of paper and handed it to Bixie.

With much fanfare the little redhead began reading out what the others had written. "I might have known you'd guess something like this, Clarke. Clarke says that it's the drink you have after you've had your nightcap. Wrong, wrong, wrong!'' While the others laughed, she tore up the prosecuting attorney's slip of paper. ''Barbara defines noctule as a type of short nocturne played only on toy pianos.''

''Makes as much sense as anything else,'' Justin said.

''Ha! Justin says it's a mushroom and—'' She opened up another bit of paper and then stared down at it blankly. ''Bird.'' She glanced around. ''Who wrote this? There's no name on it.''

''I did,'' Francy admitted in a low voice. Her nails dug into her palms and her spine felt as if it were made of ice.

Adam tipped his head back so that he could look up at her. ''Just bird?''

Francy shrugged tightly. ''I guess I'm not good at this game.''

''Actually,'' Bixie said into the uncomfortable silence, ''so far she's closer to getting it than any of you.'' She read the rest of the fanciful definitions and then opened the dictionary and read the real one. ''A variety of large brown bat of Europe and the British Isles.''

''You *were* the closest,'' Adam said to Francy, but there was still a perplexed expression in his blue eyes.

She knew that he was wondering why she hadn't played the game properly. Of course, you weren't supposed to write down four-letter words, like a child in grade school. You were supposed to write outrageous things that everyone would find amusing. Miserably she clutched her ballpoint pen. Her palms were so damp that the slick plastic surface seemed to slide against her skin.

Bixie handed Clarke the dictionary. ''Okay, smarty, your turn next.''

With a mock-evil laugh, he began to flip through its pages. "Eureka!" he cried. "The word is peduncle." He printed it out and raised it high. "Take that!"

Once again everybody began to jot down answers and pass them in.

"Adam thinks it's a type of wart that's found only on the end of your big toe," Clarke read. "Sorry, pal." He opened another slip of paper. "According to Bixie it's an uncle with large feet. Silly girl! And Patricia thinks a peduncle is a bicycle with square wheels."

"That's the best idea I've heard so far," Justin inserted. "I thought it was an exercise machine to strengthen weak toes."

Clarke opened and read out the other silly definitions and then began to look around him. "I'm missing one, aren't I? Francy, where's yours?"

"I don't know. It must have gotten lost," she fibbed. Actually the blank piece of paper lay crushed in her damp palm. How much longer could this game go on, she asked herself. Was there any way she could escape? But how?

"What was your answer?"

"I thought it was a flower," she guessed wildly.

Clarke grinned. "Francy's closest again." He opened the dictionary. "The botanical definition is the stalk of a flower cluster. Since she guessed it, she should choose our next word." He got to his feet, and carrying the dictionary, started to walk around toward Francy.

Horrified, she raised a protesting hand. "Oh, no, I'm not good at this sort of thing. I won't pick a good word. Somebody else should play next."

Wildly she looked around in search of a volunteer. But they were all smiling encouragingly at her.

"I'm sure you'll pick a better word than peduncle," Adam told her as Clarke laid the enormous dictionary on her lap. "Almost any word is better than that."

"Really, I . . ."

"Oh, come on," Clarke said with a laugh. "Just open it and write down the first word you see. Knowing this bunch's vocabulary, it probably won't get recognized unless it's spelled with three letters."

Needles of panic exploded inside Francy. Through a mist, she gazed helplessly at Clarke. Patricia was sitting just to one side of him. Suddenly Francy saw the speculative expression in her narrowed eyes. *She knows!* Francy thought. *She's guessed!* Her stomach seemed to twist into a thousand knots.

With fingers that felt like chunks of ice, she opened the dictionary and looked down at the tiny print. Before her it swam into a gray obscurity.

"See anything?" Adam finally queried, a note of impatience in his voice.

How long had she been staring silently at the page, Francy wondered. A minute? Five minutes? Ten minutes? She had no idea. Someone coughed and there were rustles as the other players shifted their positions on the floor. What were they thinking about her? Were they wondering if something was wrong with her?

She turned the page, but it was no different from the last. Francy looked up and saw the eyes staring at her— curious eyes, pitying eyes, scornful eyes. It was just the way it had been in grade school, only worse. Much, much worse!

Francy started to tremble. With a jerky movement, she pushed the dictionary off her lap so that it fell to one side on the white silk couch. "I'm sorry, I can't do this," she said through her chattering teeth. Then she jumped to her feet and, stumbling over Adam who sat gaping up at her from his position on the floor, she lurched through the crowd of players and ran from the room.

Out in the hall she heard Adam call her name. Ignoring it, she continued her headlong flight. She didn't care that it was still raining. All she wanted was to escape this house and those staring eyes.

Outside a streak of lightning lit the sky, showing up the dark shape of the pool and the wet litter still left on the table from dinner. Water seemed to tumble from the heavens in thick streamers. As Francy ran around the side of the house it splattered her head, turning her long hair into cold wet ribbons that clung to her neck and forehead.

She had made it out onto the driveway before Adam caught up with her. When she heard his feet pounding after her, she tried to run faster. But her soggy, high-heeled sandals hadn't been made for a race on a muddy gravel driveway. They twisted and squelched so that she fell against the hood of Adam's car.

Behind her, his hands seized her shoulders and spun her around. "My God! What are you doing? What's wrong?"

As she gazed up at him, another streak of lightning blazed across the sky, throwing the expression on his face into sharp relief. His blond hair, made dark by the water, was plastered to his head. Water beaded his eyebrows and lashes as he stared at her in baffled amazement. When she didn't answer, his hands tightened on her cold, wet shoulders. "Francy, why are you acting this way? Come on, this is crazy. Let's go back into the house and get out of the rain."

At the suggestion, Francy flattened her hands against the soaked fabric of his shirt and began to push. "No! I won't go back there," she shouted through her chattering teeth. "Take me home, Adam! I want to go home!"

"Now? Like this?"

"Yes, now! Take me home!"

## CHAPTER THIRTEEN

"MY GOD, WHAT HAPPENED TO YOU?" Teresa exclaimed. She and Gus were watching television with Mama and the kids. Now they stared at Francy who had to walk past the living room to get to the stairs. She looked as if she'd been half-drowned. Her wet dress hung shapelessly around her knees, her hair drooped in wet question marks around her shoulders, and her ruined shoes dangled from her hand like dead fish.

"Nothing," she mumbled dully and then turned and fled up to her room.

Teresa and Gus, who were sitting next to each other on the worn couch with Rosy on Gus's lap, stared at each other and then across the room at Mama.

"What's wrong with Aunt Francy?" Jerry queried from the corner where he was playing with a coloring book. "She looked sick."

"Yes, she did," Teresa agreed. "Oh dear. I guess maybe she didn't have a good time at the dinner party."

On the second floor Francy pushed open the door of her bedroom and then shut it behind her. Without putting on the light, she went to the window. Adam's sleek black car was still parked next to the curb with its lights on and its motor running. Though she couldn't see him behind the rhythmic shimmy of his windshield wipers, she could easily imagine the baffled expression he must still be wearing.

"Francy, talk to me. Tell me what's wrong," he'd pleaded on the long, horrible drive back to Little Italy. But in her misery and defeat she'd only curled into a tight, defensive ball.

Now, as she stood in her darkened room, she looked out the rain-spattered window and whispered, "Go away, Adam! It's over."

As if he'd heard her, the Mazda slowly pulled away from the curb and drove down the street. When its red taillights disappeared around the corner, Francy turned and plopped weakly on the edge of her bed. Her shoes fell to the floor with a squishy thud. She felt sick and hollow inside.

Out in the hall, someone tapped gently. "Francy?" It was Mama's worried voice. The door opened a crack and her curly gray head, outlined by the light in the hall, appeared around the edge. "Why are you sitting there in the dark like a mushroom?" She switched on the overhead fixture so that Francy winced as the room flooded with instant brightness. "And how come you haven't taken off those wet clothes? You want to catch pneumonia?"

Francy glanced down at her dress, which clung to her legs and breasts in a clammy embrace. Before she could think of an answer, Josephine bustled forward and tugged at her arm. "Here, stand up so I can get that thing off you."

Obediently Francy got to her feet and allowed her mother to undress her. After Josephine had wrapped her youngest daughter in a freshly laundered nightie and cotton robe, she sat her back down on the bed and bustled out to the bathroom in the hall. She returned bearing a thick towel and, in a no-nonsense fashion, began to vigorously rub Francy's wet hair. "What happened?'' she demanded. ''Did that Adam treat you bad?''

Dully Francy shook her head. ''No. Adam always treats me like a queen.''

''Then what happened to make you like this? Wasn't his mother nice to you?'' Josephine put the towel aside and reached for a comb.

Francy lowered her head, only dimly aware of the comb's long, soothing strokes. With a sigh, she began to describe the evening at Spruce Valley.

''This place sounds like a palace,'' Josephine commented.

''Yes, it was gorgeous, all right. A swimming pool and everything.''

''So why are you coming back all upset? Were the people at the party snooty? Did they make you uncomfortable?''

''A little, but I was doing okay until it started to rain, and we all went into the house.'' Expressionlessly Francy told Josephine about the dictionary game and her wild flight out into the storm.

Josephine listened in silence, her hand never wavering as she continued to comb through her daughter's tangled ebony locks.

''Oh, Francy!''

''Yeah, I know. I made a big fool of myself. You were right.''

''What do you mean? Right about what?''

''Going to Bermuda with Adam. I should have just stayed home where I belong.''

For the first time the comb paused. ''I'm not so sure about that.'' She kissed the top of Francy's head and then put her arms around her drooping shoulders. ''Honey, I'm real sorry.''

"Yeah. Oh, Ma!" Tears leaked from Francy's dark eyes and rolled down her cheeks. When Josephine sat down on the bed next to her, she collapsed against her mother and wept. "Oh, Ma, I feel so awful!"

"I know, honey, I know. You just cry all you want. It's okay by me."

Even after Francy's first storm of anguish abated and Josephine finally left the tiny bedroom, Francy's tears continued to flow silently. All night she lay awake, reliving over and over again the terrible scene in Patricia Pearce's elegant east parlor. It never lost its horror and when Francy remembered the shocked expression on Adam's face as she stumbled over him in her crazy flight, her throat ached and her eyes felt like hot coals burning inside her skull. *He must think I'm out of my mind,* she told herself. She couldn't even imagine what the others thought. And she didn't want to try.

Through the long dark hours she struggled with the consequences of what had happened. It was her own fault; she knew that. She should have told Adam the truth long ago. But it was too late. Now, the only thing Francy knew for sure was that she never wanted to go back to that house. She never wanted to see those people again. It was over between her and Adam. She would tell him that—if she ever got the opportunity. For it wouldn't have surprised Francy in the least if he never wanted to lay eyes on her again, either.

About that, however, she was mistaken. The next day Adam came to the shop. He had only been to New Beginnings once before, and that had been in the early days when Francy and Teresa had just been putting the place together. It was a shock when Francy turned around and saw him standing there amid the bolts of brightly colored cloth. He was dressed in a three-piece gray summer suit and had obviously just come from the office. His lightly tanned skin was clean-shaven and his hair neatly combed, but the hint of redness in his eyes and the lines that stood out in sharp relief at their corners testified to a sleepless night.

*Just like me,* Francy thought. When she'd looked at herself in the mirror that morning, her skin had been gray beneath what was left of her Bermuda tan.

"Francy, can we talk?"

Her hands clenched on the countertop. "What are you doing here? Don't you have to be at work?"

"Yes, I'm supposed to be in a meeting right now, as a matter of fact. But I realized that my being any place but here is a waste of time," he said in his steady, deep voice. "We need to straighten this thing out."

Teresa came out of the back room carrying a pile of remnants. She took one look at Adam and stopped short. "Oh, hello, there. Umm, I think I'll go over to Gus's and help him unload a crate of pineapples. I'll be back in half an hour."

"No, Teresa, please..."

But Teresa deposited her remnants on the counter and hurried out the door, leaving Francy and Adam alone in the shop.

She took a deep breath. "I'm busy, and I'm expecting a customer any minute."

"Francy, stop it! We need to talk."

Of course he was right. But it was going to be so awful. Inwardly Francy quaked. She could hardly bear to look him in the face. "All right."

"About last night..." Adam lifted his hands and stared at her. "I don't understand what happened."

"No, of course you don't. How could you?"

"I didn't get any sleep. All I could do was pace back and forth trying to figure it out. I never did. I feel more confused now than ever."

Francy fingered one of the remnants that Teresa had left, nervously tracing its flowered pattern with the tip of her thumb. "Did you go back to Spruce Valley after you dropped me off?" It was morbid curiosity. At one point while she lay awake the night before she had pictured Adam and his friends sitting in that pink parlor speculating about her bizarre behavior. "Maybe she's a schizophrenic, or maybe she's got some sort of terrible health problem and was having an attack," she'd imagined Bixie saying.

"No," he told her, laying at least that fear to rest.

"You must have talked to your mother. I mean, she would wonder what happened when we both disappeared that way."

"She did call me late last night," he admitted.

Francy laughed sharply. "I bet she's got a theory or two about my behavior." When Adam was silent, Francy looked at him inquiringly. "Well, she does, doesn't she?"

"She thinks you might have some sort of emotional problem."

"What do you think, Adam?"

"God, Francy, I don't know what to think."

They stared at each other. With a kind of desperation, Francy's eyes drank Adam in. What a fine man he was, she thought, standing there so tall and strong and yet so vulnerable. She registered all the tiny details about him, the way his hair waved over his ears, the exact tint of his eyes, his hands, which were a little too large and yet were so capable and, at times, so sensitive. All these things she stored away because she knew that she was about to lose him forever.

"Well, your mother's partly right," she said dully. "Only it's not an emotional problem, it's a mental problem."

"What?" He took a step forward, but Francy held up her palm.

"No, I'm not telling you that I'm crazy. Adam, I couldn't play that game last night because I couldn't read that dictionary."

"You couldn't?" He frowned. "Do you have some difficulty with your vision? Do you need glasses?"

Francy shook her head. "I couldn't read the dictionary because I can't read. Adam, I can't read."

She might as well have told him that she couldn't grow hair. He stared at her, his expression uncomprehending. "I don't understand."

"I never learned to read," she ground out. "I can't read, and I can't write. Last night I couldn't write down something witty to amuse your friends because I only know a few simple words."

He shook his head as if to clear it. "But that doesn't make sense. You've read Faulkner and Hemingway. We've discussed their books. You've even quoted Shakespeare."

Francy's hands clenched on the edge of the counter. "Every week I go to the library and take out cassette recordings of different books. I have an excellent memory. I was deceiving you when I talked about those novels. I never read them, I just listened to them."

"Francy, this still doesn't make any sense to me. You went to school. You were in high school."

"Yes, but I never learned anything there except how to cheat and cover up. After a while that didn't work, and I had to drop out."

"You're taking a literature class now. You told me so."

"Every Tuesday and Thursday I go to an adult reading class. So I'm still trying, but, as you can tell from my performance last night, I'm making very slow progress."

Again, Adam shook his head. "Everybody learns to read. A smart person like you—"

"Not everybody, and I'm not so smart. I have a learning disability." Francy felt as if tiny bits of her were being steadily chipped away. Just standing and watching the expressions of shock and disbelief come and go on Adam's face was torture. Her legs were beginning to tremble. "It isn't as if I didn't try to learn, but I couldn't. I'm dyslexic. My father was dyslexic, too, and so is my nephew. It runs in our family."

"Dyslexic? Francy—" He looked thunderstruck.

Suddenly she had reached the end of her strength and couldn't bear it any longer. "Adam, will you just go? It's not going to work out between us. You must see that now. Just go."

"What do you mean? What are you saying?"

From the corner of her eye, she spotted Mrs. Caldo crossing the street toward the shop. There was a finished order for her in the back room, which she had an appointment to pick up. Francy gathered the ragged remnants of her strength. "There's no place for us to go from here. I can't marry someone like you, and you can't marry someone like me. From here on out it's just a dead end for us, and I don't need any more dead ends in my life. Just go."

The bell on the door tinkled, and Anna Caldo hurried into the shop. "Oh, I was so glad when you called to say my curtains were ready. I can't wait to see how that pattern looks in my living room," she declared breathlessly. She stopped short, gazing curiously from Francy to Adam as she began to take in the tense atmosphere in the room.

Decisively Francy turned her back on Adam and walked over to her customer. "Your drapes are all ready to go. I wrapped them up for you last night."

"I'm not in that much of a rush. You can finish waiting on this gentleman."

"I'm finished with this gentleman. He was just leaving. I'll go back and get your order now."

After Francy had walked quickly past Adam without looking at him, she took her time finding the order. For several minutes she stood breathing deeply, waiting for her hands to stop trembling. But she couldn't hide in the back of the shop forever. At last, she gathered up the plastic-covered fabric and went out. Mrs. Caldo was alone in the store.

ADAM SAT IN HIS CAR, staring blindly at the steering wheel. He felt as if he'd been hit with a cement-wrecking ball. Francy couldn't read? It was impossible for him to accept. Everyone he knew could read.

Painfully he searched his memory, going back to his grade-school days. Had there been anyone who hadn't picked up reading? He remembered Norm Walters, who as late as third grade had stumbled over words of more than one syllable when asked to read aloud. Norm had never been any great shakes as a scholar. But eventually even he'd learned to put letters together well enough to get by. Now he ran his own construction business.

Adam thumped the steering wheel with his balled fist. "Everyone learns to read," he repeated aloud. Then he stiffened, as another more recent memory came to mind. It wasn't true that everyone he knew could read. What about J.D. Pike? Poor, pathetic J.D. who the local hooligans liked to play cruel jokes on. One of the reasons the guy got into so much hot water was because he'd never been able to decipher a line of print.

"Oh, my God!" Adam muttered. His mouth set in a grim line, he dug out his car keys and jerked on the ignition. Pulling out into the traffic, he headed the Mazda west toward Catonsville. He'd already played hookey on one important meeting and would miss another if he didn't make it back to his office pronto. But instead of driving straight to the large brick building outside Ellicott City where he had his headquarters, Adam parked on Frederick Avenue in front of the sprawling Catonsville public library.

Inside, he went straight to the information desk and told the woman who sat behind it, "I want all the material on dyslexia that you've got."

THAT NIGHT when Francy finally closed up the shop, she felt limp with exhaustion. It wasn't just lack of sleep. For almost twenty-four hours her emotions had been stirred into a cauldron and set to boil. As she locked up New Beginnings and then began a slow, slump-shouldered walk in the direction of home, she told herself that she was too tired to have any feelings left.

But feeling came in a sharp, painful stab when she saw that Adam's sports car was parked outside her row house. The car was empty so he must be inside. Doing what, she wondered. Teresa and the kids were out with Gus. Was he in there talking to Mama?

Francy quickened her stride. But when she'd thrown open the door and hurried into the living room she stopped short again. Sure enough, Mama and Adam were sitting across from each other, their tense faces turned toward the entry.

Mama was the first to speak. "Adam came here to see you, Francy."

"I don't want to see him."

"Yes, you do." Mama stood up and wiped nervous hands on her apron. "I'm going into the kitchen and finish fixing dinner. Adam is invited to stay, if he wants. Now you talk to him, Francy, and listen to what he has to say."

Francy cast a rebellious look at her mother, but Josephine only hurried past and went down the hall. A moment later the clang of pots and pans began filtering from behind the closed kitchen door.

Adam waited until they were alone and then got to his feet. He looked the same as he had that morning only paler and more drawn. They were both being run through the same wringer, Francy realized, and felt the urge to comfort him, to smooth his brow with her fingertips. Then she saw the determined glint in his eyes, and her spine stiffened. Comfort was something she could no longer offer Adam Pearce—not if she loved him.

"You didn't think it was all over when I left your shop this morning, did you?" he queried.

"If it wasn't, it should have been."

"No, Francy." He began to walk toward her. "We have a lot more to say to each other. You might be interested to hear how I spent the afternoon."

"How?" As he drew nearer, Francy felt a knot tighten in her chest and her eyes began to burn. She wanted so badly to reach out to him.

"I've been in the library, reading about dyslexia. I'm in a lot better shape to talk to you about it now than I was this morning."

"But I'm not, Adam. I'm not in shape to talk to you. Or anyone, for that matter."

"We can't just let this thing hang between us. Francy, what you've got is a learning disability that has nothing to do with basic intelligence. It's just something that needs to be overcome."

"Where have I heard that before?"

"Don't you see? It has nothing to do with us."

"Doesn't it?" When he was only a step away she hurried to the opposite corner of the room. There she almost threw herself into the old lounge chair where her father had liked to sit and watch television. In the protection of its cushions she drew up her knees and avoided Adam's eyes while she smoothed her skirt around her ankles. "You're wrong," she said tensely. "It has everything to do with us. We aren't going to make it, Adam. It isn't going to work."

"Francy, don't say these things. Don't make it sound as if we haven't got a future. I love you. I want to marry you."

How horribly ironic to hear those words now, when the taste of them was like ashes. While her hands clenched the sides of the chair, she stared down at the hem of her skirt. Beneath it her knees were trembling again. "When we were in Bermuda, you talked to me about children. Have you thought about the sort of children you'd have with me? They'd probably inherit my learning disability."

"Then we'd see to it that they got the right kind of help as soon as they needed it. I'm worried about us, Francy, not children that haven't been born yet. If only you'd told me about the reading before. That whole scene at my mother's place needn't have happened."

"You're right," she said on a ragged sigh. Francy struggled to gather her shredded strength. "Adam, I didn't tell you about my problem before because I wanted your respect. But that was a terrible mistake. If I'd let you read the menus in the fancy restaurants for me, if I'd let you point me to the ladies' room so I wouldn't walk in the wrong door, if I'd let you stand between me and all the situations that a person like me can get into in your world, then I would have realized a lot sooner just how impossible we are together. Adam, don't you see?"

"My world? What's that supposed to mean?"

"Yes, your world!" she threw out. "I do okay here where I know my way around. Here nobody expects me to play dictionary games or puts labels on the bathrooms that only a yacht owner would understand. If you came from my neck of the woods and were willing to stay there, maybe it would be okay for us. But you don't and you're not. And when I cross the line into your territory I'm constantly putting my foot into bear traps."

"You're talking about that party last night. But that was just an isolated incident."

"No," Francy said hotly. "You don't know what I've had to go through to eat in restaurants with you and meet your friends. I'm always uptight, afraid I'm going to make an idiot of myself. Well, last night I really did it, didn't I?" She jabbed at her eyes, hating the tears that were beginning to spill out of them again. "Maybe it wouldn't be so bad if that was all there was to it. But it's going to get worse.''

"Francy!''

"No, Adam, you know that I'm speaking the truth. You're smart and strong and ambitious, and you're going places. You're going to run for national office.''

"But I probably won't get elected.''

"Maybe not this time, but eventually you will. And you should be. I think you'll make a wonderful congressman, and I wouldn't stop there, either. But that means you'll be associating with powerful people. You'll need a wife who can handle herself in those circles, not someone like me. I would only handicap you. And eventually that would tear us both apart.''

Adam knelt in front of her and reached for one of her cold hands. "I don't believe that for a minute. But if you really feel this way, I'll withdraw from the campaign. It won't be hard at this point.''

"No.'' She yanked her fingers from his. "Don't you understand what I'm saying? I couldn't bear it if you stopped being who you are and doing the things you want to do because of me.'' Francy's expression was tormented. "But I'm who I am, and I can't change that, either.''

"I love who you are. Don't you understand? I love you.''

She met his anguished gaze. "I love you, too, Adam. I do. But I'm not going to marry you, and I'm not going to see you again, either. It's over between us.''

Before he could react, she had jumped out of the chair and pushed past him.

"You can't mean that,'' he cried as she bolted from the room. But when he got to his feet and followed after her, she'd already run up the stairs and slammed her bedroom door behind her.

He was about to follow, but a hand tugging on his forearm distracted him.

"She's all upset," Mrs. Rasera said. She stood behind him, a dish towel in one hand and a troubled expression on her lined face. "Maybe you should just wait. Maybe she'll feel different in a couple of days."

"You think so?"

"Sometimes things look different after a day or two. Francy always takes things so serious, but she's got a good head on her shoulders. Give her some time to think."

His shoulders slumped. "I don't know. Maybe you're right."

"You're a good man. I see that now. She's smart. She'll see it, too." Reassuringly Josephine patted Adam's arm. "I got some lasagna made fresh. I'll put it in a dish, so you can take it home and heat it up for supper tonight, okay? Everything looks better with a full stomach."

He managed a wry smile. "Okay."

Fifteen minutes later, holding a plastic container in one hand, Adam pushed open the Raseras' front door. Immediately the brooding expression in his blue eyes changed to one of consternation. In front of him the Mazda slouched at an uneven angle. Its tires had been slashed.

# CHAPTER FOURTEEN

"I'M SORRY, I CAN'T."

"I have to see you. Let me come over tonight." Adam's voice on the other end of the line was taut with urgency.

"No, I'm busy."

"Francy, please, we have to talk again."

She glanced over her shoulder and then steeled herself to say what had to be said. "Talking doesn't do any good. It's over. Please, please... just give up."

"Francy—"

Gently she depressed the switch hook and then, instead of replacing the receiver, lay it down on the counter.

"That must be some obnoxious salesman if you're willing to leave the phone off the hook so he can't call back."

Francy turned toward Jimmy Alonzo. The thin, dark-haired young man was hunched over the kitchen table, his elbows propped on a stack of books and a quizzical expression in his hazel eyes.

Unconsciously Francy raised her right hand to her chest, as if she could quell the ache of her heart beneath the soft flannel shirt she wore loose over her jeans. "Yes," she said dully. "He's been very persistent."

Which was certainly an understatement. For two weeks now, ever since their stormy scene in the living room, Adam had called every day. Mostly it was Mama or Teresa or one of the kids who took the calls. Tonight, however, Francy was the only Rasera at home. Maybe if Jimmy Alonzo hadn't been with her she would have just let the phone ring. But she didn't want to have to explain such bizarre behavior to her guest, so, with her heartbeat accelerating nervously, she'd picked up the receiver. Her throat had contracted when she'd heard Adam's voice on the other end of the line. It was bad enough that she thought about him night and day. Did he have to torture her with the sound of his voice, too?

"What's the guy trying to sell?" Jimmy queried.

Francy's smile was twisted. "Daydreams."

"What?"

"Really, it's not important. Let's get back to work." Making a show of eagerness, Francy crossed the kitchen floor and sat down next to her old school friend. Jimmy had made good on his promise to help her with her reading.

"Okay," he said, handing her the book they'd been working with, "start there."

Francy smoothed the page and began struggling through the sentence at the top. "The f-i-e-r-c-e..." She hesitated, trying to put the sounds together. "Fierce?"

"That's right," Jimmy encouraged.

"The fierce dog ru-sh— Rushed?"

"Yes, you should trust yourself a little more. Most of the time you're getting them right, Francy. Don't be so unsure."

Easy for Jimmy to say, Francy thought wryly. He hadn't spent ninety-nine percent of his life being wrong.

But instead of commenting out loud, she continued to labor through the sentence and then the paragraph following it.

"Finish the page and we can take a break."

"Slave driver."

Jimmy quirked his expressive eyebrows. "You want to learn, don't you?"

"Yes," Francy told him earnestly, "more than anything."

"Well, you're going to. We've only worked together twice and already I can see that you're making progress. Now, back to work."

Obediently Francy resumed the battle, doggedly sounding out the unfamiliar longer words and trying to commit the shorter ones to memory. It took her a full fifteen minutes, but she finally made it through the whole page.

"Congratulations," Jimmy told her as he shut the book and pushed it to the other side of the table. "That was quite a performance. You really are getting better."

"Do you think so?"

"I know so. You know it, too, don't you?"

She nodded. "Yes, but—oh, how long do you think it will be before I'll really be able to read?"

"You can read now. It's just very slow, and you have so little confidence that almost anything rattles you."

"Don't I know it." Yet again, Francy thought back to the horrible dictionary game at Spruce Valley. That night was seared permanently on her memory.

"Francy," Jimmy queried, "maybe it's none of my business, but I can't help wondering...is something wrong? Something besides the reading?"

She was jerked from her brief, painful reverie. "What do you mean?"

"Oh, I don't know," Jimmy replied with his customary tact. "It's just that you seem sort of melancholy. And there are shadows under your eyes, as if you're not getting enough sleep." He reached out to lay a gentle finger on her cheekbone. "They're very attractive shadows, but they don't belong there. Your face was made to be happy."

Francy looked away. "Maybe I've been putting in too many hours at the shop."

"Maybe," Jimmy said doubtfully. "You certainly work yourself to the bone at that place. But I have a feeling that's not really the trouble. I have a feeling that some guy has made you unhappy." He waited, but when she said nothing, he shook his head ruefully. "You're not going to tell me, are you?"

"It's nothing, Jimmy. I'm okay, really."

He sighed. "If you say so. But remember, if you need a shoulder..." He brushed some imaginary lint off his sleeve. "It's not much, but it's all yours."

Francy managed a smile. "You're a nice guy, Jimmy. You always were, and you haven't changed a bit."

"That's not the only thing that hasn't changed, beautiful Francy. You still want to be just friends. I've got that right, haven't I?"

She looked at him anxiously. "Oh, Jimmy, yes, that's right."

"I was afraid you were going to say that." Melodramatically he clutched at his heart. "The pain! The pain!" Then he gave her his endearing lopsided grin. "Okay, but no more Mr. Nice Guy. Back to work."

As he reached for the book, Francy studied his boyish profile. Why couldn't she have fallen in love with someone like him, she asked herself. Jimmy was bright and kind and quick, and he knew all about her. With him she didn't have to pretend to be anything but exactly what she was. Yet much as she liked Jimmy, she didn't love him and never would. She loved Adam. And it was going to be a long, long time before she got over him. That was pathetically clear.

Francy had been at work on a new page for less than five minutes when the front door banged open. Laughing voices filled the hall and a moment later Gus, Teresa, Mama and the kids spilled into the kitchen. As they greeted Francy and Jimmy they were all breathless and smiling.

Grinning from ear to ear, Mama bustled over to the cupboard to unload her armful of groceries. Gus, looking sheepish but happy, followed her with more bags filled to the brim with fresh produce from his store. While the kids accepted the apples and pears Mama handed out, Teresa stood in the doorway as if caught in a delicious trance.

Francy gave her sister an inquiring once-over. It had been a long time since she'd seen her look quite this pretty. With her flushed cheeks and eyes glowing like dark stars, she could almost have passed for the teenage beauty she'd been in her youth.

"What's up, Teresa? You look as if you've had some good news."

"Sort of," she replied with uncustomary shyness. Her blush deepened and so did the shine in her eyes.

Beaming, Mama turned and planted her feet wide. "Gus and Teresa have an announcement to make."

The kids started to giggle. "Yeah, they're going to get married," Mike shouted.

His grandmother gave the boy a light thwack on the head. "Now you be quiet. This is for your mama and your new papa to say."

Francy's jaw had dropped open. "Married?"

Teresa nodded and then crossed the floor to take Gus's hand. Plainly both proud and thunderstruck, he was standing wedged in the corner next to the refrigerator. "Yes," Teresa said. "Gus and I have decided to tie the knot. We want to be a family." She turned and kissed the greengrocer squarely on the mouth.

He turned a brilliant shade of red, but he looked pleased. When Teresa moved away, he gave Francy an uncertain look. "I love your sister very much," he said in a voice husky with emotion. "I think I've been a little in love with her for years. I hope you don't mind having someone like me for a brother-in-law."

"Mind?" Francy cried. "Gus, I'm going to love having you for a brother-in-law." She scrambled off her chair and rushed over to give him and then her sister a big hug. A moment later Jimmy added his congratulations while he shook the older man's hand.

Hugs and kisses all around followed, with the children dancing around the embracing adults' feet shouting high-pitched questions and exclamations. When things finally settled down a bit, Jimmy said, "This calls for a celebration. How about I take you all out for beer and pizza at Vivo's?"

Gus, Teresa and Mama looked at one another. "I was going to make linguine," Mama said.

Teresa shook her head. "This is a special occasion. You deserve a night off from cooking." She smiled at Jimmy. "That sounds like fun. Let's do it. Only I warn you, these kids can stuff down a lot of pizza."

"I ate four slices the last time we went out," Jerry bragged.

Jimmy ruffled the youngster's hair. "I'll challenge you to a pizza eat-off."

"You're coming aren't you, Francy?" Teresa queried.

"Sure," Francy answered. "I just have to go upstairs and change my top." She flicked the hem of the flannel shirt she wore with a deprecatory finger. "I'll be ready in a minute."

Upstairs, Teresa soon joined her sister. "Well," she said after she'd closed Francy's bedroom door so that they could have some privacy, "what do you think?"

As she pulled a lilac knit top out of a drawer, Francy shot Teresa an uncertain look. "I think that if you're happy, I'm happy."

"Oh, Francy, I really am happy." Teresa sat down on the edge of the bed and clasped her hands in her lap. "I know it's hard for you to believe that I could really love someone like Gus, but I do. I don't even know exactly when it happened. It sort of grew on me."

"It's not hard for me to believe that you could love Gus. He's a very lovable guy."

"Yes, like a big old teddy bear," Teresa agreed with a soft little smile. "But he's not handsome and romantic like your Adam. He's not Prince Charming."

"Yeah, well, maybe Cinderella needed to have her head examined," Francy answered gruffly. "Anyhow, what's Adam got to do with anything? You know that's over. The people who count here are you and Gus." She dropped down next to her sister and gave her another warm hug. "Congratulations, hon. I'm really happy for you."

"I just wish you were happier for yourself."

"I'm not the important one tonight. You are. Let's concentrate on you."

"Okay, tonight's my night. Yours will come, though. I just know it."

They both got up and started to walk out of the room. But Teresa paused with her hand on the door. "Maybe," she whispered hopefully, "you'll get over Adam and get interested in Jimmy Alonzo. He seems like such a nice guy."

"He is a nice guy," Francy agreed. But that was all he could ever be to her. She wasn't sure what the line was between a friend and a lover. What made your heart do flip-flops over one man while another just as good left you unmoved? But whatever that mysterious line was, Adam had crossed it immediately and Jimmy never would.

Downstairs the others waited in the living room. Gus bounced Rosy on his lap while Jimmy looked through a storybook with Jerry. Mama rushed around plumping pillows and ordering the kids to put away their scattered toys and schoolbooks.

"Finally!" Mama said when Francy and Teresa appeared at the foot of the stairs. "What were you two doing up there, giving each other home permanents?"

"Just trying to make myself attractive. Brides need to look their best, you know," Teresa replied gaily. She took Rosy off Gus's lap, kissed the plump little girl's cheek and then set her down and linked her arm through her fiancé's. "Lead me to this pizza. I'm hungry."

Vivo's was an unpretentious neighborhood place with scarred wooden booths and a black and white tile floor. They served good pizza, though, and that night everyone but Francy filled up on the cheesy treat. It had been weeks since she'd had much of an appetite and the viscous mozzarella seemed to stick in her throat. But not wanting to spoil her sister's celebration, she did her best to hide the fact and forced herself to join into the lively banter around the crowded table.

"What kind of dress are you going to wear to the wedding, Mom?" Jerry queried. "Will it be a long white one?"

"No," Teresa replied, "but it will be nice." She winked at Francy. "I have my own personal dressmaker."

"Yes, and her name is Teresa," Francy returned. "You can sew perfectly well when you put your mind to it."

"Can I wear a pretty dress?" Rosy wanted to know.

"Of course," her fond grandmother assured. "You're going to be the flower girl."

It was late when they left the eatery, and the streets were dark. On the narrow pavement that led back to the Rasera row house, their little group split into natural divisions. Walking arm in arm, Gus and Teresa led the procession. Shepherding the kids, Mama followed, and Jimmy and Francy tagged behind.

"When do you want to work again?" Jimmy asked.

"Tomorrow night I go to my class, but Wednesday is good."

"Fine, I'll come over at the usual time."

She glanced over at the obliging young man. "Are you sure? I mean, you must have better things to do."

"No." He shook his head. "I'm new in town, remember, and except for you, all my old friends are gone. It's kind of a lonely situation. Believe me, when I have better things to do, I'll do them."

She was still gazing across at him doubtfully when a subtle change in the atmosphere made her glance ahead to the others. Teresa was looking over her shoulder and her eyes, as they met Francy's, were anxious. Ahead of her Francy could make out the shape of a tall man standing in front of their house. Beneath the streetlight his hair glittered. Francy drew in her breath. It was Adam.

Her steps slowed and, for the first time that night, she linked her arm through Jimmy's.

"Who's the guy waiting in front of your place?" he asked in a low voice. "Someone you know?"

"Uh, yes."

Through his teeth Jimmy gave a low-pitched whistle. "Doesn't look as if he's from this neighborhood."

"No, he isn't."

Teresa and Gus had already drawn abreast of Adam. They greeted him politely and walked past and up the stairs to the house. Mama and the kids, after an uncomfortable little exchange, did the same.

Through the darkness Adam stood staring at Francy and Jimmy's linked arms until she felt as if her skin was burning wherever it came into contact with her old friend's.

"You want me to stick around?" Jimmy queried.

"No," she told him. "Maybe you'd better go now. I'll see you on Wednesday."

"Sure."

He gave her a searching look, and then with a jaunty salute, he turned and walked down the street. As his footsteps died away, Francy stood eyeing Adam. He wasn't wearing anything fancy, just jeans and a white shirt with a horizontal stripe across the chest. But Jimmy was right—you knew immediately that he didn't belong in this neighborhood. What was it? The hair, the crisp clean line of his profile? He looked as if he'd just stepped out of the pages of a yachting magazine.

Obviously totally unconscious of this effect, Adam strode toward her. There was nothing that suggested yachting in his expression. His features were grim, and the moon glittered in his eyes.

"Who's the guy you were with?" he asked starkly.

"An old friend." Francy would have liked to bristle, but she couldn't because all she really wanted was to reach out and touch Adam, to assure herself that he was real and not something she had imagined. Just once more she wanted to feel the solid warmth of him.

"You had your arm through his."

"Did I?"

Adam stared at her, his jaw working. "I don't understand what's happened to us. I really don't understand it."

Francy's hands clenched at her sides as she forced herself to remain calm. "There's nothing complicated."

"Isn't there? Then maybe you can explain it to me."

"Oh, Adam, we should never have gotten started. We're too mismatched. We're just not compatible."

"Mismatched, not compatible? Those are just empty words. They don't mean a thing!" He gestured over his shoulder toward his car. "We have to talk, Francy. We have to! Won't you let me take you someplace where we can have some privacy?"

"Your apartment, maybe?" She had no trouble imagining what would happen if she went to Adam's apartment. Right now, standing here outside on the street, she wanted to throw herself into his arms and cling. But that wouldn't be fair to him or to herself.

"It doesn't have to be my apartment. I'll take you any place you want. We just need to have a rational discussion."

"No."

"No?" His voice rose on a note of baffled desperation.

"No, it's over, Adam. I don't want to see you again."

She could feel him struggling for control. "Francy, you can't mean that."

"I do mean it."

For a long, tense moment he stood there, breathing hard, his nostrils flaring. Inwardly she felt as if she were slowly shriveling, yet she forced herself to meet his caustic scrutiny.

"Is it that guy you were with? Is it because of him?" Adam said tightly.

"It has nothing to do with Jimmy."

"Jimmy? How cozy."

"Leave Jimmy out of this. He's a nice person."

"Yeah, I'll bet he's just great." Adam's voice was rough with repressed emotion. "All right, Francy, have it your way. Sorry I bothered you." He turned and strode rapidly to his car. A moment later the powerful engine sprang to life and the low-slung automobile pulled sharply away from the curb.

As the taillights grew smaller in the distance, Francy jabbed at her eyes. They were wet with tears, and she didn't even know when they'd started to fall.

"I'M WORRIED ABOUT YOU, PAL. Do you ever go home, anymore?" Clarke stood in Adam's office doorway, eyeing his friend. Adam, as usual, was behind his desk, pouring over a mile-high stack of papers. He'd long ago removed his tie, and his shirtsleeves were rolled up. Be-

hind horn-rimmed glasses, his eyes were red with exhaustion, and his face looked drawn.

"There's no reason for me to go home, and I have
work to do."

"You always have work to do, and it's going to get
worse now that you've decided to go political. Hey, it's
quitting time. How about coming with me and getting
a decent home-cooked dinner?" Clarke eyed the remains of the fast-food burger and fries pushed to one
side on Adam's desk. Most of the cold food had been
left untouched and, if Adam ran true to form, would
wind up in the trash.

"Thanks for the invite, but I'm too busy. Anyhow,
I'll be dining in style tomorrow night."

"Oh, yes, how could I forget? Tomorrow night you
announce your candidacy formally and start the fried-
chicken circuit. Nervous?"

Adam took off his glasses and looked at them
thoughtfully. "A little, but I think it's the right step."

"Well, you've got my vote. That is, if you live long
enough to be elected. What do you hear from your
mystery friend?"

"Nothing, actually. Since he slashed my tires, if he
was the one who did it, there's been no action at all.
Maybe he's had enough fun and games with me."

"I hope so," Clarke said. "But something tells me it
isn't over yet." He eyed Adam. "Are you going to this
dinner tomorrow night solo?"

"Yes," Adam replied bleakly.

"It's going to be an important occasion for you. I
could name a half dozen pretty ladies crazy to be your
date and share the glory."

"There's only one pretty lady I'd like to take, and
she's not interested."

Clarke sighed. "I know you don't want to hear this, but how long has it been since Francy gave you the brush-off?"

"Three months."

"Maybe you'd better give up on her, Adam."

"Thanks for the advice, but maybe you'd better get going. I wouldn't want Janet's dinner to get spoiled." Pointedly Adam put his glasses back on and returned his attention to the papers on his desk.

Clarke hesitated another moment, but then shrugged his round shoulders, picked his briefcase up off the floor and disappeared down the hall. When he was gone, Adam dropped the document he'd been pretending to scrutinize and stared into space. He knew he'd been rude to a friend who was only trying to help, and he was sorry. But he didn't think he could stand any more well-meant suggestions about his personal life from people like Clarke and his mother. Only yesterday he'd walked out on Patricia when she'd tried to arrange a dinner date for him with her idea of an eligible female.

"Maybe Clarke is right, maybe I should give up on Francy," Adam muttered to himself. But somehow he hadn't been able to do it. Oh, he'd finally given up trying to get her to see him, though several times he had driven past her row house at night, staring up at the lighted window on the second floor that he imagined might be her bedroom. Was he going crazy, he wondered—turning into some kind of Peeping Tom? Once he'd even gotten a haircut at the barbershop across from New Beginnings, hoping to catch a glimpse of her through her store window. The haircut hadn't been bad, actually, but he hadn't seen Francy.

All he had now was the memory of the way she had looked in the shadows with her arm linked through another man's. At the thought, Adam ripped the document he'd been studying in half. "Damn!" he muttered as the sharp sound of the tearing paper shattered the heavy silence in the office, and he realized what he'd done. Maybe he really was going crazy! Now he'd have to tape the thing together, photocopy it and start all over again.

"WELL, WHAT DO YOU THINK?" Teresa preened like a runway model, moving her hips this way and that as she showed off the ice-blue wedding dress that she had made.

"I think you look great."

Teresa pursed her lips. "Francy, put down that book. Honestly, whenever I try to talk to you now you're either bent over a sewing machine or have your head stuck in some kids' book."

"Well, we've had a lot of orders to fill at the store," Francy defended herself, "and being able to read any kind of book is pretty exciting to me."

"*Nancy Drew and the Mystery of the Iron Gate*?" Teresa arched a black eyebrow.

"It's taken me an hour to get through five pages," Francy said, checking her watch. "I'll probably have gray hair before I find out who did it." Laughing ruefully, she dropped the book on the sofa, stood up and walked around her sister, eyeing the new dress critically. "It hangs well, the seams are straight, looks to me like you did a pretty good job. Now aren't you glad you ran it up yourself instead of making me do it for you?"

"You really think it looks okay?" Teresa asked shyly.

"I think it looks great, and so will Gus when he sees you on your wedding day."

Mama, closely trailed by the kids, bustled in with a bowl of popcorn. "Time for the evening news," she said, switching on the set.

Francy groaned. "I think I'll take Nancy Drew upstairs. I promised Jimmy I'd have a chapter read by the time he came over for our next lesson."

"When's that?"

"A week from Wednesday. He can't come as often as he used to. I think he's met a girl."

Both Teresa and Mama shot Francy an inquiring look. She knew what they were thinking. They'd both hoped that she'd get over Adam and take more than a friendly interest in her old school pal. But she'd known from the beginning that wasn't going to happen, and she was glad that Jimmy was beginning to meet new people.

Francy picked up her mystery. A moment later she froze as the voice of the newscaster filled the room.

"Rumors have been flying that Howard County's charismatic State's Attorney, Adam Pearce, would enter the campaign for the third district congressional seat. Last night at a VFW fund-raiser, Pearce made it official." The camera cut away from the announcer to a scene at a long banquet table. In the center Adam stood in front of a microphone speaking earnestly.

"I want to represent you and the people of Maryland in congress."

At his words the audience burst into approving shouts and applause. As he listened to the enthusiastic response, Adam smiled into the camera, the image of a confident man facing what had to be a brilliant future.

Once again, Mama and Teresa looked anxiously at Francy. She was staring at the TV set and thinking that now it really was over. It was as if Adam had crossed to the other side of a chasm that could do nothing but grow wider and deeper.

# CHAPTER FIFTEEN

IT WAS WINTER, but the little storefront tucked into a hilly side street in Ellicott City hummed like a hive in springtime. People came and went carrying posters, buttons and stacks of campaign literature. The cars parked in front all bore patriotically striped bumper stickers that read, Pearce for Congress! Pearce is the Man! and Make Your Vote Count—Pearce!

"There he is!" Barbara Kains called out as Adam appeared in the doorway. "Our leader!"

As the others in the little room cheered, Adam smiled sheepishly. After he'd announced his candidacy he'd been amazed by all the people who'd rallied around to work for his campaign. Who would have guessed that he had so many friends and supporters? Even J.D. Pike had offered his services.

"I think every unmarried secretary in this building is wearing a Pearce for Congress button and spending her weekends distributing your campaign literature door to door," Clarke teased. "Doesn't it boost your ego to know that they all hero-worship you?"

"Maybe they're helping out because they think I'm the best candidate," Adam argued.

"Maybe," Clarke had shot back. "But I'll bet it has more to do with the way you comb your golden locks."

Now as Adam faced the cluster of beaming volunteers who'd all but taken over his life during the past few months, his smile was apologetic. "Sorry I'm late, ladies. And gentlemen," he added as he caught sight of J.D. coming out of a back room loaded down with a box of freshly printed posters. "I got held up at the office."

Barbara came forward in her brisk way. "Well, now that you're here, Adam, I want to go over this list of speaking engagements with you. Requests have been coming in all afternoon."

For the next hour Adam worked with his staff, confirming dates, calling to thank contributors and going over the seemingly endless lists of things that needed to be done. Barbara, with her well-organized efficiency, was a godsend, he thought. It had surprised him when she'd called to ask if she could help out with the campaign. Considering the awkwardness between them over Francy, he'd even been reluctant to accept her services. But in the end it had seemed ridiculous to turn down a capable worker and offend an old friend further just because they were no longer intimate. So he'd welcomed Barbara. Now he wondered how he would have ever managed without her.

"Thanks," he told her with a grateful smile as he handed back a list of potential contributors. "I think you missed your calling. You should be running a multinational oil company. Only yesterday Ben Catlett was telling me how impressed he is with the way you keep things operating so smoothly."

Barbara flushed with pleasure. "I've been enjoying myself, I really have." She cocked her head. "I'm not sure the same could be said for you, though."

"What?"

"You look pale and tired, Adam. What's wrong? Aren't you getting enough sleep?"

He hadn't slept well for months. "Gearing up for a long, tough campaign doesn't leave much time for sleep," he said.

"And I bet you're not eating right, either. In fact, I know you aren't—snatching meals here and there. I've watched you when you speak at these banquets. You hardly touch your food."

"I'm too busy trying to remember my opening joke. And it's hard to look a drumstick in the face these days," he agreed.

Barbara looked thoughtful. "Have you eaten dinner yet?"

"No, I thought I'd grab something on the way home."

"I have a better idea." She checked the thin gold watch on her wrist. "It's past quitting time. Why don't you come home with me and let me cook you a decent meal? As a matter of fact, I happen to have a nice thick steak in the freezer. Just the thing for a man who's been overdosed on fried chicken." She smiled at him.

As he looked down at her, Adam was tempted. Standing there in a full-skirted rust jersey dress that accented her fair coloring and underlined her femininity, Barbara was an appealing sight. He'd always liked her and enjoyed her company. Lately he'd been so lonely and depressed. Yet he hesitated.

"Come on," she said. "Just a meal between old friends. I won't try and seduce you or anything." She laughed self-consciously. "I only want to feed your face."

Adam grinned. "How can I turn down an invitation like that? Okay, I'll be there."

An hour and a half later, he parked his car in an underground lot and rode the elevator up to Barbara's condominium. As he watched the lighted numbers over the tiny cubicle's closed doors change, he reflected that last spring when he'd taken this trip he'd been thinking of asking Barbara to marry him. Then he'd walked into her living room and seen Francy and everything had changed. Now that pivotal afternoon felt like a lifetime ago.

Adam's sense of déjà vu sharpened when Barbara let him into her apartment. She'd changed out of her rust-colored dress and into a green silk outfit. He didn't normally pay that much attention to women's clothes, but he had the feeling she was wearing something similar to what she'd had on the fateful last time he'd visited her place.

"The steaks are thawing in the kitchen," she told him. "How about we have a nice relaxing drink before I put them on the grill?"

"Sounds good." He loosened his tie. "It's been a long day."

"I know it has," she said as she led him into the living room. "Really, Adam, I'm concerned about you. You're running yourself ragged."

Barbara gestured at the couch and then went to the bar. But instead of sitting down, Adam stood surveying the beautifully appointed room with its cool, elegant color scheme.

"It looks nice," he said. Crossing over, he laid a hand on one of the club chairs by the window.

Barbara glanced up from the cocktail pitcher. "Yes, I don't believe those slipcovers were on when you were here last."

"No."

"Francy made them, you know."

"Yes, I know."

"She did a beautiful job, don't you think?"

"Yes, beautiful." He stared down at the chair, his hand lightly stroking the smooth fabric.

"Adam," Barbara said, "Patricia told me that it's been months since you and Francy saw each other."

"Did she?" He put his hand in his trousers pocket and looked up. "Did she also tell you that it was Francy's idea to call it quits, not mine?"

"When she talked to me, your mother seemed confused about your relationship with Francy. All she really understands is that you've been very unhappy lately, and that you seem to be angry with her. She's worried about you."

Adam sighed. "Yes, well, I suppose I haven't exactly been the dutiful son of late. Maybe it's not my mother's fault, but I can't help thinking that if she'd made things a little easier for Francy we'd still be together. But she never approved of her. You're the kind of girl she wanted me to marry."

"Yes, well, there was a time when I had similar ideas," Barbara said softly.

Adam was instantly contrite. "God, I'm sorry." He passed a hand over his eyes. "That was a stupid, insensitive thing for me to say."

Barbara came out from behind the bar bearing two martinis on a silver tray. "I forgive you." She smiled gently. "In fact, I forgave you a long time ago. If you hadn't dumped me, I wouldn't have met Justin."

"Barbara, I didn't dump you. It was just—"

"I know, I know. You took one look at Francy and fell like the proverbial ton of bricks. I think I knew that from the first, really. All I had to do was look at the two of you together." She sat down gracefully and took a sip of her cocktail.

After a moment, Adam joined her on the couch and picked up his own drink. "Are you and Justin getting serious?"

"Yes," Barbara answered simply. "He's out of town on a buying trip. That's why I could invite you."

Uncomfortably, Adam swirled his martini. "If my being here is any kind of a problem—"

"Oh, don't be silly! Of course it isn't. I only meant that if Justin weren't out of town I'd be cooking dinner for him. But I'm glad to have this opportunity to clear the air between us, Adam. I think it's time, don't you?"

"Yes."

"You know," Barbara continued, "Justin's background is almost as different from mine as yours is from Francy's. Your mother thinks that's a handicap, but I believe she's wrong. The trouble with us was that we were too much alike. Isn't that right, Adam?"

"I don't know," he answered honestly. "All I know is that when I saw Francy, I realized that she was the one for me." He sighed. "Unfortunately, she shares my mother's point of view about backgrounds. She thinks we're too different to make it work. At least, that's what she said when she sent me packing."

"If she really loves you, she'll change her mind," Barbara said gently.

"That's what I tried to tell myself," Adam answered. "But it's been so long. I'm beginning to think that she never really cared, not the way I did about her."

Barbara tried to reassure him, but as he listened to his own words, Adam realized how true they were. From the first Francy had received his advances coolly, he acknowledged. Oh, yes, there had been times when he'd thought that she must love him, times when she'd lain in his arms returning his ardent kisses with a fervor that had convinced him she cared. She'd even told him she loved him. But he must have been mistaken. Otherwise, would she have cut him adrift this way?

Later while Barbara cooked their food, she and Adam continued their conversation in the kitchen. With her customary unruffled efficiency, she produced a delicious dinner of steak, tossed salad, asparagus and crisp French bread. They ate it on the smartly set table in the dining room, talking of many things—Barbara's work at the art gallery, local news, Adam's campaign and the people working for it.

"You know," Barbara said as they enjoyed their after-dinner coffees, "a while back Clarke mentioned that you were being harassed by some sort of weirdo. That isn't still going on, is it?"

"No," Adam replied. "It's been months since he's made trouble for me, so that's all over."

"Well, I certainly hope so." She shivered. "Just the thought of something like that gives me the creeps."

"Me, too," Adam told her with a smile. He could laugh it off now, but it had been damn disturbing while it was going on, he thought. For a while there he'd felt like a tethered goat being stalked by some unknown creature of the night.

When dinner was finally over, Adam folded his napkin and cleared his throat. "That was delicious. I really enjoyed it. But maybe I'd better get going."

"You wouldn't like to stay for a brandy?"

He gazed across the table, thinking what a restful person Barbara was to be with. No hassles, no problems, everything smooth as the cool green silk she had on. But she wasn't the one he wanted, and she never would be. "No," he said. "I'm tired. Think I'll go home and get some shut-eye."

"Maybe that's a good idea," she told him gently. "You do look tired, Adam."

They parted with a handshake and a friendly peck on the cheek. Adam rode down alone in the elevator. A deep depression settled around him, and when the elevator opened on the underground parking garage, he stepped out into the chilly night air slowly. Instead of going directly to the spot where he'd left his car, he stood for a moment in the dimly lit concrete cavern. It felt as lifeless as the moon, he thought, and perfectly suited his bleak mood.

He started to turn, but at that moment a sharp report shattered the eerie stillness. Adam clutched at his head and then slipped unconscious to the floor. A trickle of blood stained his temple.


"AREN'T YOU GOING TO DANCE anymore, Aunt Francy?"

Breathlessly Francy sat down next to Jerry. The youngster's dark curls were slicked back, and he was dressed in a new pale-blue suit. Next to him his sister Rosy, resplendent in a pink organdy confection sprinkled with silk rosebuds, was a vision of dark beauty. Spoiling the effect somewhat was the wedding cake and ice cream that now smeared both children's faces.

"Jerry, you look like a little prince who's fallen into an ice-cream machine. How many pieces of that cake have you two had?" Francy demanded.

Jerry looked guilty while Rosy merely beamed, showing the gaps where she was beginning to lose her baby teeth. "This many," she said, holding up all the fingers of one hand.

"Five? Oh, Rosy, you'll be sick."

"They were just little pieces," Jerry argued, "and besides, it's a special occasion when your mom gets married."

"That's true," Francy admitted. She looked out at the area that had been cleared to make a dance floor in the center of the church basement. Teresa, in her ice-blue dress, and Gus, looking like a stranger in a new pearl-gray suit, were doing a slow waltz, all the while gazing lovingly into each other's faces. Several other couples were dancing around them. But Gus and Teresa only had eyes for each other.

As she watched them, Francy felt a pain tighten around her heart. She was happy for her sister, but at the same time she felt like a kid who'd been locked outside in the cold away from the Christmas tree. That was a feeling she'd had for much of her life, she reflected. But now that she'd lost Adam, the sense of being always on the outside of things was much worse.

"Maybe you haven't lost him," Teresa had argued only the day before. "I'm sick of watching you pine for that guy. Now that you're doing so well with your reading, you needn't let that stand between the two of you. Why don't you call him?"

"I've been thinking about that for weeks," Francy had admitted.

"For heaven's sake, then why not let him know how you feel?"

"Because I'm afraid. It's been so long. He's bound to have found someone new."

Now, as Francy looked across the room, she remembered how Teresa had thrown up her hands in exasperation. Maybe her older sister was right, she thought. Maybe it was time to find the courage to call Adam.

"Mom looks pretty," Rosy said to Jerry.

"Yeah, but..."

"But what?"

"But I don't see why they can't take us to Florida with them."

"Want to see Disney World," Rosy piped up.

Chuckling, Francy reached over and wiped a crumb off the little girl's dimpled chin. "They'll take you to see Disney World another time. Right now your mom and your new dad need some time alone together."

"Maybe," Jerry grumbled.

"No maybes about it," Francy retorted. She ruffled the little boy's hair and then returned her attention to the dance floor. Jimmy Alonzo and his pretty date, Linda, were also up dancing. Since Christmas Francy had been seeing a lot less of her old friend. Now he could only find time to come over and coach her every other week. But Francy didn't mind. It was the concentrated help with phonics that he'd given her through the fall that had really made all the difference.

A few minutes later the music stopped and Teresa announced that she was going to throw her bouquet. Francy tried to hang back, but her older sister would have none of it. "You stand right there," she said firmly and then got up in a chair and dumped the sweet-smelling arrangement of roses and baby's breath right on top of Francy. There was no way she could avoid catching it without looking like a spoilsport. Teresa kissed her on the cheek and whispered, "You next, kiddo. I just know it."

Not long after that, Gus and Teresa, ducking under a shower of rice and confetti, ran to Gus's new Chevy and disappeared down the street headed for the airport.

"Well, that was the best wedding I've been to," Jimmy said, putting an arm around Linda's waist.

"It was fun," the smiling math teacher with the wavy brown hair agreed.

Over the top of Linda's head, Jimmy looked at Francy. "Any time you want to get back home, you and the kids have a ride with us."

"Thanks. I appreciate that. The older ones are going to stay and help clean up. But I think Jerry and Rosy are about ready to call it a day. So whenever it's convenient..."

Obligingly Jimmy brought his old rattletrap of a station wagon around and Francy and the kids piled into the back while Linda slid in beside him in the front. It was only a short drive from the church to the Raseras' row house, but the streets were congested with slow-moving traffic despite the late hour.

"If you don't mind, I'll switch on the news," Jimmy said, reaching out to depress the knob on his radio.

Francy didn't mind at all. A fog seemed to have crept into her head, and she was suddenly feeling too tired to join in the conversation flowing so brightly between Jimmy and Linda.

What was it about people who were falling in love that made them witty raconteurs, she wondered. But she remembered only too well. When you were with that other special person it was as if you were charged with energy. The whole world became a brighter, sharper, more colorful place. You wanted to know everything about them and share all the best things about yourself. It was only when you were alone and likely to stay that way forever that you felt as she did now—empty, drained. What if she did call Adam? Even if he turned her away, as he had every reason to do after the way she'd behaved, at least she would have heard his voice one more time. Francy laced her fingers together tightly. *I'll do it,* she thought. *Tomorrow I'll stop putting it off because I'm afraid and do it.*

The children, exhausted from the merrymaking and filled to the teeth with cake and ice cream, had already dozed off. Wearily Francy leaned her head against the station wagon's cracked vinyl headrest, closed her eyes and let the radio announcer's static-punctuated voice roll over her.

There was a weather and traffic update and news about a robbery on North Avenue. Then his tone sharpened. "This report just in. State's Attorney for Howard County, Adam Pearce, was found shot."

Francy's eyes flew open.

"Pearce, who announced his bid for Congress late last year, was found in the parking garage of Heritage House where he'd been having dinner with one of his campaign workers. He was taken to Johns Hopkins hospital where his condition has not been listed yet."

Francy jerked forward, clutching the back of Jimmy's seat with frantic fingers. "Did you hear that?"

"Yes," he said over his shoulder. "That's the guy you were—"

"Yes." Francy cut him off. "Oh, Jimmy, can you take me to the hospital?"

"Of course," he told her as he put on the turn signal. "Just give us the key to your place. Linda and I will stay with the kids until your mother gets back. Don't worry about a thing."

"ARE YOU A RELATIVE?" The woman at the reception desk looked at Francy coolly.

"No, I'm a friend. I just want to know how Adam, how Mr. Pearce is."

"You and half of the rest of the world. Since he came in an hour ago we've been inundated with calls. But I'm afraid there's no news on his condition yet. He's still in surgery." Another phone rang and she turned away to pick it up.

Trying not to choke on the sharp lump that clogged her throat, Francy waited for the receptionist to finish the call. When she finally hung up, Francy pressed her palms together. "Oh, please, when do you think they'll know something?"

The woman glanced up from the notepad where she'd been scribbling a message. Light glinted off her wire-frame glasses. "I have no idea, miss, but if you'd care to wait." She gestured out at the cavernous lobby. It was a quarter filled with people whose faces had been turned greenish by the fluorescent lighting. They milled aimlessly or sat staring vacantly into space.

Shoulders drooping, Francy nodded and turned away. This was a nightmare! Was it only an hour ago that she'd been catching the bouquet at Teresa's wedding?

She found a chair by a pillar and huddled there for several minutes, shivering. It wasn't so much the temperature as the atmosphere of the hospital at this late hour. Somewhere in the depths of its antiseptic bowels Adam was lying injured, perhaps fighting for his life. *Oh, God, don't let him die!* Francy wailed inwardly. It was horrible now to think of all the weeks and months that she'd missed being with him—and all because of her stupid pride.

The minutes lengthened. Several times she went back to the reception desk. But the woman only shook her head. "No word yet."

As Francy walked back to her chair, a man hurrying toward the door stared at her hard. Suddenly she realized what an incongruous picture she must make dressed in her wedding finery, a spray of baby pink roses pinned to her white coat. *Like a bride at a funeral,* she thought, and then almost stumbled and fell as the implications of that idea tore at her vitals.

Desperate for some distraction, she glanced around. A little way down the corridor she could see the entrance to a cafeteria. Maybe if she got herself a cup of coffee it would help.

The cafeteria was a huge place filled with Formica tables, its walls lined with machines, which at this time of night were the only things operating. Francy went to one labeled Beverages and fumbled in her purse for the right change. On any other occasion she would have congratulated herself on not having to search for a picture to know that this was the machine she wanted. Now the thought never even crossed her mind.

After she'd pressed the right button and watched an orange and yellow paper cup fill with hot liquid, she gingerly plucked it out of its window and headed toward an empty table. She had plenty to choose from as the place was almost deserted. The table she was passing was occupied by another lone woman. She, too, was huddled over a cup of coffee, her blond head lowered as if a weight were pressing down on the weak stalk of her neck.

Suddenly Francy stopped short. The woman was Patricia Pearce.

"Mrs. Pearce," she said uncertainly.

Patricia looked up, blinking at her from reddened eyes. "Francy?"

"Yes, I—I heard the news on the radio. How's Adam?"

"I don't know. They won't tell me anything. All I know is that he lost a lot of blood before they found him." She clutched at a napkin. "To think of him lying all alone in that parking garage, bleeding and with no one to help him!" Her face crumpled and she turned away and covered her eyes.

Stricken, Francy stood gazing down at her. "Do you mind if I sit here, or would you rather be alone? I can understand if you don't want to talk to anyone." She felt pretty unsociable herself, but it didn't seem right to just walk off and leave Patricia alone at this table crying.

"No, no, please sit down." Patricia took her hand away from her face, and began to dab at her eyes. "Barbara is upstairs waiting for news. She said she'd come down if anything happened."

"Oh." Francy ran a finger along the edge of her cup. "It was Miss Kains's building where Adam was shot?"

"Yes, they'd been having dinner."

So Adam had gone back to seeing Barbara. Though Francy wasn't surprised, her misery thickened around her. It was what she'd expected, after all. They'd always seemed so right together. "Why would anyone shoot Adam?" she muttered aloud. "I don't understand."

"I don't either. According to Barbara some crazy man has been harassing him for months. And he never told me." Once again Patricia dabbed at her eyes. "I'm his mother, and he never tells me anything. I feel so shut out! He's my only child. He's more important to me than anything in this world. And now I might lose him!''

Francy gazed at the older woman in consternation. At this moment she bore little resemblance to the immaculately groomed matriarch who had been so intimidating in Bermuda and then at Spruce Valley. Now, with her hair in disarray, her eyes red from weeping and lines of stress bisecting her face, she looked old and frightened. *Under the skin we're not so different,* Francy thought. *We both love Adam and we're terrified of losing him.*

"I'm glad you're here, Francy," Patricia said. "Please sit down."

"You are?" Hesitantly Francy pulled out a chair and perched on the edge of it.

"I've been thinking we should have a talk."

"Oh?" Francy took a sip of her coffee. It was still scalding hot and burned her tongue.

"I know that you and Adam have stopped seeing each other."

"Yes, long ago."

"Adam hasn't been himself lately. He's been upset. And he's been very cold to me."

"Well, running a campaign and all—"

Patricia shook her head. "That's not it. I still don't understand what happened the night you ran out into the rain from our place, but he seems to blame me for it in some way. It wasn't my fault, was it? I didn't do anything to upset you, did I?"

So Adam never told his mother about the reading. Why not, Francy wondered as she gazed at the older woman. Patricia certainly hadn't tried very hard to make her feel comfortable. But the dictionary game hadn't been her fault, either. And Francy knew that without the diabolical game, she would have made it through that evening all right.

"No, it's not your fault. It was all my fault. You see, the reason I ran away was because I hadn't been honest with Adam, and I felt humiliated by that game we were playing." Clutching her paper cup as if it were a support, Francy explained about the reading and her dyslexia.

"You mean you actually couldn't read?" Patricia's blue eyes stretched wide in amazement.

"No, I couldn't. Though I was taking an adult class at the time, trying to overcome my disability."

"Are you still trying?"

"Yes," Francy replied. "In fact, I've even made some progress."

Patricia didn't respond. She was staring past Francy's shoulder, her face paper white. Turning, Francy saw Barbara hurrying toward them. She must have word about Adam, Francy thought as she leaped to her feet. A second later Patricia did the same and scrambled around the table, knocking over a chair in her haste.

"The news is good," Barbara said as soon as she was within earshot. "The doctor says it was close, but he'll be okay."

"Oh, thank God!" Patricia flew into Barbara's arms, and the two women hugged.

As she hung back, tears of relief stung Francy's eyes. "Thank God," she muttered, repeating Patricia's words.

"Do you want to go upstairs and talk to Dr. Eberhard?" Barbara was saying.

"Oh, yes," Patricia cried, an eager note in her voice. "Oh, let's go now! I want to hear what he has to say."

With their arms around each other's shoulders, the two women hurried off.

Through reddened eyes, Francy watched them go. She knew they weren't being deliberately impolite. Barbara had been so eager to tell Patricia her news that she probably hadn't even noticed Francy standing there. And Adam's mother was too overwrought to think about anything but her son at this moment. Still, as the two women disappeared around the corner, Francy felt more than ever like an outsider. Should she follow them, she wondered, so she might hear what the doctor had to say? But now that she and Adam weren't together anymore and he'd gone back to Barbara, what right did she have to intrude? For now, it was enough merely to know that he was going to be okay. "Thank God," she repeated again as she turned away.

## CHAPTER SIXTEEN

THE PICTURE ON THE FRONT of the postcard showed a couple clad in bathing suits strolling hand in hand on a deserted sandy beach. Francy turned the card over and read printed in large block letters, "Gus and I are having a wonderful time. Must admit I don't wish you were here. Kiss the kids for me. Love, Teresa."

Smiling wryly, Francy put the postcard down and glanced at the scene outside her shop window. Leaden clouds scurried across the sky and a frigid wind knifed down the street making stoplights sway and street signs clatter. Only a few people were out braving it. In the distance a slender woman clutched the collar of a fashionably cut coat, her blond head lowered against the wind as if she were trying to push a boulder uphill.

Francy's dark eyes narrowed. There was something familiar about that woman. A moment later the blonde crossed the street and headed toward New Beginnings. It was Barbara Kains.

The bell above the door jangled and Barbara blew in along with an icy blast of wind.

"Whew, what a day!" she exclaimed as she smoothed back her tousled hair. "Hello there, Francy."

"Hello, Barbara. How are you?"

"Fine." Loosening her scarf, she glanced around, taking in the warm country decor. "This is the first time I've been to your shop. I love the way you've decorated it. That little print wallpaper is so attractive. From the looks of things, you must be doing well."

Warily Francy nodded. "So far my sister and I have managed to make a go of things. It's not easy getting a new business off the ground."

"Oh, I can imagine."

Francy stood staring at Barbara. What was she doing here? Did it have anything to do with Adam? More than anything Francy wanted to ask about him. Yet she hesitated, uncertain whether she had the right. Every day she'd called the hospital to inquire about his condition, so she knew that he was doing well. But there were so many other things she wanted to know, things that Barbara might rightfully resent being asked to tell.

A fleeting expression of uncertainty crossed Barbara's face, and she fidgeted with the ends of her silk scarf. "I suppose you're wondering why I'm here."

"It's a pretty cold day to be out looking at curtains."

"I'm not here because I need curtains. I want to apologize for not saying hello at the hospital. Frankly I was so upset that I didn't even register your presence until Patricia mentioned it later."

"Oh, I understand. Please don't bother about it."

Barbara hesitated. "Francy, Patricia asked me to come and talk to you."

Francy took an anxious step forward. "Is it Adam? Is there something wrong? I thought that he was doing okay."

"He is. In fact, he's going to be released from the hospital tomorrow."

"Released? But it's so soon—only a week." Francy's brow furrowed. "And that madman is still on the loose."

"No, they've caught the man who shot Adam. I heard it on the radio before I left this morning."

"They have?" Francy's voice was filled with relief. "Who is he?"

"I don't know, but they're certain they've got the right man, thank God. And it's really best for Adam to leave the hospital. He hates it there. It will be much more pleasant for him to recuperate at Spruce Valley. Of course he'll have a private nurse."

"Oh, that's good." Francy twisted her hands. "How is he?"

"That's what his mother wanted me to talk to you about," Barbara said. "Adam is young and strong and physically he's doing very well. But he's depressed." She pulled off her kidskin gloves and stuck her hands in her pockets. "Francy, while he was unconscious he was asking for you, calling your name."

"He was?" Her jaw dropped, and a little thrill of gratification shot down her spine.

"Yes, he was. When Patricia told him that you were there at the hospital the night he was injured, his eyes lit up. He hasn't said much about it, but she knows he's disappointed because you haven't visited him. I told her you must care a little, or you wouldn't have gone to Johns Hopkins that night. I don't know why you've stayed away, but won't you go see him now?"

"Care a little?" Francy repeated in amazement. "Of course I care about Adam. But I thought that you and he—"

"What?" Barbara lifted her brows.

"They said that he was having dinner at your place the night he was shot. I thought that you and he were back together, and I didn't want to interfere."

"Interfere?" Emphatically Barbara shook her head. "Adam Pearce isn't in love with me, Francy, and he never was. He's in love with you. You're the one he wants. You're the one who's broken his heart."

"YOUR MOTHER SAYS we can't stay for more than ten minutes, but I knew this was a story you'd want to hear," Clarke Burdette said.

The round-faced lawyer perched on one side of the hospital bed that had been set up in Adam's boyhood room, while Ben Catlett stood on the other. Between the two, Adam, pale and still swathed in bandages, lay propped against the pillows. "Okay, I'm listening."

"We've caught your assailant. Remember the Gary Johnston case?"

"Of course, but Johnston is behind bars for the murder of Thelma Murdock."

"Yes, but his brother isn't. Or rather, wasn't."

Adam blinked. "You mean Gary Johnston's brother shot me?"

"And made your life miserable for several months before he finally got around to aiming his gun." Clarke rubbed his hands together in satisfaction. "We've charged the guy with attempted murder—we've got the weapon and everything. We've even got a witness willing to testify that Al Johnston bragged about harassing you."

"What kind of witness?"

"His cell mate."

Adam pushed himself up on his elbows. "His cell mate!"

"This is beautiful. The reason you hadn't heard from Johnston for several months before he got you in that parking garage was because he'd been locked up on a burglary charge. As soon as he was released he bought himself a gun and went after you.''

Adam fell back against the pillows. "My God!" He passed a hand over his bandaged brow. "There really was someone out there all that time planning to kill me. What a feeling!"

"It's a feeling politicians have to learn to live with," Ben Catlett interjected. "Tell me the truth, Adam, after all this are you still interested in running for that seat in the House?"

Adam turned his head away from Clarke and gazed thoughtfully at the older man. "More than ever. But I'm going to lose some time. It'll be at least another month before I'm on my feet and ready to tackle the fried-chicken circuit again."

"Take all the time you need. We've got an early start and you've built yourself a strong and loyal organization. And to tell you the truth—" Catlett grinned "—I don't think this little incident will hurt your chances. If you weren't already a hero in the eyes of a lot of voters, you are now."

Clarke chuckled. "Just can't seem to get away from the hero image, can you, pal? Here and at the office the phones have been ringing off the hook. I think every woman in Howard County has called to ask how you are. When you're on your feet again, they'll be all over you."

Instead of looking amused, Adam gazed at his friend soberly, the shadow of pain lingering around his eyes. "Did Francy call?"

"No, sorry." Clarke shook his head.

Adam's nurse, Mrs. Camp, popped her frizzy head around the door. "I'm afraid I'm going to have to ask you gentlemen to leave. Mr. Pearce needs to get some rest.''

"I feel perfectly fine," Adam protested.

But Clarke had already gotten to his feet and walked around to where Ben Catlett stood.

"I'll be back next week when you're a little stronger," Catlett said. "We can talk strategy then."

"And I'll keep you posted about Johnston," Clarke added. "But I don't think you have anything more to worry about where that bozo's concerned."

A few minutes later both men departed, and after Nurse Camp fluffed up Adam's pillow and straightened his sheets, she left him alone.

He supposed he should follow her advice and take a nap. But he didn't really feel like it. Instead, he lay idly glancing around the room where he'd grown up. Many years had gone by since he'd last spent any time in it, and it had been repainted and redecorated. Yet it was still much the same. The network of oak branches outside the window hadn't changed much. He remembered the time he'd used them for an escape route and almost broken his neck. His gaze shifted to the bureau where a high-school picture of him preparing to hit the water during a swimming meet still sat. The miniature birchbark canoe that had been a souvenir from a Canadian camping trip with his scout troop decorated the top of the bookcase, and his leather baseball mitt hung from the doorknob on the closet.

His gaze lingered. It was a good mitt. His father had given it to him for Christmas when he was ten, and he'd always thought he'd like to pass it on to a son of his own some day. Would he ever marry and have children, he asked himself. Right now the prospect seemed remote.

The thought brought Francy to his mind. It had been so long since he'd seen her, yet her image was as clear and fresh as if she stood before him. He'd been so elated when he'd heard that she'd come to the hospital that night. And he'd been convinced that she'd come back and they would be reconciled. All during visiting hours he'd waited tensely, listening for her footsteps in the corridor outside his door. But though he'd had many visitors, none of them had been Francy. She hadn't come. She hadn't even called.

Adam turned his face away and closed his eyes. Well, it wasn't going to go on this way, he told himself. As soon as he was well enough to get out of bed, he'd go see her. And he'd make her see him.

"THAT'S A LONG TRIP, LADY. I can't do it for less than thirty."

Any other time Francy would have been inclined to haggle. Now she merely gave the taxi driver a meek nod and climbed in. "Thirty dollars is okay."

"Must be pretty anxious to get out to this farm in Howard County," the driver muttered as he pulled away from the curb.

"Yes, yes I am."

Actually she was terrified about what would happen when she reached Spruce Valley. What if Adam didn't want to see her? What if he didn't want to hear her apologies or her declarations? Nervously she crossed her legs and smoothed her navy-blue wool coat over them. Well, there was no turning back now, she told herself. She was going to tell him that without him her life was empty. No matter how deeply she buried herself in her work, no matter how successful her shop might be, no matter how many books she read, she couldn't get past that fact. Without Adam, none of it seemed to matter. She had been wrong to push him away. That move had been dictated by her pride, not her heart. Now, whether or not she could fit easily into his world seemed unimportant. The only important thing was how much she loved and needed him.

They rode in silence through the city and suburbs. "You make a right here," Francy told the driver as they approached the turnoff on Route 29.

"Yeah, I know. Howard County sure has changed. Used to be farmland. Now it's all fancy developments." The cabby, suddenly more talkative, glanced out the side window and shook his head.

"The area we're going to is still rural."

"Oh, yeah? Hey, this is where that guy Pearce comes from, you know, the one who was shot last week. They had it on all the news stations."

"Yes, I remember."

"They caught the jerk who tried to knock him over. I heard it was the brother of a murderer Pearce put behind bars a while back. Something, huh?"

"Yes." Francy shivered.

"Got to hand it to Pearce. If he still has the guts to run for Congress, he's got my vote."

"Mine, too," Francy agreed.

Following her directions, the driver turned down another road. There were no suburban developments. Gradually the route began to wind through fields alternating with stands of tall trees. As the miles passed the butterflies fluttering inside Francy's stomach beat their wings more frantically. To calm herself, she took a deep breath and then looked around her carefully. When Adam had driven her out here it had been deep summer. The trees had been in full leaf and the fields lush with corn and hay. Now the ground was frozen and the trees etched the pale blue sky with bare branches. But Francy had an excellent visual memory.

"I think the driveway's coming up here pretty soon," she warned the cab driver. They swung around a curve and she pointed. "Yes, yes, turn right into there."

"Not much of an entrance," he grumbled. Nevertheless he did as he was told and a moment later they were rumbling up the long driveway that led to Spruce Valley.

"Hey, this place is something else," the man exclaimed as the house loomed into view.

"Yes, it is, isn't it." Francy's voice was small. Against the winter sky the house looked less startling than it had the first time she'd seen it outlined by a purple and red sunset. But with its turrets and gingerbread, it was still impressive. As she gazed up at it, a wave of emotions swept over her and her throat closed. When she'd fled this place last summer, she'd never wanted to see it again. *But here I am,* she thought. *And I'm not going to leave until I've got what I came for.* Francy opened her purse and took out the thirty dollars she'd promised the cab driver.

"How are you going to get back?" he queried when she handed him the money. "Want me to wait?"

She hesitated, tempted to say yes. What if Adam refused to see her, or for some reason he wasn't there? But she shook her head. There was no turning back now. "No, thanks. I'll manage."

Outside the overheated cab, the frigid air bit into her hands and she stuck them deep into her pockets. Listening to the click of her heels against the icy flagstones, she walked up the path that led to the porch.

At the carved oak door with its sidelights, stained glass fanlight and ornate brass knocker, she looked around for a buzzer. There didn't appear to be one so she picked up the handle on the knocker and let it drop against its metal plate. It sent out an echoing thud. But the sound seemed no louder than the deafening pound of her heart.

The door swung open, and a woman in a nurse's uniform looked out, an expression of polite inquiry on her freckled face.

"Hello. I'm Francy Rasera. I've come to visit Mr. Pearce."

"Oh, I'm afraid he's sleeping right now and can't be disturbed."

"I've come a long way, and it's very important that I speak to him. Can I come inside?"

"Oh, yes, of course." Looking none too welcoming, the nurse stepped back reluctantly.

When Francy was in the foyer and the door shut behind her, she glanced up the staircase with its curving dark wood banister. Adam was up there some place. She *had* to see him.

"Perhaps it would be better if you came back later," the nurse was saying. She consulted her watch. "He should be awake by five."

That was three hours from now. Francy's heart sank. She knew she should have called first, but she hadn't had the courage. "Could I wait?" she asked. "I took a taxi out from Baltimore, so you see—"

"Who's at the door?" a voice called out from the room across the hall.

Francy turned just as Patricia Pearce emerged from the arched entry that led into the front parlor. She was wearing beige slacks and a matching cashmere sweater.

Gold-rimmed glasses perched atop her nose and her hair was once again immaculate.

At the sight of Francy, her face lit up. "Francy," she cried, coming toward the younger woman with a welcoming smile and hands outstretched. "Oh, I'm so glad to see you! Adam is going to be thrilled!"

ADAM WAS DREAMING, and the dream was beautiful. In it a beloved face came toward him. Velvety brown eyes smiled lovingly into his, and hair like black silk caressed his cheek. As he gazed up into that delicious face, a sigh of pleasure escaped him. He loved every feature on it, the beautiful eyes fringed by sooty lashes, the neat, slightly upturned little nose, the smooth, creamy cheeks, and then there was that full mouth—so soft, so enticing.

*Kiss me, Francy,* he wanted to say. But the words were frozen in his chest. Yet she seemed to understand. With a quickening of her breath, she lowered her mouth to his. And at the touch of her lips, all the sweetness in the world seemed to enfold him, soothing away the pain like a healing balm.

"Francy," he murmured.

"I'm here, Adam."

How he wished it were true. But though he was still half asleep, he knew he'd only been dreaming. The voice was fantasy. The soft hand he felt curling around his was surely only wish fulfillment, and when he opened his eyes he would be alone. With a faint groan, Adam reluctantly lifted his lids.

He blinked and stared. The vision in his dream was sitting on a straight chair next to his bed, one slim hand resting over his on the sheet.

"Francy?"

"Yes." She took her hand away and folded it in her lap. "How are you?"

"I'm..." He stopped, at a loss for words.

After a second or two of taut silence, Francy filled the gap. "The nurse didn't want me to wake you, but your mother said it would be all right for me to come up to your room. I hope you don't mind."

"No, I don't mind." His eyes wandered over her. She looked paler and thinner than he remembered. Against the dusky richness of her eyes and level brows her skin was the creamy color of antique satin. She wore her hair differently. It was drawn away from her face with silver combs and hung in a long swathe of midnight against her neck. He remembered what it had been like to lift that hair and kiss the soft hollow at the back of her neck. It had been like touching his lips to warm panne velvet. "Never cut your hair," he heard himself say.

"What?" For the first time Francy smiled. "From time to time I have to. Otherwise it would reach my knees."

"That would be all right with me. Then I could wrap myself in it." From his pillow he stared at her, making no attempt to hide what he was feeling. "Francy, thank God you're here. Why didn't you come sooner?"

*Why didn't I?* she asked herself. *Why was I so afraid?* A half an hour ago when she'd climbed the stairs and tiptoed into his room, her knees had been shaking and it had been an effort to breathe. But then she'd seen Adam lying there asleep, his head bandaged. The sight of him had hit her with the force of a rough blow. She'd never seen him like this before, hurt, looking so pale and alone. It made tears start from her eyes, it made her want to rush forward and cradle him in her arms.

Instead, she'd taken off her shoes and padded across the wide plank floor. As silently as possible, she'd drawn up a chair on the Oriental carpet and sat down close to his bed. While the silent minutes ticked past, she'd studied him, listening to his quiet breathing and watching the shadows beneath his gold-tipped lashes.

When she had first met Adam she had thought him almost too handsome, too perfect. Now, as he slept, she could see the strength in his face. There was an uncompromising sternness beneath the set of his features that his waking expression disguised. It was the face of a man who forced himself to live up to some very high standards, who did not give up easily, and who had known pain.

It was all too easy to read trouble in the lines around his mouth and eyes. Some of those lines were new, she was certain. "Oh, Adam," she breathed. She wanted to lean forward and kiss the pain away. Instead, she gently lay her hand over his.

It was then that he had awakened and looked at her with clear blue eyes that hid nothing and made her heart squeeze tight in her breast.

"I didn't come before because I couldn't," she finally said in answer to his question.

"Couldn't?"

"Oh, Adam, when I heard that you'd been shot, I rushed to the hospital, and I didn't leave until word came that you were all right."

"Yes, my mother told me that. It gave me such hope to hear that you still cared. But then I waited, waited for you to call or come see me. You never did."

"I phoned the hospital every day to get a report on your condition."

"The hospital? But why not me? Francy, are you involved with that guy I saw?"

"Jimmy? Oh, no! I was going to call you and tell you that I was sorry for the way I behaved and that I loved you and wanted you back. But then you were shot. I didn't come to see you in the hospital because I thought—" She twisted her hands together. "I heard you were having dinner with Barbara Kains before it happened, and I thought—"

"Oh, my God! You thought that the two of us were back together?" Emphatically he shook his head. "No, no, that will never happen. Since I met you there hasn't been anyone else for me."

"I know. Barbara told me. She came to the shop yesterday and talked about you."

Adam looked surprised and then wary. "Did she suggest that you come see me?"

"Yes."

He frowned and turned his face away. "Is that why you're finally here, out of pity? Because if that's it, it won't do. I want more from you, Francy."

She gazed at his averted profile and then glanced over her shoulder at the tall bookcase next to the window. "I love you, Adam. I didn't come out of pity, but partly to show you something." She pushed back her chair, got to her feet and crossed to the bookcase. After a moment's indecision, she lifted out a beautifully bound green and gold book. When she returned to her seat, she flipped it open.

Adam watched her curiously. "That's Henry Thoreau's *Walden*," he said. "My father gave it to me when I graduated from elementary school."

"It's beautiful. The pictures are lovely." Francy ran her finger over the smooth vellum page and studied the woodcut of a tree at the top. Then her eyes shifted down to the print. "'Let us spend one day as deliberately as Nature, and not be thrown off the track by every nutshell and mos...'" She paused, but then continued. "'Mosquito's wing that falls on the rails. Let us rise early and fast, or break fast gently and without pertur...'" Again she stumbled. "'Per-tur-ba-tion.'" She took a deep breath. "'Let company come and let company go, let the bells ring and the children cry,—determined to make a day of it. Why should we knock under and go with the stream?'" Francy stared down at the page a moment and then gently closed the book. "I would pick one with hard words in it," she said.

"You can read." His voice was warm.

"A little, yes." She looked up at him shyly, but with a conscious lift to her head. "I've been working very hard on it all these months."

"You must have been."

"That's one of the reasons why I couldn't come to you before, Adam. I couldn't come to you until I was a whole person, and then I was afraid it was too late."

"But you've always been a whole person, and the reading didn't matter to me, Francy!"

"Yes, it did." Firmly she shook her head. "It mattered to both of us, and I had to do something about it."

He eyed her. "Put the book down and come here, Francy."

A little uncertainly, she did as he bade. When she was perched on the edge of the bed at his side, he reached up and laid a finger on her cheek. "I was dreaming about you. I was dreaming that you were kissing me. Kiss me now, beautiful Francesca."

"Oh, Adam!" She lowered her head and brushed her lips against his.

Their mouths melded, and for long, sweet moments they savored the rich closeness. Francy's hands clasped the ridge of Adam's broad shoulder and then rested against his chest where she could feel the steady drum of his heart. Adam's fingers came up to stroke her cheek and then the long graceful line of her throat. When finally their lips parted, she felt him shudder with strong emotion.

"I love you, Francy," he whispered huskily. "I loved you the moment I saw you, and I adored you more with every day I got to know you. Nothing could change that. I don't care whether you can read or not. All I care about now is hearing you say that you love me, too, and that you won't leave me."

"I do love you," she whispered fervently. "I felt that way almost from the first, too. It was just that it seemed too good to be true, and I was a coward. I couldn't believe that it was real."

"Oh, it's real all right." Possessively Adam's hand stroked down the length of her arm. "I want you in bed with me. I want to make love to you right now."

"Adam!" Francy pulled back, her expression half-shocked, half-pleased. "Your mother's downstairs and you're sick. I don't want you to have a relapse."

He grinned wickedly. "I'm not going to have a relapse. Having you back in my arms is going to make me get well real fast." His expression grew serious and his eyes searched her face. "You are going to stay, aren't you? You won't walk out on me again? I'm not sure that I could take it if you did."

"I—I'm not sure what you mean," she said uncertainly.

"I'm saying that I love you, Francy. I want you with me for the rest of my life. I want to marry you. As soon as possible, I want you to be my wife."

There was a brief, stunned silence. All at once Francy's eyes were wet. "Oh, Adam, I love you so much. I want to be with you. But—"

"But what?"

"We still have a lot of problems."

"Such as?" His tone was gruff, almost belligerent.

"Children, for one thing. My dyslexia is inherited."

"And so is my left-handedness. If our children inherit either one, we'll just have to love them and do the best we can for them. That's all parents can ever do for their children."

"But what about your career in politics? You know that I'm not exactly the ideal political wife, Adam."

"You're the only one I want, and if my running for office is a problem for you, I'll back out of the campaign."

"You don't want to do that, do you?"

"No," he admitted.

"Then I don't want you to do it, either." She threw her arms around his neck. "Adam, I love you so much."

"Then make me whole again, Francy. Give me a present to cherish and a future to look forward to. Say you'll marry me."

"Yes," she whispered through lips that quivered with happiness. "Yes—I'll marry you."

# EPILOGUE

FRANCY STOOD BACK to admire her handiwork. The cut of the jacket pinned on to the tailor's dummy was unusual, she thought, and would make a very nice addition to the collection she was putting together for her fall catalog. "What do you think?" she asked Lou.

The plump seven-month-old was sitting in his high chair eating banana slices, most of which wound up on the floor. "Da da da da," he commented.

"Daddy isn't going to be home for at least another couple of hours. He has a senate committee meeting."

"Da da da da!" Lou repeated and cheerfully hurled a chunk of banana across the room.

The door banged and feet pounded down the hall. "Mom!" Seven-year-old Patsy skidded into the room with her usual verve. "Mom!"

"Yes, honey." Lovingly Francy smiled at her beautiful blue-eyed, black-haired daughter.

"Is Grandma here yet?"

"No, Grandmother Pearce isn't supposed to pick you up until six, remember?"

Patsy heaved a gusty sigh of relief. "I forgot when she was coming, and my stupid old piano lesson took so darn long."

"I hope you did okay at your stupid old piano lesson."

Patsy shrugged. "I guess. But I have to go pack now. I need all my riding clothes. I hope Rusty hasn't forgotten me."

"I'm sure Rusty hasn't forgotten you. After all, it's only been two weeks."

But Patsy was already running upstairs, her mind obviously on the weekend and on riding her fat chestnut pony stabled at Spruce Valley.

Francy shook her head. Who would have ever thought that a daughter of hers would be a budding equestrian? But then, who would have imagined that she would be a senator's wife and live in a beautiful house in Bethesda, or that she would own a flourishing dress-design business as well as a partnership in the drapery shop that Teresa now managed so successfully in Baltimore?

"And who would have guessed that I'd have such a gorgeous, intelligent son?" she playfully asked Lou.

"Da da da da!" he repeated emphatically and then popped the last slice of banana into his mouth.

Chuckling, Francy took a damp paper towel to his chubby face and hands and then lifted him out of his chair and gave him a big squeeze. "Time for your bottle, my man!"

When the phone rang ten minutes later, Francy was rocking Lou while he lay in the crook of her arm contentedly downing the last of his milk.

"Hello?"

"Sweetheart?"

Her face lit up. "Adam, are you out of that meeting already?"

"All done, and raring to celebrate. I think I'm going to get that bill through the barricades yet. Any chance you could round up a sitter for Lou? I'd love to take you dining and dancing someplace special, just the two of us."

"Sounds like it might be worth my while to give Jenny a call." Francy's oldest niece, now a student at Georgetown University, was usually willing to baby-sit if she didn't already have a date for the evening.

Francy was in luck and Jenny was free. "Sure, I'll take care of Lou," she told her aunt. "I have to study tonight, anyway, and since I'm going home tomorrow to see Jerry star in his high-school play, I'd better take advantage of your nice quiet house and hit the books."

"It won't be quiet until you put Lou to bed."

"Oh, I know, but he's such a sweetie, I don't mind."

"I wish I could see Jerry's performance, too, but I promised I'd be a hostess at the Senate Wives' Charity Tea."

"That's okay, you can go up to see him next week-end."

"I'll plan on it," Francy promised.

When Adam came home later that evening, he brought Jenny with him. "Have a great time, you two," she told her petite dark-haired aunt and tall, handsome uncle as they left the house for a night on the town. "And don't worry about Lou. We always get along great."

Outside, Adam smiled down into Francy's eyes. "You look beautiful tonight."

"Thank you, kind sir. This morning when I stepped on the scale I had a nice surprise. I've lost all the weight I gained when I was pregnant with Lou."

Adam cast an admiring glance over her neat figure. "To me you always look great."

"Even when I was shaped like a bowling ball?"

"Especially then." Before opening the car door for her, he leaned down and kissed her tenderly.

After Adam settled her into their Volvo station wagon and pulled away from the curb, Francy glanced at him sideways. There were touches of silver in his hair now, but they only made him look more distinguished. Was this wonderful man really hers? Sometimes she still had to pinch herself to believe it was true. Oh, she knew now that he had weaknesses and vulnerabilities, just like she had. But he possessed so many strengths, and she was so proud of him. Already he had made a name for himself in the senate, and who knew where he might go from there. But, more important as far as Francy was concerned, somehow he managed not to sacrifice his family life to his career of public service. He was an adoring father and a loving husband—a very loving husband, she thought with a small, satisfied smile.

"Where to?" he asked.

"Anywhere you like. I'm at your command."

He took her to La Colline, a French restaurant on North Capitol. After they dined there on fresh salmon, they went to some of the night spots in Georgetown. It was late when Adam finally returned from taking Jenny back to her dorm. When he came upstairs, Francy had just donned a lacy, low-cut nightgown and was waiting for him in bed.

"Obviously you read my mind," he said closing the door behind him as his gaze played over her warm flesh.

Francy laughed, but there was a hunger in her dark eyes. It wasn't true that married lovers grew bored with each other—at least it certainly hadn't happened between her and Adam. She still melted at his touch, and judging from the haste with which he was now removing his clothes, he was far from losing interest in her.

"Watch you don't tear off the buttons," she teased as he flung his shirt on the carpet and strode toward her quite unabashedly naked.

"If you don't want me to pop my buttons, you shouldn't sit around in that lacy thing looking so gorgeous and so sexy," he growled as he climbed in next to her. He took her in his arms and kissed her passionately.

"Oh, Adam," Francy breathed. "I love you so."

"More with every day that passes," he murmured. "There aren't enough words in the dictionary to tell you how much."

She smiled at the irony of that, but then his lips went to her breasts and she gasped with the pleasure of his loving caress, all words forgotten.

# *Harlequin Superromance*

## COMING NEXT MONTH

# ATTRACTIVE, SPACE SAVING BOOK RACK

Display your most prized novels on this handsome and sturdy book rack. The hand-rubbed walnut finish will blend into your library decor with quiet elegance, providing a practical organizer for your favorite hard-or soft-covered books.

*Only $9.95*

**Approximately 16" x 8" when assembled**

**Assembles in seconds!**

To order, rush your name, address and zip code, along with a check or money order for $10.70* ($9.95 plus 75¢ postage and handling) payable to *Harlequin Reader Service*:

Harlequin Reader Service
Book Rack Offer
901 Fuhrmann Blvd.
P.O. Box 1396
Buffalo, NY 14269-1396

*Offer not available in Canada.*

*New York and Iowa residents add appropriate sales tax.

BKR-1A

**Lynda Ward's**

# LEAP THE MOON

... the continuing saga of *The Welles Family*

You've already met Elaine Welles, the oldest daughter of powerful tycoon Burton Welles, in Superromance #317, *Race the Sun*. You cheered her on as she threw off the shackles of her heritage and won the love of her life, Ruy de Areias.

Now it's her sister's turn. Jennie Welles is the drop-dead-gorgeous, most rebellious Welles sister, and she's determined to live life her way—and flaunt it in her father's face.

When she meets Griffin Stark, however, she learns there's more to life than glamour and independence. She learns about kindness, compassion and sharing. One nagging question remains: is she good enough for a man like Griffin? Her father certainly doesn't think so....

*Leap the Moon* ... a Harlequin Superromance coming to you in August. Don't miss it!

LYNDA-1B